Born in Paris in 1947, Christian Jacq first visited Egypt when he was seventeen, went on to study Egyptology and archaeology at the Sorbonne, and is now one of the world's leading Egyptologists. He is the author of the internationally bestselling RAMSES series, THE STONE OF LIGHT series and the stand-alone novel, THE BLACK PHARAOH. Christian Jacq lives in Switzerland.

Also by Christian Jacq:

The Ramses Series
Volume 1: The Son of the Light
Volume 2: The Temple of a Million Years
Volume 3: The Battle of Kadesh
Volume 4: The Lady of Abu Simbel
Volume 5: Under the Western Acacia

The Stone of Light Series
Volume 1: Nefer the Silent
Volume 2: The Wise Woman
Volume 3: Paneb the Ardent
Volume 4: The Place of Truth

The Queen of Freedom Trilogy
Volume 1: The Empire of Darkness
Volume 2: The War of the Crowns
Volume 3: The Flaming Sword

The Black Pharoah

The Living Wisdom of Ancient Egypt

About the Translator

Sue Dyson is a prolific author of both fiction and non-fiction, including over thirty novels, both contemporary and historical. She has also translated a wide variety of French fiction.

The Queen of Freedom Trilogy

The Empire of Darkness

Christian Jacq

Translated by Sue Dyson

POCKET
BOOKS

LONDON • SYDNEY • NEW YORK • TOKYO • SINGAPORE • TORONTO

First published in France by XO Editions under the title
L'Empire des Ténèbres, 2001
First published in Great Britain by Simon & Schuster UK Ltd, 2002
This edition first published by Pocket Books, 2003
An imprint of Simon & Schuster UK Ltd

A CBS COMPANY

1 3 5 7 9 10 8 6 4 2

Simon & Schuster UK Ltd
1st Floor
222 Gray's Inn Road
London WC1X 8HB

www.simonandschuster.co.uk

Simon & Schuster Australia
Sydney

A CIP catalogue record for this book is available
from the British Library

ISBN-978-1-84983-503-9

Typeset in Times by SX Composing DTP, Rayleigh, Essex
Printed and bound in Great Britain by
Cox & Wyman Ltd, Reading, Berkshire

The Empire of Darkness

AHHOTEP, QUEEN FREEDOM

Around 1690 BC, Egypt was under Hyksos domination. But one young Theban princess refused to bear the invader's yoke any longer. Her name was Ahhotep. With very little chance of victory, she set about awakening her fellow Egyptians' consciences. Her Egyptian name, *Ah-hotep*, is made up of two words: *Ah*, the moon-god, who is sometimes aggressive and fearsome, and *Hotep*, which means 'peace', 'fullness', 'completion'. The name Ahhotep is therefore a positive programme for a reign; it can be translated as 'The Moon is Full' – in other words may heavenly power come at the end of darkness – or as 'War and Peace'.

Three men, three Thebans, three pharaohs mark the life of Ahhotep: her husband, Seqen-en-Ra, and their two sons, Kames and Ahmose. From the very start, the queen made great sacrifices to invest all her energies in the campaign of reconquest, vital to reunite the Two Lands of Upper and Lower Egypt.

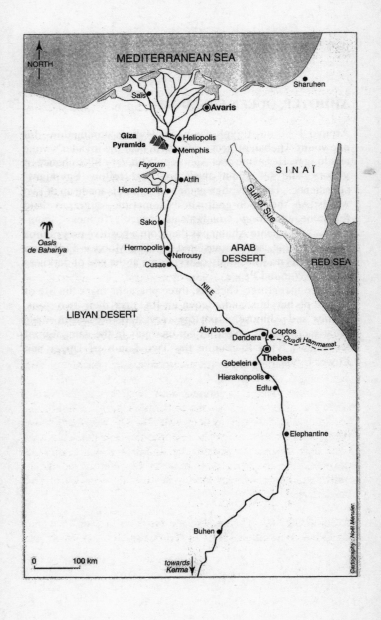

HISTORICAL BACKGROUND

During its magnificent 3,000-year history, ancient Egypt experienced troubled periods. One of these marked the end of the Middle Kingdom, an era of peace, harmony and stability which began about 2060 BC.

Danger came from the north-east, in the eighteenth century BC, in the form of the Hyksos invasion.

Who were these Hyksos, called in Egyptian 'Hekau Khasut', 'Princes of Foreign Lands?' The debate continues, but it is certain that among them were Canaanites, Anatolians, Cyprians, Asians, Caucasians and others. This was the first invasion to strike Egypt.

The Hyksos occupation was long (lasting over a century) and very harsh. The invaders established the centre of their military and trading empire in the Delta, at Avaris. Soon there remained only one small island of resistance: the small city of Thebes.

Teti the Small became queen on the death of her husband, the last pharaoh to reign at Thebes before the occupation. She needed great courage to maintain a semblance of independence in her province. But salvation came from her daughter, Ahhotep, who was under the moon's protection and determined to resist.

Was Ahhotep the Egyptian Joan of Arc? In a way she was, since she incited the Thebans to form an army of liberation and played an essential military role. But she was much more than a warrior queen, for she restored the essential values of pharaonic society. For the novelist and the historian, Ahhotep presents the image of a woman as fascinating as she is unforgettable; a woman who said 'no' to occupation and barbarism.

Around 1730 BC, Thebes was the last small island in which Egyptian civilization survived. To the north of the town, the whole country was under the yoke of the Hyksos and their leader, the tyrant Apophis. To the south, there were the Nubians, allies of the Hyksos. Thebes – the Theban province was called Waset, '(divine) Power' – was then only a provincial town which celebrated the cult of the god Amon in the temple at Karnak (it was very modest compared to the immense temple-city that tourists visit today). As yet there was only one temple, built by Senusret I (XIIth dynasty). This temple no longer exists, for the pharaohs of the New Kingdom re-used the ancient blocks of stone as symbolic foundations for their own monuments. But digs have enabled archaeologists to find the separate parts of a shrine called 'the white temple of Senusret I', which has been reconstructed and shows the beauty of buildings of the time.

It was the horse, an animal hitherto unknown in Egypt, that gave the Hyksos their military superiority. Its role was a vital one: harnessed in pairs to a chariot, horses could carry four soldiers into battle, one driving the vehicle, the other three using bows or throwing bronze-headed spears. The Egyptians in turn adopted this 'weapon', as was seen many generations later at the battle of Kadesh, won by Ramses II.

The battle fought by Queen Ahhotep with her husband, Pharaoh Seqen, against the Hyksos was a ruthless one. The most moving testimony that has come down to us is the disfigured mummy of the young Seqen, known as Seqen-en-Ra, 'Valiant One of the Divine Light', whose face and head carry terrible wounds. The embalmers did not remove these signs, as they wished to preserve the memory of the fierce battle in which the heroic king was killed. At Ahhotep's side, he was the first pharaoh to resist the Hyksos occupation, because he wanted to see Egypt free again and reunified.

KEY DATES

Ancient era (dynasties I and II) *c*. 3150–2690 BC

Old Kingdom (dynasties III–VI) *c*. 2690–2180 BC
The time of the great pyramids. The most famous pharaohs are Sneferu, Djoser and Khufu.

First intermediate period (dynasties IX–XI) *c*. 2180–2060 BC

Middle Kingdom (dynasties XI–XII) *c*. 2060–1785 BC
Rule of the Amenemhat and Senusret dynasties.

Second intermediate period (dynasties XIII–XVII) *c*. 1785–1570 BC
Hyksos invasion and occupation.

New Kingdom (dynasties XVII–XX) *c*. 1570–1070 BC
Among the most famous pharaohs are Hatshepsut, Akhenaton, Seti I and Ramses II.

Third intermediate period (dynasties XXI–XXV) *c*. 1070–672 BC

Low Era (dynasties XXV–XXX) 762–332 BC

Greco-Roman period 332 BC–AD 395
This includes Alexander the Great's conquest and the rule of the Ptolemies (including Cleopatra), then that of the Roman emperors.

Thebes, the last free place on Egyptian soil, 1690 BC

1

Ahhotep had not moved for more than half an hour. When she saw the last guard walk past the main gate of the palace, the beautiful brown-haired girl took advantage of the few minutes before the guard was relieved, and scurried into a thicket of tamarisks, where she hid until nightfall.

Ahhotep was the eighteen-year-old daughter of Queen Teti the Small, and she bore a strange name which could be translated as 'The Moon is Full', 'The Moon Has Been Appeased', or even as 'War and Peace' for, according to the sages, the moon was a warrior-god embodying the mystery of death and resurrection.

War . . . It was the only way to rid the land of the Hyksos who controlled it all – with the exception of Thebes, the sacred city of the god Amon. Thanks to his protection, the Temple of Karnak and the town nearby had been spared by the barbarians, but for how much longer?

The Hyksos had flooded in through the Delta, forty years before, like a mighty swarm of locusts. Asians, Arabs, Canaanites, Syrians, Scythians, Minoans, Cyprians, Persians, Anatolians and yet more races, all armed to the teeth. They used strange four-legged creatures called horses, which had large heads and were bigger and faster than donkeys. The horses drew wheeled vehicles which moved incredibly swiftly, and which had enabled the attackers to massacre Pharaoh's soldiers.

Ahhotep cursed the softness and cowardice of the feeble Theban army. True, it could not hope to measure up to the large, powerful forces of occupation, with their terrifying new weapons; but failure to act would result in annihilation. When Apophis, the Hyksos's supreme commander, eventually decided to raze Thebes to the ground, the Egyptian soldiers would run away, and the population would be massacred, with the exception of pretty women, who would be used by the brutish soldiers for their pleasure, and sturdy children, who would be sent into slavery. The last free men on Egyptian soil would bow their heads, incapable of dong anything.

What was left of the wondrous realm of the pyramid-builders? A province caught between the occupying power in the North and its Nubian allies in the South, a temple built by Senusret I and left abandoned, and a palace which now looked anything but royal.

Without Teti the Small's resolution, even the House of the Queen would have been destroyed, and the Thebans, like all other Egyptians, would have become servants of the Hyksos. But, trapped in her isolation, Teti was beginning to weaken, and the supporters of Theban independence saw their numbers fall every day.

If there was only one rebel left, that person would be Ahhotep. The young girl had no fear of battle, suffering or death. Even with a dagger at her throat, she would still refuse to submit to the Hyksos yoke.

The courtiers mocked her as mad, regarding her as amusing rather than dangerous. They were wrong. Today was the start of the war for freedom. With an eighteen-year-old rebel as its only soldier, and a well-sharpened flint knife as its only weapon.

The guard had been changed, and Thebes was asleep. It was a long time since any banquets had been held or music played in the reception hall, with its faded paintings. And there was no longer a pharaoh to take his seat upon a desperately empty throne.

Ahhotep wanted to forget this heart-rending sight, and she ran towards the landing-stage. At the quay lay a half-derelict cargo-barge, once used to transport blocks of stone from the quarries, which the Hyksos had closed down, and a few small sailing-boats.

Among them was one small boat in good condition. This was the means of transport Ahhotep planned to use to leave the Theban enclave. She jumped nimbly down into the boat and seized the oars. As she was heading north, the current would be in her favour.

No one travelled on the river at night, for there were many dangers: hippopotamus, crocodiles, whirlpools . . . but Ahhotep had no choice. 'And when we have no choice,' she often declared loudly, 'we are free.'

Determinedly, the princess began to row.

Since no one could tell her precisely where the free area ended and Hyksos-occupied territory began, she would find out for herself. The queen's frightened advisers assumed that the Hyksos had made great progress since Apophis's seizure of power – and Apophis's reputation for cruelty exceeded his predecessors'. They were urging Teti to leave Thebes without delay.

But where could she live in safety?

As far as Ahhotep was concerned, the only refuge was in attack. The first skirmish would take place on the demarcation line and, if necessary, the princess herself would command the tattered remnants of the Egyptian army.

In the past forty years, thousands of her compatriots had been massacred. The Hyksos believed they could act with complete impunity and continue their reign of terror over the Two Lands of Upper and Lower Egypt. Ahhotep would soon show them that they were very wrong.

Never had an Egyptian princess, accustomed to the luxury

of court, been forced to wield heavy oars like this, at the risk of spoiling her hands. But the survival of the country was at stake, and the pretty brunette thought only of the goal she must attain.

The boat bumped hard against something and almost capsized, but by great good luck it righted itself. Ahhotep glimpsed a dark form moving away, its powerful tail thrashing in water. She had disturbed a crocodile.

Refusing to be afraid, Ahhotep rowed on. Thanks to her excellent eyesight and the light of the full moon, she avoided the wreckage of a boat and a grassy islet where pelicans were sleeping. On the banks the peasants' houses stood abandoned. Fearing that the invaders were coming, the people had taken refuge in Thebes.

Not far away, she saw smoke.

Ahhotep slowed her pace, steered the boat towards the bank and hid it in a papyrus thicket, disturbing a cloud of sleeping egrets. Fearing that their cries might give her away, she waited some time before moving. When she eventually climbed up the sloping bank, she found herself in an abandoned field.

Was the smoke coming from a burning farm or from a Hyksos camp? Whichever the case, the enemy was very close.

'Well, well, little girl,' barked an aggressive voice, 'what are you doing here?'

Without a moment's hesitation, Ahhotep swing round and, brandishing her flint knife in her right hand, hurled herself at the enemy.

2

'Kill it,' ordered Apophis.

The young donkey saw its death approaching. Its large, soft eyes were filled with incomprehension. Why kill me? it thought. Since the age of six months, it had constantly carried loads so heavy that they had hollowed its back. It had guided its companions in misfortune along every track and had never once lost its way. It had always obeyed orders without hesitation. But its owner, a merchant from the Arabian peninsula who had been in the Hyksos's service, had just died of a blood clot, and it was the invaders' custom to sacrifice a caravan-leader's best donkeys and throw their remains into a makeshift grave.

Indifferent to the slaughter, Apophis climbed slowly up the steps leading to his fortified palace. It stood at the heart of the citadel that dominated his capital, Avaris, which had been built in a fertile area of the north-eastern Delta.

Apophis, supreme commander of the Hyksos, was a tall fifty-year-old with a prominent nose, flaccid cheeks, a pot-belly and thick legs. His manner was icy and his voice harsh, and the mere sight of him was enough to inspire fear. People forgot his ugliness and spoke of his unfathomable gaze, which could catch a man unawares and enter his soul like the blade of a dagger. It was impossible to know what he was thinking, this man who had terrorized Egypt for twenty years.

5

*

Whenever he thought of the Hyksos invasion, Apophis felt a surge of pride. Had it not put an end to thirteen centuries of Egyptian independence? Chariots and horses, then unknown to the pharaoh's army, had caused panic and made the conquest easy and swift, all the more so since many collaborators, like the Canaanites, had been happy to resort to treachery in order to win the conquerors' favour.

Although well paid, Pharaoh's hired mercenaries had turned their weapons against the Egyptian footsoldiers, who had thus been attacked from within as well as without. And there were too few forts in the Delta to stem the flood of invaders.

'A fine journey, my lord,' exclaimed Khamudi, Apophis's most trusted henchman, bowing low.

Khamudi had a moon face, jet-black hair plastered to his round head, slightly slanting eyes, plump hands and feet, and a heavy frame; he looked much older than his thirty years. He hid his aggressive nature beneath a feigned unctuousness, but everyone knew he would not hesitate to kill anyone who got in his way.

'I trust you have put a stop to those regrettable incidents?'

'Oh yes, my lord,' confirmed Khamudi with a broad smile. 'No more peasants will dare rebel, you can be certain of that.'

Apophis never smiled. The only time his face brightened was when he witnessed the death-throes of an adversary who had been insane enough to oppose Hyksos domination.

In this instance, a small village close to the new capital had recently protested against the unbearable burden of taxation. Khamudi had immediately unleashed his dogs of war, Cyprian pirates whom the Hyksos had recruited from Egyptian prisons. Despite orders, they had not spared even the children. When they left, nothing remained of the village they had attacked.

'What about the harvests?' asked Apophis.

Khamudi's face fell. 'According to first reports, they aren't very good.'

Cold anger filled Apophis's eyes. 'Do you mean they'll be worse than last year's?'

'I fear so, my lord.'

'The peasants are mocking us.'

'I'll have a few villages burnt. Then they'll realize that—'

'No,' interrupted Apophis. 'It's pointless killing slaves whose labour may be useful. We must find another solution.'

'Believe me, they're frightened.'

'Perhaps too frightened.'

Khamudi was dismayed.

Apophis began climbing again; Khamudi followed, keeping one step behind his master.

'Fear is a good counsellor,' Apophis went on, 'but dread can paralyse. And we must have more wheat and barley to feed our officials and our soldiers.'

'None of them will consent to work in the fields.'

'I don't need to be reminded of that.'

Khamudi bit his lip. A lover of food, good wines and voluptuous women, he sometimes had a tendency to talk too much.

'We have conquered Egypt,' Apophis reminded him, 'and that miserable Theban enclave, populated by cowards and old men, is certainly not going to pose a threat to us.'

'I was about to suggest that you destroy it without delay.'

'That would be a mistake, my friend, a grave mistake.'

'I don't understand.'

Soldiers armed with spears bowed as the two men passed by. Heading along a low-ceilinged, narrow passageway lit by torches, they reached a small room which had been constructed at the very centre of the fortress. Apophis was certain that no one would overhear them here.

He sat down on a low, plain chair made of sycamore wood. Khamudi remained standing.

Apophis said, 'Not all our allies are reliable. I am counting on you, my efficient and devoted friend, to put our own house in order.'

'Have no fear, my lord.'

'Use any means you like – yes, you heard me correctly: any. Whatever the circumstances, I shall approve and support your actions. The only thing that matters to me is the result. I do not wish to hear even one more dissenting voice in the Hyksos coalition.'

Khamudi almost drooled with delight. Those who had dared criticize him, even in their thoughts, had just been condemned to death.

'We still have a great deal of work to do to erase the remaining traces of the pharaoh's former regime,' Apophis continued. 'We must show the people of Egypt that the Hyksos revolution is all-powerful, and can never be reversed.'

'Then Thebes must die.'

'Of course, but first it must unwittingly serve my ends. The key to total victory is collaboration. Traitors helped us invade Egypt, and other traitors will help us to bring her to heel. Let us allow the last rebels to believe that Thebes represents a real hope, while insinuating a worm into the fruit.'

'The peasants . . .'

'If they harbour hopes of liberation, however distant, they will work with renewed ardour, little knowing that not one ear of corn will reach the rebels. And you, my friend, must demonstrate your skill in the art of lying and disinformation. Organize false networks of opponents, and then arrest a few members so that no doubts remain, and whip up the yokels' fervour.'

'My lord, I shall be obliged to kill a few of our own officers.'

'Concentrate on the Canaanites – they're a little too noisy for my taste.'

'As you wish, my lord.'

'Khamudi' – Apophis's tone made his henchman shiver – 'you're the only person who knows my real intentions. Make sure you don't forget that.'

'It is an immense privilege, and I shall prove myself worthy of it, my lord.'

3

Teti the Small was beside herself with worry, for there was no denying the facts: Ahhotep had vanished without trace. The headstrong girl was neither in her bedchamber nor in the library, where she spent hours reading stories written during the glorious Middle Kingdom period. Nor yet was she in the garden, where she loved to play with her enormous dog, Laughter, a half-wild creature which obeyed no one but her. In her absence, the guards had tethered the huge animal to the trunk of a sycamore tree.

'But, Qaris, you must know where she has gone.'

Qaris, the queen's steward, was the very soul of politeness, a plump, round-cheeked fellow who kept calm in all circumstances. He had taken on the difficult, if not impossible, task of maintaining some semblance of comfort in the royal palace at Thebes, which seemed destined for rapid decay.

'Alas, Majesty, I do not.'

'I am sure she has confided in you and you do not wish to betray her.'

'Truly I know nothing, Majesty. The guards have been informed.'

'The guards! A band of cowards who will die of fear before the Hyksos even arrive.'

Qaris could not deny this. He said, 'I have also alerted the army.'

Teti sighed. 'Does it still exist?'

'Majesty . . .'

'Attend to lunch, Qaris. Let us continue to pretend to live like a royal court.'

Shoulders bowed, the steward went off to attend to his duties. He had long since given up trying to comfort the queen with fine words he did not believe himself.

Teti was tired. She went to the throne chamber, which had been hastily created forty years earlier, when the court had fled the Memphis region and taken refuge in the small insignificant town of Thebes, 'the Iunu of the South.'

On the death of her husband, a pharaoh who had lacked true power, Teti had chosen not to be crowned as his successor. What was the use of bestowing inflated titles upon herself? That would only have attracted the anger of the Hyksos, who at present were too busy bleeding the country dry to crush wretched little Thebes beneath their heel.

The queen's strategy had worked. The invaders had forgotten the sacred city of Amon, convinced that it was peopled only by harmless old priests celebrating outmoded cults. And that was indeed the message Teti wished to send to the new capital, Avaris, in the hope that the Hyksos would leave the last free Egyptians to die in peace.

What else could she have done? The Theban army was nothing but an incompetent, ill-armed rabble. The soldiers' training amounted to grotesque parades which no longer even entertained the children. Experienced officers had given up hope, and limited themselves to maintaining the fabric of their barracks.

When the Hyksos eventually attacked, as they must surely do, both soldiers and guards would lay down their arms and try to pass as civilians in order to escape the ensuing massacre. And the most senior general, an old man in failing health, would be incapable of maintaining even a semblance of discipline among his troops.

11

From time to time, Teti convened the ghostly relic of a council, at which people spoke without laughing of a 'Theban kingdom'. For in theory Thebes still governed a few ruined provinces, each of which retained a governor and a scribe whose task was to proclaim the pharaoh's decrees. But no one believed in this masquerade any more. At the first sign of a threat from the Hyksos, all the governors would declare that they did not support Thebes in any way and that its queen was a dissident who should be severely punished.

Teti was surrounded by people who were insignificant, incompetent or corrupt. She had not even appointed a tjaty, since he would not have had the power to do anything. The only official posts remaining were those of the ministers for agriculture and finance, which were held by elderly courtiers who provided their dispirited staff with directionless leadership.

Loyalty had disappeared, and people thought only of themselves. By some miracle, the Thebans had agreed to retain the royal family, albeit in greatly reduced form, as if they were reluctant to forget the past. Thanks to Qaris's tireless efforts, Teti, Ahhotep and those close to them did not go hungry, even if the food put before them would have seemed pitiful to the monarchs of glorious ages gone by. Each day, the queen wept. Shut up in her paltry palace, which seemed more and more like a prison, she lived on memories and dreams, in which the future had no place.

Teti bowed before the empty throne, which no pharaoh would ever occupy again. Horus, the falcon of heaven, had flown away, never to return to the Earth from his celestial paradise. The happiness of the Two Lands, symbolized by the union of the plants of North and South, was no more than a mirage.

Although the queen hid her despair behind a mask of carefully applied face-paint – and it was scarce now – she had already thought several times of killing herself. What use was a queen without a crown, helpless in the face of a barbarian revolution?

The only thing that gave her the courage to go on living was gazing up at the stars. In them shone the immortal souls of reborn kings, who trod the path of righteousness for all time, beyond the reach of doubts and despair. And so Teti carried on her obscure existence as the last Queen of Egypt.

Qaris's discreet cough broke into her thoughts. 'Majesty,' he said.

'What is it?'

His voice unsteady, he said, 'The guards are asking to speak to you.'

'Can you not deal with it?'

'Their commander will speak only to you.'

'Very well. Show him into the audience chamber.'

Qaris's gaze was fixed on the empty throne. 'Majesty, were you thinking of . . .?'

Teti smiled sadly. 'Of course not.'

'If we only had a pharaoh again . . .'

'Banish that thought from your mind, Qaris.'

Slowly, the queen closed the door of the throne chamber. From now on it would be left to its silence.

'If you wish, Majesty, I will have the floors cleaned and try to brighten up the paintings,' suggested Qaris.

'That will not be necessary.'

The queen went to her bedchamber to check her appearance in a bronze mirror, and put on a fine gold crown which other Great Royal Wives had worn before her. (Her last woman of the bedchamber had tried to steal it, but Teti had done no more than dismiss her.) The queen of the Theban enclave must continue to look like a queen. Fortunately, she still had a few dresses worthy of her rank and she took great care of them, for presenting a truly regal appearance was the one thing that sill made an impression on the forces of law and persuaded them that a governing authority still existed, however limited it might be.

Today, she chose a pink linen gown and golden sandals. As she put them on, for a moment the queen imagined that her province was a real country and that she was going to address a real representative of the law.

Surprised by the queen's noble bearing, the guard commander was silent for a few seconds. Then he bowed low and said, 'Majesty.'

'What is it, Commander?'

'It is a serious matter, Majesty, very serious.'

'Does it concern the safety of Thebes?'

'I fear so. Your daughter . . .'

The queen paled. 'Have you found her?'

'Not I personally. It was a border guard.'

'Is she . . . alive?'

'Oh yes, Majesty – no one could be more so! As for the guard, the princess wounded him in the arm with her knife.'

'Her knife? Are you mad?'

'The report is quite clear, Majesty. Princess Ahhotep tried to kill the guard who arrested her. She was so wild that he had to call for reinforcements to control her.'

Teti was struck by a terrible thought. 'Was she . . . harmed?'

'No, Majesty, for she identified herself immediately. At first the guards did not believe her, but her vehemence shook them. They were afraid of making a mistake, so they decided to tie her up and bring her to me.'

'Then this ridiculous matter is now closed.'

The commander met her eye. 'I fear not, Majesty.'

'What do you mean?'

'We cannot consider this incident a simple altercation.'

'Why not?'

'Because it is clear that the princess was leaving Theban territory to join the Hyksos.'

'How dare you!'

'The guards and I accuse Princess Ahhotep of treason. Given her rank an emergency court must be convened as a matter of urgency.'

'Do you realize that—'

'She will be condemned to death,' said the commander with relish. 'What could be more appropriate? If we do not make an example of her, there will be chaos.'

Teti swayed. 'No, it's impossible. You must be mistaken.'

'Facts are facts, Majesty.'

'I wish to see my daughter.'

'The interrogation was carried out properly, Majesty, I assure you.'

'Has Ahhotep confessed?'

'We will have her confession soon.'

Teti the Small drew herself up to her full height. 'I am the Queen of Thebes, and I demand to see my daughter immediately.'

4

The contrast between the two women was striking. Teti the Small was like a precious statuette, so slender she looked as though she might break; Ahhotep was tall, majestic, her hair hanging loose, her green eyes flashing with anger. They were equally beautiful, but had nothing else in common save the fact that they were both members of the royal family.

And the fact that they were being watched with cruel amusement by the guard commander and his four men, who held the princess bound and gagged. Teti knew she was embarking upon a decisive battle. If she lost, those who favoured collaboration with the Hyksos would strip her of her few remaining powers and deliver up the city of Amon to the invader.

'Release my daughter!' ordered the queen.

'She is dangerous, Majesty,' said the commander. 'We cannot take any risks.'

'I gave you an order,' she reminded him coldly.

The officer hesitated. He could sweep away this frail, defenceless creature with one swipe of his hand, and seize the palace's last few riches. But to take power that way would provoke hostility from both soldiers and priests, and no one would emerge victorious from the ensuing conflict.

'Let us be cautious, Majesty, and just remove the gag.'

Two guards untied the strip of coarse linen.

'Are you hurt, Ahhotep?' her mother asked.

'Only by these idiots' stupidity. It took five of them to overcome me – what fighters!'

'They accuse you of trying to escape and of treason.'

Everyone was expecting an explosion of anger, but the young woman remained strangely calm. She stared at each of the guards in turn, and each took a step backwards.

'Who,' said Ahhotep, 'dares tell such a lie?'

'You cannot deny that you were trying to escape,' said the commander defensively.

'Are these men really border guards?'

'Yes, my lady.'

'I was arrested at Mount of the Quails, was I not?'

'Indeed, but—'

'Is the border really that close to Thebes?'

'Of course not!'

'Then kindly explain why your guards were there, and why they had lit a fire.'

One of the men could not hold his tongue. 'We were there on our commander's orders – we're not responsible for anything.'

'And what were those orders?' asked Ahhotep angrily.

'Say nothing, you fools!' hissed the commander.

'You looted and burned a farm, didn't you? Instead of doing your duty and guarding the forward positions, you took advantage of your uniforms to rob unfortunate people who had taken refuge in the free area.'

The guards huddled together; their commander unsheathed his short-sword.

'Surely you aren't afraid of two women,' sneered Ahhotep. There was no answer.

'You are the one who is guilty of treason,' she went on, 'and the queen demands that you bow down before her.'

Teti the Small gazed disdainfully at the accused man. 'Put up your sword and prostrate yourself before me.'

He burst out laughing. 'You are nothing now, Majesty, and your daughter's hands are bound. You should thank me for offering you a quick death.'

A menacing growl drew everyone's attention. Wheeling round, the ruffian saw Ahhotep's huge dog, Laughter. He raised his sword, but the attack was so swift that he had no time to use it. The dog sank its teeth into its victim's arm, and the man roared with pain.

'Untie me,' ordered Ahhotep, and the guards hastily obeyed.

Ahhotep stroked her dog, which looked up at her with gentleness and a satisfied expression, as if extremely proud of its latest exploit.

'How did that creature manage to get free?' whined the wounded man.

'A court shall indeed be convened urgently,' the princess informed him, 'but it will sit in judgement on you, a traitor who dared raise his hand against his queen and threaten her with death.'

The commander sobbed, 'You must forgive me. I didn't wish Her Majesty any harm.'

'A coward as well as a traitor,' said Ahhotep with contempt. 'Guards, throw this vermin in prison.'

Only too glad to be let off so lightly, the guards did not need to be told twice.

Tongue lolling out, Laughter stood up on his hind legs and put his enormous front paws on the princess's shoulders.

'So you were tied up and yet managed to free yourself, did you?'

The dog was incurably honest, and Ahhotep saw in his eyes that he had had some vital help.

'I shall solve this problem,' she promised.

'Ahhotep,' whispered Teti.

Seeing that her mother was on the point of collapse, the princess hurried to her and helped her to a chair.

The Empire of Darkness

'So much violence,' said Teti, 'even here, in my palace. I no longer have the strength to bear such horrors.'

'Of course you have. You ought to rejoice.'

'Rejoice? Why?'

'Because the commander made such a huge mistake. That useless creature has at last shown you just what he's capable of. Replace him as soon as possible.'

Teti began to see her daughter in a fresh light. Although Ahhotep was already a woman, and a very attractive one at that, up to now the queen had regarded her as an undisciplined child, who thought only of escaping into her own imagination so as to forget her country's death-agonies.

'Ahhotep, I'm so tired.'

'Majesty, you have neither the right nor the time to be tired. It is only because of you that Egypt survives. If you give up, the enemy will have defeated us without even fighting.'

How sweet it would be to close my eyes for ever, thought the queen. But she knew her daughter was right. Aloud, she said, 'Do you really think we have a chance of defeating an enemy like the Hyksos?'

'Yes, if we really want to.'

Teti gazed at her thoughtfully for a moment, then said, 'Why did you venture so far from the palace?'

'To find out the precise location of the border of what we dare to call "the Theban kingdom". But I failed, so I shall have to try again.'

'It's too dangerous.'

'But it's vital, Majesty. We cannot organize resistance if we don't know the enemy's positions.'

Teti took off her crown and laid it on her knees. 'The situation is desperate, Ahhotep. We have neither a pharaoh nor an army, and our only chance of survival is to persuade the Hyksos that Thebes is just a small town populated by harmless old men who spend their time praying to dead gods.'

'That will do excellently,' declared the princess. 'As long as the invaders regard us as utterly negligible, they won't attack us.'

'But we *are* negligible,' Teti sighed. 'May the sky-goddess permit us to die here, on our own land, in the illusion of freedom.'

'No.'

The queen stared at her daughter in astonishment.

'I will not accept as inevitable an outcome that is nothing of the kind,' Ahhotep continued passionately. 'If Amon has preserved Thebes's independence, it must surely be because he has a mission for his city. If we hide ourselves away, quaking with fear, we shall close our ears and no longer hear his voice.'

'Not a single man will have the courage to fight the Hyksos,' said Teti.

'Then the women shall do it.'

'Have you taken leave of your senses?'

'Mother, you are the earthly representative of Ma'at, are you not?'

The queen smiled faintly. Ma'at, goddess of harmony, righteousness and justice; Ma'at, depicted as a woman crowned with the rectrix, the feather that enabled birds to steer their flight; Ma'at, the foundation upon which the pharaohs had built both their civilization and the statues of the reborn, whose mouths, eyes and ears were opened by the priests.

'Even Thebes is no longer fit to welcome Ma'at,' lamented Teti.

'Of course it is, for you are the queen and Ma'at is made flesh in the office you fulfil.'

'That is nothing but a dream now, Ahhotep, a distant dream which has almost faded away.'

'Ma'at is nourished not by dreams but by reality,' said Ahhotep firmly. 'That is why we must reconquer our land and

The Empire of Darkness

give it back to her.' She knelt before the queen. 'Majesty, I have taken up arms. All I have is a flint knife, but that is not such a bad start. If handled well, it is very effective.'

'Ahhotep! Surely you aren't thinking of fighting?'

'I have just done so, Majesty, and I shall do so again.'

'You're a young woman, not a soldier.'

'And where are they, those valiant soldiers of ours? If no one jolts them out of their stupor, they will sleep on for ever. It is our task to awaken them.'

Teti closed her eyes. 'It is insane, my dear daughter. You must forget these mad thoughts.'

The princess got to her feet. 'They are my only reason for living.'

'Is your determination really so strong?'

'It is as strong as granite.'

The queen sighed again. 'In that case, I shall help you with every last shred of my strength.'

5

Ten peasants were trudging slowly through the marshes, not far from the Hyksos's new capital. They were long-haired and unshaven, and dressed only in kilts made from reeds. They led four fat oxen towards a small island where juicy galengales grew.

Their leader, a man with a big, bushy moustache, growled to a straggler, 'Faster.'

'Haven't you had enough of playing the slave-master?'

'Take a look around you,' advised a third fellow, who had plastered himself with mud to guard against mosquitoes. 'It's a beautiful day, with a clear sky and a light northerly breeze. Why are you so bad-tempered?'

'Because the Hyksos have taken my land,' replied Moustache.

'Yes, but a man can get used to anything in time. Looking after oxen isn't so bad.'

'If you aren't free, everything is bad.'

Moustache thought of the hours he had spent irrigating his land, looking after his tools, sowing, harvesting, arguing with scribes at the Finance secretariat to get his taxes lowered – all that toil wasted. And then there was the struggle against nature, which could be generous one moment and merciless the next. He bemoaned his lot constantly, and dreaded what the future might hold in store for him.

Not content with having ruined him, the Hyksos had forced him to become leader of this miserable band of ox-herds, who habitually grazed their charges in an area which was often flooded. Quarrels were frequent, and the atmosphere oppressive.

'We're going to have grilled fish to eat,' announced a plump-cheeked fellow, licking his lips. 'I caught it before dawn, and we're not going to tell the officer.'

Each morning and evening, Hyksos soldiers counted the oxen. In exchange for their toil, the herdsmen were allowed just one spelt flatcake, some onions and – once a week – some dried fish, which was often inedible.

'If they see the smoke, they'll beat us,' said another man worriedly.

Plump-Cheeks shook his head. 'We're too deep into the marshes for them to spot it.'

Everyone's mouth watered at the thought of the feast.

'Watch out, all of you! There's someone on the little island.'

A strange, turbaned man with a large black beard was sitting on a papyrus mat, roasting a fish.

'He's an odd-looking fellow,' said Moustache.

'I bet he's an evil marsh-spirit. Let's get out of here.'

'No, let's go and take over his fire,' advised Plump-Cheeks. 'He won't stand a chance against all of us.'

As the oxen and herdsmen approached, the stranger stood up slowly and turned to face them.

'I tell you, we should run away,' said one of the ox-herds. 'He's not human,' and in panic he turned to flee.

But the stranger pulled out a slingshot and began to brandish it, whirling it round his head at an incredible speed. A stone flew out of it and struck the man on the back of the neck. He instantly collapsed into the murky water and would have drowned if Moustache hadn't dragged him out by the hair.

'Come here, friends,' said the stranger. 'You have nothing to fear.'

The ox-herds, scared to death as they were, found this difficult to believe. But Plump-Cheeks decided to obey, and his comrades followed suit.

'Don't forget your oxen,' their host reminded them with an ironic smile.

One of the animals was tired; it bellowed and refused to go any further. However, a few blows on its back with a stick soon changed its mind.

One by one, the peasants clambered up on to the little island. The Oxen shook themselves and were at last able to graze.

'Who is your leader?' asked the bearded man.

'He is,' replied Plump-Cheeks, pointing at Moustache. 'And who are you?'

'You may call me "Afghan".'

The peasants exchanged looks. None of them knew the word.

'What's an Afghan?' asked Plump-Cheeks.

The stranger reached into the pocket of his brown tunic and took out a blue stone. When he held it out to them, the ox-herds saw that it contained flecks of what looked like gold. The marvel dazzled them.

'That must be worth a fortune,' breathed Plump-Cheeks. 'It looks like lapis-lazuli.'

'There is nothing more beautiful,' agreed the Afghan. 'Where have you seen a stone like this before?'

'My cousin was a priest of Ptah. When he died, his colleagues gave him a heart-scarab made from lapis-lazuli, and I was allowed to admire it before it was placed on the mummy. How could I forget something so gorgeous?'

'Lapiz-lazuli comes from my country, Afghanistan. When a pharaoh ruled Egypt, my countrymen delivered it to him in large quantities, in exchange for gold. Only temples were

24

allowed to work it. Today, everything has changed. The Hyksos invaders aren't interested in rites of symbols – or in buying lapis-lazuli, either. They would simply take it, as they take everything else. Because of them, Afghanistan has lost its main source of wealth.'

'So you're an enemy of the Hyksos, are you?'

'I'm the enemy of anyone who impoverishes me. My family owns the main seam of lapis-lazuli. They used to live on a splendid estate, had many servants and owned so many head of livestock that they had lost count of them. Since the loss of the trade with Egypt, they have been living in poverty. Last year my mother died of despair, and I have sworn to take revenge on those responsible for her death.'

'You mean . . . the Hyksos?'

'They have ruined me and condemned my people to poverty. I belong to a race of warriors, who do not tolerate such insults.'

'You'd do better to go home while you can,' advised Plump-Cheeks. 'Pharaoh's army has been wiped out, and there is no longer any opposition at all to the invaders.'

'Aren't you forgetting Thebes?' protested Moustache.

'Thebes?' Plump-Cheeks shook his head. 'That's just a mirage.'

'But isn't it the sacred city of Amon?' asked the Afghan.

'Yes, it is,' said Moustache. 'But nowadays it houses only a queen with no power at all and a few old priests who spend all their time praying – but that's only what people say.'

'You mean it's not true?'

'I hope not,' said Moustache fervently.

'Is there any organized resistance to the Hyksos?' asked the Afghan.

'If there was,' cut in Plump-Cheeks, 'we'd know about it. Why are you so interested, anyway, stranger?'

'You still don't understand, Egyptian. I want to sell my lapis-lazuli, become rich again and restore my tribe's fortunes. That is my only goal, and I shall devote my entire life to it, whatever the risks may be. If the Hyksos had been honest businessmen, I would have come to an understanding with them. But they will never sign a trading-agreement, for they're nothing but lawless predators. There's only one solution: to drive them out and support the return of the pharaohs – a pharaoh would never alter the rules of the game to suit himself.'

Plump-Cheeks burst out laughing. 'You're the funniest man I've ever met, Afghan. I bet nobody gets bored in your country.'

'My father delivered lapis-lazuli to Thebes – and was paid handsomely, I may say. He told me that Amon isn't the only god of the region, that he has an ally, Montu, represented by a bull strong enough to destroy any enemy.'

'The gods have left the Two Lands,' said Moustache sadly.

'Why shouldn't they come back?'

'Because soon there'll be no one left to welcome them.'

'Not even the Prince of Thebes?'

'It's a queen, not a prince, who rules the city, and no one knows if she's still alive.'

'Then the rebellion shall have its birth here,' said the Afghan, 'right here in this marsh.'

'And who's going to start it?' asked Plump-Cheeks worriedly.

'Those of you who agree to help me.'

'But . . . You're completely mad!'

'Any enemy can be beaten – especially if he thinks he's invincible. Just one little wasp causes great pain to the giant it stings, doesn't it?'

Moustache was intrigued. 'What's your plan?'

'To create a swarm of wasps. But sit yourselves down and let's smoke a plant from my country which relaxes the mind and makes one see things more clearly.'

Abandoning the overcooked fish to Plump-Cheeks – who

guzzled it down in one mouthful, much to the dismay of his comrades the Afghan brought out and lit some little rolls of hashish, which he handed out to the peasants.

'Inhale slowly, and then let the smoke emerge from your nostrils and mouth. Little by little, you will forget your fear.'

At first they all coughed, but they soon got used to it.

'This isn't a marsh, it's a peaceful garden,' declared Plump-Cheeks.

Several of the other ox-herds agreed. Only Moustache seemed to have reservations.

'Smoking this plant doesn't just open the doors to dreams,' said the Afghan. 'It has another quality which will be very useful to us.'

'What quality?' asked Plump-Cheeks, whose pupils had dilated.

'It compels traitors to betray themselves.'

'Really? How does it do that?'

'They lose control, sweat profusely, stammer inconsistent explanations and eventually confess. Confess that they have been spying on their comrades for the Hyksos – as you have, for example.'

'What? Me?' stammered Plump-Cheeks. 'You're saying . . . you're just saying anything that comes into your head.'

'I saw you yesterday with a Hyksos officer,' said the Afghan. 'You took me for a beggar, so you weren't wary of me. You promised him you'd denounce the ox-herds as rebels, one by one, in return for a reward.'

Looks of hatred were turned on Plump-Cheeks.

'No, that's not true, comrades – at least, not completely. You don't understand. I lied to the officer, of course, I'd never betray you and—'

Vengeful hands seized him by the hair and plunged him face down into the marsh. He struggled for a few moments, then his corpse sank down into the mud.

'Now,' declared the Afghan, 'we can talk safely about the

Christian Jacq

future. All of us here present shall become rebels. In doing so we'll be risking arrest, torture and death. But if we win we shall become very rich men.'

28

6

As Queen Teti and Princess Ahhotep left the palace, protected by Laughter, a young man stepped into their path.

'I'm the one who did it,' he declared proudly.

To Ahhotep's surprise, Laughter did not bare his teeth.

'My names is Seqen, Princess, and it was I who freed your dog so that he could come to your aid. Seeing him tied up made me realize you were in danger. So I did what I could.'

Seqen was clearly very nervous, and delivered his speech in a great hurry. He was a rather thin young fellow, scarcely older than Ahhotep, and his only obvious assets were his piercing eyes, which drew attention away from an unattractive face and an oversized forehead.

'Well done,' said Ahhotep. 'You saved Her Majesty's life.'

'And yours, too, Princess.'

'But you should bow before the Queen of Egypt.'

The young man did so, rather awkwardly.

'Stand up straight,' ordered Teti. 'I have not see you at the palace before, my boy. Where do you live?'

'On the southern outskirts of the city. I came here from the country to learn how to fight.'

'Have you been accepted into the army?' asked Ahhotep eagerly.

'Unfortunately not. It seems I'm not strong enough. So I

have found work as a gardener's assistant. The gardener works me hard, and that pleases me a lot because soon I'll have the strong muscles I need.'

'How did you know Laughter is my dog?'

'The gardener told me,' said Seqen. 'He advised me to go home and forget that I had seen the guards' commander tie it to a tree.'

The dog placed an enormous front paw on Seqen's chest and almost knocked him over. It seems that Laughter's memory was not short.

Ahhotep said, 'I don't suppose your lodgings are very pleasant.'

'I am not unhappy, Princess. The widow who rents a room to me is a charming old lady, and I love listening to her talk about the happy times.'

'If her Majesty consents, from now on you shall live in a house belonging to the palace, and you will take charge of the poultry, the cats, the stewards' donkeys and, of course, my dog.'

Seqen looked thunderstruck. 'Princess, I . . .'

'Agreed,' said Teti.

'You are to begin immediately,' said Ahhotep. 'Laughter needs a long walk.'

Still in a state of shock, the young man scarcely felt the dog's thick pink tongue gently licking his hand.

'Laughter does not like being on a leash,' added the princess, 'but take one anyway, in case he meets someone unpleasant. He is rather demonstrative, and he is not used to hiding his feelings.'

For the moment, Ahhotep was in the queen's good graces. Not only had Teti not sent her away, but she had even listened to her daughter's plans for reforming the Theban government and making preparations for the reconquest of Egypt. How right, the princess thought, she had been to embark upon this adventure. By the sheer power of her own belief, she would awaken sleeping forces and give Teti back her will for victory.

'Where shall we begin, Majesty?' she asked.

'With the most important thing of all.'

'Are we going to appoint a commander-in-chief at last?'

'No, I'm talking about something vital,' said Teti.

'What could be more important today than a good leader and a good army?'

'Today, just as it was yesterday and will be tomorrow, the most important thing is the temple. If you persist in this insane struggle, you must enter its heart. But it is not without danger.'

'I am ready to take any risk.'

'The ancient pharaohs built dwellings for the gods and knew how to converse with them. Compared to those giants, we are less than dwarves.'

Ahhotep was undaunted, even though she could tell that the ordeal the queen was evoking would be formidable.

'Giving up would not be cowardice,' said Teti.

'How should I prepare myself?'

'In a different age, you would have had leisure to converse with wise men. But today time is short.'

Ahhotep had never heard her mother speak with such authority.

'I shall follow where you lead, Majesty.'

Ever since the golden age of the great pyramids, the Theban site had been held sacred; but not until the rule of Senusret I did Karnak become a temple worthy of that name,* although

* It was pharaohs of the Middle Kingdom, the Montuhoteps, who founded Karnak or, more likely, developed an ancient shrine erected on the site. Amenemhat I (1991–1962 BC) built a temple there, then Senusret I (1962–1928 BC) created remarkable monuments which we shall recall. The celebrated and magnificent 'white temple' still exists, rebuilt using stone blocks found in the third pylon at Karnak.

it was still much less imposing than the buildings at Iunu, Memphis or Elephantine.

The Hyksos invasion had interrupted building work on the temple. Since Pharaoh no longer ruled, the construction sites had been closed; like other shrines, however magnificent, modest Karnak was sinking into a deathly sleep.

In fact, according to the sages' teachings every building was to be regarded as a living being, in a perpetual state of growth; therefore each king must continue and augment the work of his predecessors, and no temple could ever be considered finished.

But the craftsmen's tools no longer made the stones ring, and not a single stone-cutter was at work. The only people living at Karnak were four 'Servants of God', four ritualists and ten 'Pure Priests', whose job was to carry out basic tasks; all were so old and so uninterested in the outside world that they had not ventured beyond the wall of sun-baked brick for several years.

Teti halted before the temple's main door, which was made of Phoenician cedar-wood. 'It is so long since it was opened to bring out the god's statue,' she said sorrowfully. 'And so long since a pharaoh celebrated the dawn ritual to awaken the divine energy. Yet Amon is still present, because a few of the faithful still worship him.'

'What danger could possibly threaten me in a place of peace and meditation like this?' asked Ahhotep in surprise.

'Do you know the name of the goddess who is the Wife of Amon?'

'Yes, Mut, the universal mother.'

'Her name also means "death",' revealed the queen, 'so she is represented as a terrifying, raging lioness. Her statue contains all the forces of destruction that we have failed to dispel since the invasion.'

'Why don't we use them against the Hyksos?'

'Because they would destroy everything in their path, Thebes included.'

'And yet it is Mut whom I must confront?'

'Only if you wish it, Ahhotep. No other power can make it possible for you to fight an enemy whom you have no chance of defeating. Alas, this power is too violent to be mastered.'

So, thought Ahhotep, that was why her mother had brought her to the temple: to make her see how foolish her plans were. Aloud, she said, 'You wanted to teach me a lesson, didn't you?'

'Surely you are intelligent enough to realize that your rebellion will lead only to bloody failure?'

Ahhotep stared at the temple wall for a long time. 'Are you forbidding me to confront Mut?'

Teti stood very still. 'So my warnings were in vain.'

'I want to fight, Majesty. And if a goddess can help me I must not refuse her help.'

'You are mad, child! Mut will destroy you.'

'It would be a fine fate to die by a goddess's hand.'

Resignedly, the queen led Ahhotep to a little door guarded by a Pure Priest, and told him, 'Take the princess to Mut.'

'Majesty, surely you are not serious?'

'Obey.'

'But you know that—'

'Such is the will of Princess Ahhotep, and no one will make her change her mind.'

Visibly shaken, the Pure Priest took off the princess's shoes, then washed her hands and feet with water from the sacred lake. When he had finished, he said, 'I must tell the High Priest. Wait for me here.'

The thought of exploring the interior of the Karnak temple delighted Ahhotep, though the fear of facing Mut was strong within her breast.

'Farewell, my daughter,' said Teti sadly. 'At least you will not know the humiliation of the final wave of Hyksos invasion as it submerges Thebes.'

'Do you really think I have no chance?'

'Farewell, Ahhotep. May eternity treat you gently,' and she kissed her daughter tenderly.

As the queen was leaving, an old man who walked with a stick appeared. He came slowly over to Ahhotep and asked her, 'Are you the princess who dares defy the goddess with eyes of flame?'

'I am not defying her,' said Ahhotep. 'I wish to beg for her strength.'

'Have you lost your mind?'

'Quite the reverse. This is the only rational way of enabling Thebes to regain its dignity and courage.'

'You have both – but you lack self-awareness.'

'Are priests always so talkative?'

The old man gripped the head of his stick. 'As you wish, Princess. Face the bloodthirsty lioness, since that is your decision. But, before you do, behold the sun for the last time.'

7

For a moment, Ahhotep was simply a frightened girl, daunted by the thought of losing her life in an insane venture. But as soon as she saw the old priest's ironic smile she forgot her fears.

She said, 'The sacred songs say that the sun will rise every morning for the just, don't they?'

'Would you claim to be among the just, Princess?' asked the priest.

'Yes, because my only wish is to free my country from the Hyksos.'

'Then follow me.' Leaning heavily on his stick, the Servant of God led her past a magnificent limestone shrine whose breathtakingly perfect carvings were dedicated to the regeneration festival of Senusret I. There Pharaoh communed with the gods, who gave him the vital power to transform the One into many and thus create the provinces of Egypt, at once diverse and indivisible.

'I would like to stop here for a few moments,' said Ahhotep.

'There is no time.'

With regret, Ahhotep followed the priest to a formal garden in front of the main Karnak temple, which was formed from two porticoes built by Senusret I. One had square pillars; the other had pillars supporting colossal statues of

35

Osiris, his arms folded across his chest and holding the sceptres of resurrection.

Here, before the Hyksos invasion, the king had acted as 'Master of the Accomplishment of Rites', and at dawn each day he had awoken the Hidden God, Amon, who was one with Rā, the primeval creative Light.

'Gaze upon the eternal East which is present upon this earth, Princess, the isle of the flame where, without human involvement, Ma'at continues to vanquish injustice, evil and chaos.'

'Then all is not lost,' breathed Ahhotep.

'No pharaoh has been crowned since the Two Lands became prisoners of darkness. That is why this temple works alone, as though we no longer existed. No one, today, knows how to master the magic of the gods.'

'Why does no one try?'

'Because Mut has erected insurmountable barriers. Owing to our cowardice and incompetence, she who was our mother has become our death.'

'And you accept this defeat without protest?'

'We are only ritualists, Princess; we cannot alter destiny. If you dare enter this shrine, you will not come out again. The fire of Mut's anger will consume you, and all that will remain of you will be ashes.'

Ahhotep was fascinated by the noble statues of Osiris, proof of the triumph of life over death. The divine power itself had guided the sculptor's hands.

The young woman walked towards the central gateway of pink granite.

'Go no further, Princess,' implored the priest.

'My mother has bidden me farewell. Since I am already dead in her eyes, I have nothing left to fear.'

When Ahhotep entered the temple, the old man turned and went back to his official house, beside the sacred lake. To see youth and beauty sacrificed like this caused him anguish, but he could do nothing to save her.

36

*

Silence. True silence, without a whisper, without a breath.

Ahhotep had stepped into an unknown universe where limestone and granite reigned. She was encouraged to continue on her way by wall-carvings depicting the coronation of Pharaoh, whose name was written on the tree of life. True, the offertory tables were empty, but the food engraved in the stone continued to feed the invisible power. And the golden ship, on its plinth, sailed into realms inaccessible to humankind.

Yes, this temple was intensely alive, beyond misfortune and baseness. It exuded power in its own right, the power of its enclosed world, and Ahhotep had the feeling that she was an intruder whom it would reject quickly and with great violence.

But she did not turn and run away. Perhaps her very presence had broken the spell condemning Thebes to immobility.

Ahhotep walked through another granite gateway and into a pillared hall partially open to the sky. A diffuse, almost unreal light shone there, conducive to meditation. The place was so peaceful that she no longer wished to leave. Surely, she thought, true happiness was to be found here, at the heart of these living stones. All she had to do was sit down, forget outside reality and allow time to annihilate itself.

The first trap!

Ahhotep leapt to her feet, furious with herself for being so lethargic. An old sage, in the evening of his life, might have the right to savour a moment like this, but she most certainly did not.

Forcing herself to be alert, the princess pushed open the door of the roofed temple, which lay in darkness. Instinctively aware of stepping into another world whose laws were unknown to her, she halted on the threshold and bowed before the Invisible One.

'My father Amon,' she prayed, 'I know you have not abandoned us. But why does your voice not ring out?'

The only answer was silence. But it was not the silence of the dumb, for Ahhotep sensed a presence like that of a landscape which spoke to the soul, using words only a loving heart could hear. The shrine was becoming accustomed to her; it was not driving her away.

At that moment, the princess hesitated.

She did not know the words of power that would permit her to open the doors of the three inner shrines and see the gods embodied in their statues. If she did not conduct the proper rituals, would she profane the temple?

Opening these final doors might unleash a destructive fire which would ravage Thebes more viciously than any invasion. But turning back seemed an even more unforgivable form of defeat and, besides, it would mean she would never know if the gods' powers would have consented to become her allies.

Ahhotep thought hard. The central shrine must be reserved for Amon, who would remain veiled in mystery until his city was victorious; so one of the other doors must be Mut's. She chose the one to the right of the Hidden God. She broke the seal and drew the bolt slowly across.

Then she hesitated. The legends told of formidable guardians with the faces of crocodiles or snakes, who cut off the heads of the curious with a single slash of their knives. But, she told herself, they were no crueller than the Hyksos – and at least she would die at the heart of an intact temple, in a place which had not been violated.

Ahhotep pushed open the door of the shrine.

In terror, she saw the lioness about to spring on her and devour her. But the great beast, whose eyes were carved with incredible realism, merely glared at her ferociously.

'I come in peace, O Mut,' she prayed. 'Grant me your strength, so that Thebes may at last fight against the empire of darkness.'

Falling from a skylight in the roof-slabs above, a ray of light lit up the granite statue, which was taller than the princess. On Mut's robe were five-pointed stars, drawn inside a circle. The goddess held a gold sceptre, whose head was that of the god Set, while the other end was shaped like a fork.

It was the *Was*, the sceptre of power that had given the Theban province its name of Waset, 'the Powerful'. Ahhotep gazed in awe at the sacred emblem of Amon's city, which only the gods had the skill to wield.

'Mut, will you permit me to use this sceptre?'

The lioness's eyes grew red.

'I will make good use of it, I swear.'

But the moment she tried to take the *Was* from Mut's hand, a terrible sensation of burning made her let go. And the lioness's mouth opened wide to devour the helpless girl.

'You must eat at least something, Majesty,' urged Qaris.

'My daughter has gone to her death, and you wish me to eat!'

'Perhaps the goddess will have taken pity on her youth and beauty.'

'Do you really think the flame of Mut feels that kind of emotion?'

The steward hung his head. Ahhotep had been the last smile of a dying royal court. Without her, Teti the Small would soon lay down her crown, and the supporters of the Hyksos would at last offer up Thebes to the invaders.

Since he could not help the queen, Qaris withdrew. As he was leaving the queen's apartments, he bumped into Seqen, with Laughter beside him.

'A priest from Karnak wishes to see Her Majesty,' said Seqen.

'I shall inform her.'

Teti received the grim-faced old priest immediately.

'Quickly, speak!' she ordered.

'The gods are the gods, Majesty, and no one can transgress their laws.'

'My daughter . . .?'

'Did she not know how dangerous her insane actions were?'

The queen almost collapsed in tears, but forced herself to remain composed and dignified, as her office demanded.

'No matter what state her corpse is in, I want to see it. And I shall conduct the funeral ceremonies myself.'

8

Apophis was justly proud of Avaris,* the capital of the Hyksos Empire. It was by far the largest city not only in Egypt but in all the neighbouring lands, too. Dominated by an impregnable citadel, the mere sight of which was enough to deter would-be attackers, it occupied a strategic position as the north-eastern gateway to the Delta. It was built on the eastern bank of the 'waters of Ra', at the junction of the roads and waterways that gave access to the eastern end of the ocean, and to Syria, Canaan and Lower Egypt. To the north, an opening in the vast drainage system created by the ancients at the heart of a succession of lakes made it possible to join the Path of Horus, which led to Sinai.

Controlling Avaris meant ruling the world.

As soon as the Hyksos arrived, the town's foreign inhabitants had given them enthusiastic support. And the new masters of the land had given the monuments and the Egyptian quarter as pasture to the sand-travellers, sworn enemies of pharaonic power.

The new principal temple was dedicated to Set, god of thunder and lightning, the expression of absolute, invincible

* In Egyptian *Hut-Waret*, 'the Castle of the Sloping Land' or 'the Royal Foundation of the District'; the city covered more than 250 hectares.

power. Concluding that violence was the best policy, the Hyksos had wiped out a thousand-year-old civilization. It was from Set's unfettered power that Apophis drew the ability to vanquish any enemy.

From the heights of the citadel, he gazed down upon the streets, which were laid out at right-angles. This rigid arrangement made it easier to keep watch on the various groups of houses, the least ugly of which were reserved for high-ranking soldiers.

The river port of Avaris, the largest in Egypt, was home to both warships and merchant craft, whose incessant to-ing and fro-ing had turned the bustling city into the trading centre of the Hyksos Empire.

In Apophis's eyes, nothing was more beautiful than the formidable citadel, whose buttressed walls were nearly twenty cubits thick at their base. He loved to climb to the top of the watchtower that guarded the northern approach to the fortress, and gaze out over his domain. He, who had risen from nothing, an Asian of no family or fortune, had become the master of Egypt, and his sphere of influence was growing by the day.

A small smile lit up his ugly face when his eyes rested on the tree-filled garden in the inner courtyard, sheltered by the fortifications. It had been a whim of his wife, an Egyptian woman from the Delta, a willing supporter of the Hyksos and one who loathed her fellow Egyptians.

Soon, Apophis would receive foreign envoys from the four corners of the empire. They would prostrate themselves before him, acknowledging his supremacy and his dazzling success. This happy event would be accompanied by a spectacular announcement, which would raise him to the summit of fame.

As luck would have it, the night was pitch black and the port of Avaris lay cloaked in darkness. Clouds hid the waxing moon and, if he were not to get lost, a man needed a good knowledge of the area where the grain silos stood.

The Hunchback had been born there, and he knew every nook and cranny of the district. Goods had once been freely exchanged there – without the knowledge of the tax-collectors. The pharaohs' rule had been bad enough, but Hyksos rule was turning out to be downright disastrous. It bled workers dry, reducing them to utter poverty.

A talented trader, the Hunchback had set up a secret market which the Hyksos knew nothing about. Nor did they know that his fabrics, sandals and ointments were destined – albeit in inadequate quantities – for the last free city in Egypt: Thebes.

Although his mother was Syrian, the Hunchback adored Egypt and hated the invaders, a set of drunkards who brought the common people closer to destruction each day, and who thought of nothing but strengthening their dictatorship. Living in Avaris was becoming a nightmare.

So when a man from Edfu, a town in Upper Egypt which was loyal to the Theban cause, had contacted the Hunchback to try and deliver grain to the resistance, the Hunchback had responded with enthusiasm. The first consignment was due to leave tonight, on an old boat which, according to its documentation, was carrying pots. The crew were trust-worthy, apart from a Canaanite oarsman who would be killed during the journey.

It was many long years since the Hunchback had been so elated. At last, a few Egyptians were showing their heads above the parapet. They were a pitiful minority, it was true, but their first success would undoubtedly bring in other recruits.

The Hunchback's first task was to open the doors of several adjoining silos, remove some of the grain and send it to Thebes, which was desperately short of supplies. And then he must repeat the process as often as possible.

An owl hooted. Or, to be precise, someone imitated the bird's cry.

The Hunchback hooted in reply, stressing the high notes.

The other person responded, accentuating the low notes.

The Hunchback and his contact made their way towards each other.

'Have you got the right keys?' asked the man from Edfu.

'Yes, I have, and all the transport documents are in order. The boat will have no difficulty passing through the military blockades and the great customs post at Khmun.'

'The crew are ready to load the grain. We mustn't waste a moment.'

The two men set off down an alleyway which led to the quayside.

'I don't understand,' exclaimed the Edfu man when they got there. 'The boat's there, right enough, but where are the sailors?'

'Perhaps they've stayed on board,' suggested the Hunchback.

'But my instructions were clear.'

A man appeared on the gangplank, and walked slowly down it. It was the Canaanite sailor.

'Greetings, friends,' he said. 'It's rather late to be wandering around here, don't you think? Tell me, Hunchback, what's that bunch of keys for?'

The Hunchback froze in silent fear.

'It wouldn't by any chance be for opening silos, would it? That's a serious crime, you know. And your friend there, might he be that man from Edfu who's trying to rally poor madmen to the Theban cause? Oh yes, no doubt you're wondering about the crew. They've all been arrested and will be executed at dawn in front of the citadel.'

The Hunchback and his ally tried to run, but fifty Hyksos soldiers barred their way.

An officer put wooden shackles on them, then spat in their faces.

'You halfwits!' exclaimed the Canaanite. 'Did you really think for one moment that you'd escape Apophis's watchful eye?'

'Others will take our place,' retorted the Hunchback.

'Don't fool yourself, cripple. We've identified every single terrorist in your network. By the time the sun is high in the sky, not one of them will be left alive.'

The Canaanite took great pleasure in slitting the throat of the man from Edfu, a cunning troublemaker who had eluded him for three years.

'Kill me too, you coward,' demanded the Hunchback.

The sailor was about to oblige when the soldiers parted to make way for Khamudi.

'My lord,' said the Canaanite, 'what a pleasant surprise. As you can see, my plan has proved a total success.'

'Arrest this traitor,' ordered Khamudi.

'My lord . . . But why?'

'Because you are an accomplice of these rebels.'

'I mingled with them to unmask them,' protested the Canaanite, 'but I followed my instructions to the letter.'

'You became friendly with these people and trafficked with them,' said Khamudi. 'That's why you stabbed the Edfu man – he was about to denounce you.'

'No, my lord, there's been a mistake.'

'Are you daring to tell me I'm wrong?'

'Oh no, my lord. I only meant that—'

'By insulting me, you simply make things worse for yourself,' said Khamudi.

'I swear to you that I'm faithful to our great king, Apophis, that I obeyed my orders, that I—'

'Take him away.'

Ignoring the sailor's cries, the soldiers bound his arms and dragged him away, kicking him as they went.

'What a wonderful night,' remarked Khamudi, running a hand through his black hair, which shone with linseed oil.

'I've had an excellent dinner, and for dessert I'm going to exterminate the pro-Theban rebels. Aren't you pleased, Hunchback?'

'That Canaanite vermin was right. You're very much mistaken.'

Khamudi slapped him. 'Don't be insolent.'

'We shall never stop fighting you.'

'The rebels have been beaten once and for all, and now the people know that they must either collaborate with us or die.'

'And now everyone will know that you infiltrate spies into our networks, and the people will distrust one another. Soon you'll be both blind and deaf.'

Khamudi could happily have smashed the Hunchback's skull there and then, but the man's determination deserved better. 'Do you really believe that?'

'The breath of Amon will sweep the Hyksos away.'

'You have fought in vain and you will die in vain. But before you do you will tell me the names of your accomplices. The palace has some remarkable experts in torture. I strongly advise you to talk before I hand you over to them.'

9

'Majesty, your daughter is alive,' said the palace doctor in astonishment. 'The voice of her heart is deep and regular. I can find no signs at all of serious illness.'

'Alive?' asked Teti, equally astonished. 'Then why does she lie so still?'

'I cannot explain it.'

'There must be a treatment which will wake her.'

'I shall consult the ancient treaties, Majesty.'

'Hurry!'

Ahhotep was stretched out on her bed, her eyes wide open and staring. A ritualist from Karnak had found her lying on the threshold of Mut's shrine, and the priests had carried her body to the guard-post outside the palace.

Teti was not fully reassured by the doctor's amazing diagnosis. If Ahhotep did not emerge from this horrible oblivion, could she really be said to be alive?

A loud thud made her start. There came another, then another, like the sound of a battering-ram hitting the bedchamber door. The queen opened it, and scarcely had time to move out of the way before Laughter rushed in, lay down at the foot of the bed and began to growl. Now no one could go near the princess.

In the paved area between the citadel and the road to the

Temple of Set stood several hundred soldiers in serried ranks. Their breastplates and spears glinted in the sunshine, proud symbols of Hyksos power. The soldiers held back the crowd, who were avid for the spectacle the heralds had promised. A large part of the population of Avaris had gathered there to witness the execution of the last few rebels.

Cheering erupted as Apophis appeared, dressed in a dark-red tunic and followed by the faithful Khamudi. Although the master of the empire was taciturn by nature and had little taste for festivities, he did not mind occasionally being the object of popular adoration.

Given his great plans, this ceremony was highly opportune: no Egyptian would be left in any doubt that supreme power was being exercised with extreme thoroughness.

He turned to Khamudi and asked, 'How many Canaanites did you arrest?'

'Four. They were a good source of information, and enabled us to identify about a hundred rebels.'

'Won't they talk at the moment of death?'

'No risk of that, my lord: I've had their tongues cut out.'

Apophis approved of such efficiency. Khamudi knew how to use his initiative without impinging on his master's absolute power.

'Did the Hunchback talk?'

'Half an hour of torture was all it took.'

'Anything interesting?'

'Nothing we didn't already know, only confirmation of a few names.'

'So all resistance has at last been eradicated,' said Apophis.

'There are no more organized groups of rebels, either in Avaris or in the Delta. There may be a few isolated individuals who'll try to regroup, but informers and the measures I've taken will enable us to destroy them.'

The headsmen had finished sharpening their axes, and

were waiting for Apophis to address the crowd.

Like Khamudi, Apophis hated the sun and the heat, which made his legs swell up, whereas Khamudi suffered from palpitations. So the master of the empire's speech was extremely short.

'People of Avaris, these infamous criminals tried to undermine Hyksos rule. They are about to be executed before your eyes, and the same fate awaits anyone who follows their miserable example. Obey me, and you will have nothing to fear.'

At a signal from the officers, the crowd raised another cheer for Apophis, who withdrew while the headsmen raised their axes.

The Hunchback was the first to be beheaded. He died roaring the name 'Thebes!'

The executioners gathered up the heads and corpses, ready for throwing to the vultures. No Egyptian had a right to mummification, however perfunctory.

The Afghan and his little band had watched the slaughter with mounting horror.

Moustache was on the verge of tears. 'You see?' he said. 'The Hyksos are more ferocious than monsters of the desert. No one will ever defeat them.'

'Don't let yourself give way to despair,' urged the Afghan. 'They have the upper hand for the moment, but they must inevitably have weak points.'

'But you saw—'

'Watching that hideous spectacle was necessary. We must harden ourselves, and be aware at all times of the perils that lie in wait for us.'

'I'm not a warrior,' said Moustache miserably.

'But I am – and you will become one. I want to get rich, and you want to avenge your people and drive out the invaders. Our interests converge. That's what matters.'

49

Christian Jacq

Showing no emotion, the employees of the Temple of Set washed down the bloodied flagstones with bucketfuls of water.

From the doctor's dejected expression, Teti knew straight away that he had not found a remedy.

'I am sorry, Majesty,' he said, 'but the princess's case is beyond my skill.'

'Have you consulted the priests at Karnak?'

'They are quite clear: your daughter acted very imprudently.'

'Is there no incantation against the fate Mut has dispensed?'

'None that I know of.'

'If Ahhotep does not eat,' said Teti despairingly, 'she will die.'

'The princess's constitution is exceptionally strong.'

'There must be a magician somewhere who can break through this trance.'

'Perhaps so, but beware of charlatans, Majesty. The fact is that, with all our learning, we cannot cure the princess.'

'Get out of here!'

Affronted, the doctor bowed stiffly and left.

Laughter still stood guard, refusing all food. Even the queen could not go near Ahhotep.

Qaris came in and bowed. 'Your bedchamber is prepared for the night, Majesty,' he said.

'I shall stay here.'

'Majesty, you must rest.'

'Ahhotep might need me.'

'Am I to bring you a bed?'

'A chair with arms will suffice.'

'Majesty . . .' The steward looked distraught.

'What is it, Qaris?'

'There are rumours being spread by sailors . . . It seems

50

that appalling things have been happening in Avaris. But perhaps you would rather not know?'

'Tell me.'

10

Whenever despair filled her heart, Teti the Small put on her face-paint. If her daughter died, she would have no further reason to continue a fight which was doomed to failure before it began – Qaris's revelations had proved that.

Forcing herself to recall the rare moments of happiness she had known, the queen reached into an oval basket and took out a wooden comb, an alabaster needle for untangling hair, a face-paint applicator and a mother-of-pearl shell, in which she mixed unguents. She had almost exhausted her reserves of the luxurious cosmetics that had once taken the temple laboratories forty days to manufacture.

Teti's favourite ointment was based on crushed galenite. It cleansed her skin and protected it from the sun, while accentuating her delicate features; it also repelled insects. In happier days, skilled experts would have painted her face, arranged her hair, and tended her hands and feet. Today Teti's own fingers smoothed red ochre over her lips.

The door burst open and Qaris said breathlessly, 'Majesty, come quickly!'

'Qaris, how dare you—'

'Forgive my intrusion, but the princess—'

Teti leapt to her feet. 'Ahhotep? No, Ahhotep mustn't die, not so young!'

Qaris beamed at her. 'The princess has woken up, Majesty.'

The queen was rooted to the spot. 'Don't lie to me, Qaris. That would be too cruel.'

'Come and see, Majesty, I beg you.'

Feeling as though she were sleepwalking, Teti the Small followed her steward.

Ahhotep was sitting naked on her bed – Qaris hastily averted his eyes – stroking Laughter's head while he licked his paws assiduously. 'Where is the goddess's sceptre?' she asked, in a strange voice.

'Ahhotep . . . You're alive!'

The princess looked at her mother in astonishment. 'Of course I'm alive. You, on the other hand, look nearly dead with exhaustion.'

'Mut . . .'

'She was harsh with me, but I was able to touch the *Was*.'

'According to the priests at Karnak,' said Qaris slowly, 'the goddess has taken back her possession, Princess. It is truly a wonder that you emerged from such a deep trance.'

'We need the *Was* in order to fight, I'm sure of it.' Ahhotep got to her feet.

Teti covered her daughter's magnificent nakedness with a linen tunic and gave her water to drink. 'Don't you feel dizzy?' she asked.

'I feel perfectly well, Mother. If Mut's flame didn't burn me to death, if it showed me the path to true power, that must surely be because I am to be entrusted with a mission.'

'Don't be so eager to fight,' said Teti.

'Why not?'

'Because there's no room left for hope.'

Ahhotep took the queen by the shoulders. 'I want to know everything.'

'Are you really sure?'

'I've risked my life and I'll risk it again. Don't keep anything more from me.'

Teti sighed. 'As you wish. Qaris, you may speak.'

Christian Jacq

'Why Qaris? Why can't you tell me yourself?'

'Because I entrusted him with gathering information from our last supporters in the occupied lands.'

Ahhotep was astounded. 'You, Qaris? You took on such dangerous work?'

'I am wholly at the service of the queen and our country,' declared the steward proudly.

'Then you, like me, must believe victory is still possible.'

Sadness filled Qaris's eyes.

'Speak honestly,' said Teti.

'The words of the sages have fled,' lamented the steward, 'and the gods no longer recognize Egypt. The ships of day and night no longer sail; the sun's course has been disturbed, and in the end it will leave us for ever. Ma'at no longer rules the Two Lands, every province is desolate, and evil has imposed its tyranny everywhere.'

'These are nothing but gloomy words,' protested Ahhotep. 'The only thing that matters is the facts.'

'The traditional way of life no longer functions, Princess. Supplies of food no longer reach the temples, and even when they do, redistribution cannot be guaranteed any more. Those who produce food and all the other things we need are now earning nothing. The only ones who are making any money are the middle-men, who are in the pay of the Hyksos. The weaving-workshops are closed, linen robes are no longer made, we have no wigs or even sandals. Uncleanliness is no longer outlawed, so washermen refuse to play their trade; moreover, bakers refuse to bake bread and brewers to make beer. The thief has become rich, injustice is triumphant.'

'This distress is only temporary – and we still have Thebes.'

'But our city stands alone and isolated, Princess.'

'How can you be certain of that?'

'I shall show you.'

The steward led the queen and her daughter to a small,

sparsely furnished room next to his bedchamber. He drew back a curtain to reveal a wooden model laid out on a low table.

'It's amazing!' exclaimed Ahhotep. 'That lotus flower is the Delta, Lower Egypt . . . and that waving stalk, that's the Nile Valley, Upper Egypt. And right down there, south of Swenet, is Nubia.'

'You can see every province, with its capital and its temples,' observed Teti. 'The surveyors and map-makers have done well. Thanks to our informants, we have been able to follow the enemy's progress.'

'Thebes is still free,' said Ahhotep. 'That's what matters.'

'Thebes is only a tiny island of freedom,' Qaris corrected her. 'The Hyksos control all the Northern provinces, they occupy Memphis, the country's main trading-centre, and they have set up a guard-post at Khmun to control trade.'

'Has the sacred city of Abydos fallen into their hands?'

'That is likely, Princess. Even more worryingly, Kebet, two days' march north of Thebes, is no safer, while at Per-Hathor, a day's march to the south, the Hyksos have built a new fortress.'

'In other words,' said Ahhotep, 'we are surrounded. But haven't we a loyal ally, Edfu, further south?'

'The governor, Emheb, is indeed loyal, but is he still alive? As for Elephantine, the capital of the first province of Upper Egypt and the border town with Nubia, she labours under the enemy yoke.'

'The Nubians are whole-hearted allies of the Hyksos,' added Teti, 'and the Hyksos are constantly expanding their empire. We no longer receive gold from Nubia or pines from Phoenicia. We cannot organize trading expeditions or go to the quarries, for the Hyksos control all means of communication.'

'Is there not one single province loyal to Thebes?' asked Ahhotep.

'They have been broken down into small principalities,' explained Qaris, 'and each local ruler has to obey a Hyksos officer who commands a local force. Apophis has succeeded in spinning a spider's web from which no town or city can escape.'

'Thebes is doomed,' concluded the queen. 'She will suffocate to death – unless Apophis decides to crush her beneath his heel.'

'But we can still grow and distribute our own food, can't we?'

'The management of food supplies has become so deplorable that we shall soon go hungry, and no one seems able to halt the decline,' said Teti.

'Up till now I have held out a desperate hope,' confessed Qaris. 'But our last group of secret supporters has just been wiped out, and we can no longer gather the information we need. We are deaf and blind: how can we possibly fight?'

'This is the end,' said Teti, and her steward agreed with a nod.

Ahhotep walked slowly round the model, studying it closely. 'It is the end of our inactivity,' she declared. 'It is because we haven't tried to do anything that we're in danger of being wiped out.'

'But the reality, Princess—'

'We don't know what the reality is, Qaris – at least, not completely. Our information is fragmentary, and I can't believe that not one single group of supporters has survived. Some of them must have, and we must make contact with them. But, above all, we must have the *Was*.'

11

Teti went pale. 'Ahhotep! Surely you wouldn't dare confront Mut again?'

'I have no choice, Mother.'

'She will never agree to give you her sceptre! This time her fire will utterly destroy you, you can be sure of that.'

'Death is better than cowardice.'

'There might perhaps be another solution,' suggested Qaris.

Ahhotep's face lit up. 'What do you have in mind?'

'We always say that only gods can wield the *Was*, but in fact there is one exception: the blind soothsayer who re-establishes the correct location of the boundary stones between fields after each annual flood. Because he acts as the interpreter of divine righteousness and therefore cannot show favour to anyone, he has the right to wield a staff shaped like the *Was*. But whether it has the same powers . . .'

'Where can I find this man?'

'I do not know, Princess. He has not carried out his duties for several years, which is why there are now so many lawsuits. Today, the strong abuse the weak, and falsehood triumphs.'

'Stop lamenting, Qaris! Which secretariat employs him?'

'The land registry.'

'We shall go there at once.'

*

The land registry, which stood not far from the temple at Karnak, was a sorry sight. Most of its whitewashed mud-brick buildings looked on the point of falling down. There was no sign of anyone at work, only wild dogs which ran away when Ahhotep and Qaris approached.

'Is there anybody here?' shouted Qaris.

A gust of wind was the only answer, a gust so powerful that two branches of an old tamarisk broke with an ominous cracking which made him jump.

'We ought to leave, Princess.'

'But . . . who is dealing with the registration of land?'

'No one, as you can see. Complaints pile up, but nothing is done about them.'

'Why doesn't the minister for agriculture do something?'

'He's like everyone else. All he thinks of is safeguarding his last few privileges.'

Ahhotep clenched her fists. 'He must be thrown into prison immediately.'

'First he would have to be tried,' objected Qaris, 'and proved incompetent. But he would bribe the jurors, so even that would not be enough.'

Suddenly the wild dogs began to bark, and formed a menacing circle round them. When Qaris tried to break the circle, one of the dogs bared its teeth and he had to back away.

'If they attack,' he said nervously, 'how can we defend ourselves?'

'For now they are content, as long as we show them respect,' said Ahhotep. 'Whatever we do, we mustn't move.'

An old man emerged from the main registry building and walked very slowly towards the intruders. He had sparse hair and a bony face, and wore a long kilt which had once been costly and impressive. In his right hand, he held a gnarled staff.

'Who are you?' he asked sternly.

'I am Princess Ahhotep, and my companion is Steward Qaris.'

'Ahhotep? Queen Teti's daughter?'

'The very same. And who are you?'

'I am the keeper of the dogs that guard the registry, to prevent thieves stealing documents.'

'Are you daring to call us thieves?' demanded Ahhotep.

'Go back to your palace, Princess. There's nothing here but old scrolls and tablets.'

'And yet you risk your life to protect them.'

The man smiled sadly. 'My life has lost all meaning, Princess, since I can no longer carry out my craft.'

Ahhotep scrutinized the old man closely. 'You . . . you're blind!'

'Yes, from birth.'

'Are you also a soothsayer?'

'Indeed I am, the last blind soothsayer in Thebes. For many years, I restored to their rightful places the boundary stones the flood had moved. But in those days justice reigned. Today there is no place for me.'

Ahhotep walked between two dog, which merely whimpered, and touched the blind man's hands. 'Have you still got the staff known as "Fearsome", which only you can wield?'

'It is my most precious possession.'

'Will you entrust it to me?'

'I cannot see you, Princess, but I know that you are beautiful, very beautiful. Why should you risk destroying yourself?'

'Because I want to set Egypt free.'

'To set Egypt free? Wait here.'

Without hesitation, the blind man turned, walked quickly to a wooden hut roofed with papyrus stems, and went inside. When he emerged a few minutes later, he was holding a strange wooden sceptre-like staff; at the sight of it the dogs ran off.

'Let us sit down on the bench over there,' said the soothsayer.

Ahhotep gazed in fascination at the staff.

The old man explained. 'The head of this sacred staff is that of Set, with eyes of fire. It is he who sees the correct path, removes obstacles from it and strikes down falsehood. But the god charges a high price for his services. Any man vain enough to think he could master Set's power would be destroyed by the heavens' wrath. No one may use the gods for his own gain, especially not Set, for he dominates the powers of heaven and earth.'

'I need him,' declared Ahhotep. 'With his sceptre to guide it, my army will be victorious.'

'Set's will is unpredictable, Princess. He has become accustomed to my hand, not yours.'

'I am prepared to take that risk.'

'My lady, that is madness!'

'The only madness is to grovel before the invader.'

The soothsayer got to his feet, and Ahhotep followed suit.

'Turn round, Princess.'

The old man bound her eyes with a strip of linen, took her hands and led her to a fallow field.

'The owner of this field died a month ago,' he said. 'The flood carried away the boundary stones, and his heirs are tearing each other to pieces. I had not meant to intervene, because my skills have not been registered by a palace official. But today things are different, since you are ready to attempt the adventure and Steward Qaris's testimony will carry official status. But are you absolutely sure you want to do this?'

'Don't, Princess,' begged Qaris. 'The Staff of Set is filled with an energy which may well destroy you.'

Ahhotep shook her head. 'The blindfold will protect me from attack. Give me the staff, soothsayer.'

'If it permits you to hold it, Princess, be guided by it.'

Ahhotep did not falter, but took a firm grip of the staff. It was so burning hot that she let out a cry of pain. But she did not let go – and suddenly she saw a night sky, in which one star shone more brightly than the others. She went towards it, and it dimmed.

Three more times, the same thing happened. And each time, she followed the star. All at once the sky and the burning disappeared, and the blindfold fell away.

'The telling of the land has been carried out according to the laws of heaven,' declared the old man. 'The boundaries of this field have once again been properly established. Let Princess Ahhotep keep the Staff of Set and do the same for all Egypt.'

12

The sky was dark above the Temple of Set at Avaris. Serried ranks of clouds had drifted in from the north, threatening the Hyksos capital with a storm.

The city's principal temple was very different from the majestic Egyptian ones. It was built of brick rather than stone, and dedicated to the god of thunder and to Hadad, the Syrian storm-god. Before the temple stood a rectangular altar, surrounded by oak-trees and by ditches full of the whitened bones of sacrificed animals.

It was here that ten conspirators had agreed to meet. The most eminent of them was no less a person than the commander of Apophis's personal bodyguard. After long and careful discussion, he had succeeded in bringing together a Canaanite general, officers from Anatolia, and the lady Aberia, daughter of a Cyprian father and a Greek mother, who had been ordered by the tyrant to force prosperous Egyptian women into slavery.

All held important positions and had become rich by serving Egypt's new master unquestioningly. But in the months since Khamudi had risen to become Apophis's confidant, the situation had changed. The leading lights of the court were losing their influence, and Khamudi was doing everything he could to strengthen his power. True, he had proved his efficiency by destroying the last group of rebels;

but there were whispers that he had taken advantage of the occasion to eliminate those loyal supporters of Apophis whom he thought too ambitious.

And so the commander of the bodyguard had asked himself a troubling question: 'Whose turn will it be next?'

The question had eventually aroused a few people's interest. They all feared that Apophis and Khamudi were preparing to seek out and destroy allies they considered burdensome, who would be replaced by men who had risen from nothing and who were willing to carry out even the vilest tasks. Hence this secret meeting.

The Anatolian officer in charge of training archers made sure that the area was secure. At night, the priests of Set slept in huts far from the temple, watched by guards controlled by one of the conspirators. There really was no better or safer place in which to draw up their plan of action.

'Shall we go into the temple?' suggested the Canaanite general.

'No, let's avoid the gaze of Set,' advised the Asian. 'Let's sit near that altar over there, in the shelter of the trees.'

The conspirators formed a circle.

'I now have reliable information,' said the general. 'Our agents who infiltrated a group of rebels have all been executed by Khamudi, on Apophis's orders.'

The lady Aberia, a statuesque woman with notably long, powerful hands, looked frightened. 'How could that happen?'

'I don't know. But I do know that several courtiers have died suddenly in recent weeks and that they have been replaced by men loyal to Khamudi. They're Libyans and Cyprian and Anatolian pirates – in other words, men who will kill without a moment's hesitation. And I repeat: these are facts, not rumours.'

A worried silence fell.

'Are we to be their next target?' wondered Aberia, still looking alarmed.

'I think so,' replied the general. 'None of us is close to Khamudi, and that is an unpardonable mistake on our part.'

'Why don't we kill him?' suggested an officer.

'It would only bring down Apophis's vengeance upon us.'

'Then we'll just have to kill them both.'

'Surely not,' objected one of his colleagues. 'We should simply tell our leader about Khamudi's plot. That will be enough.'

The general smiled grimly. 'You're forgetting that Khamudi is carrying out Apophis's orders. The truth is that we are all condemned to death.'

'Apophis is beyond our reach.'

'I remind you that I'm the commander of his personal bodyguard,' cut in the Asian. 'Khamudi dislikes me, but Apophis still trusts me.'

'What do you suggest?' asked the general.

'I'll take care of Apophis, and you must deal with Khamudi. The others can deal with the ordinary guards – they'll bow to the will of whoever is strongest. We must act quickly and as one. Our coordination must be perfect and leave nothing to chance.'

'But . . . but supposing we fail?' stammered an officer.

'Unless we do something, we'll simply be slaughtered. It's vital that we take the initiative.'

'Who is to succeed Apophis?' asked Aberia.

The question was met with consternation. The Asian and the general exchanged suspicious looks.

'We have time to wait and see,' suggested another officer.

'That is exactly what we do not have!' snapped the general. 'Improvisation would be fatal. We must choose our leader now, the man who is to replace the tyrant.'

'The more risks each person takes,' said the Asian, 'the greater the reward should be. As commander of Apophis's bodyguard, and the man who will have to kill him, am I not facing the greatest danger of all?'

'No one will deny you your moment of glory,' said the general, 'but ruling the Hyksos Empire will require other qualities, starting with the ability to control the army.'

Several officers nodded their agreement.

'Only the Canaanite soldiers will obey you,' objected the Asian, 'and they're in the minority. Wouldn't the hero who killed Apophis be the best man to unite all factions?'

'Why does it have to be one of you two?' protested an Anatolian officer. 'Our mountain warriors are unequalled, and our troops won't trust anyone but a fellow Anatolian.'

'Why not choose a pirate?' exclaimed the general furiously. 'If we lose our heads before we've even started this delicate operation, we're guaranteed to fail. If we each do what we are good at, we have a chance of succeeding.'

'You're right,' agreed the Asian, 'and the most important thing is for us to remain united.'

An Anatolian officer gave a sudden start. 'I heard something.'

The conspirators froze.

'Go and see,' ordered the general, sliding his dagger out of its sheath.

The officer seemed to be gone for an eternity. Even the Canaanite general found it difficult to breathe.

At last the man returned. 'Nothing to report, sir.'

Everyone breathed a sigh of relief.

'If we cannot reach agreement,' the general went on, 'we might as well give up here and now.'

'That's out of the question,' replied the Asian. 'Things have gone too far, and we must not hesitate now. I shall kill Apophis, the Anatolian officers will take care of Khamudi, and the general will take command of the Hyksos army. Afterwards, we shall call a meeting of senior courtiers and officers and choose our leader.'

'Very well,' nodded the Canaanite, and the other conspirators followed suit.

The moon appeared between two clouds, illuminating Aberia's statuesque figure as she stood up and went over to the general.

'I congratulate you,' she said. 'You persuaded us to embark on this mad adventure, and you've managed to settle our disagreements. For that you deserve a reward.' She laid her hands on his shoulders.

For a moment he thought she was going to kiss him. But, to his horrified surprise, her powerful fingers fastened tightly round his neck.

'Die, you mangy cur!' she hissed.

He fought to escape from this she-devil, but he fought in vain: she was inexorably strangling him.

Sword in hand, the Asian rushed at Aberia, but a volley of arrows plunged into his back, while twenty Cyprian pirates came rushing out of the shadows and fell upon the other conspirators, stabbing them to death with their daggers. The Anatolians fought valiantly, but were overcome by sheer force of numbers.

At the moment when the Canaanite general died, Khamudi appeared, wearing a satisfied smile. 'This is work well done,' he said. 'The plot has been nipped in the bud.'

Aberia spat on the general's corpse, and rubbed her hands. 'Our great king should be well pleased. And I must say, I found it most pleasurable myself.'

13

Apophis stood high on the walls of the citadel, gazing down at the port of Avaris, where sailors were swarming about, unloading a host of boats. The storehouses were bursting with wine, oils, precious woods, bronze and all sorts of other wares, which had turned the Hyksos capital into an exceedingly wealthy city where everything could be bought and sold. Business was booming and people thought only of getting rich, though they always remembered to bow the knee before their new master.

The old pharaonic way, based on redistribution and unity, had been abolished. Soon every province in Egypt would see jars imported from Cyprus, recognizable by their black, polished surface decorated with white incisions. In order to ensure they were imported in large numbers – which would bring him a handsome profit – Apophis had closed the traditional potters' workshops and given the craftsmen to his officers as slaves.

Khamudi came up to him and bowed. 'My lord, it is almost time. Here are the two things you asked for.' He handed Apophis a dagger and a flask.

The dagger had been made by a Mycenaean craftsman. It had a gold handle inlaid with silver lotus flowers, and a triangular bronze blade with a sharp point. The flask had two small handles and was made of blue porcelain. Its surface bore a map of Egypt. The miniaturist had done his work with exceptional skill, even managing to show the location of each province's capital city.

'The dagger makes me invulnerable,' said Apophis. 'It has powers which no enemy can destroy. Remember that, Khamudi, and make sure everyone knows. As for the flask, do you want to know what I'm going to do with it?'

Khamudi was nervous. 'Perhaps there's no need for me to know, my lord.'

'Are you not my faithful servant, the man who will never betray me? Watch.'

With his fingertips, Apophis touched the word 'Avaris' on the flask's surface, and it began to emit a disturbing reddish light.

Khamudi recoiled in terror.

'Don't be afraid, my friend. As you see, all I have to do is lift my finger to control each part of this country exactly as I wish – a country which thought it was protected by the gods. Not one cubit of the land of the pharaohs shall escape me.'

'Not even Thebes?'

Apophis smiled. 'Thebes's madness amuses me, and it's useful, too – for the moment. I know everything that happens there, and not one of its pathetic plans will come to fruition.'

Khamudi saw that the Hyksos emperor was not like other tyrants. Not only did he have a large, powerful army, but he also had supernatural powers, which even the finest warriors had no chance of defeating.

'Today is as important as the day we invaded Egypt,' declared Apophis, his voice icy with menace. 'The Egyptians will at last realize that I am their king and that they must submit to me and abandon hope of regaining their freedom, which they have lost for ever. Eventually, like all slaves, they will come to worship me. Let us begin by receiving the homage of our vassals.'

*

Dressed in a long red robe and a belt decorated with geometrical motifs, Apophis walked slowly into the pillared reception hall, which was crowded with envoys from every country of the Hyksos Empire.

They were all watched closely by Khamudi's men, and if anyone had tried to lift a hand against the emperor he would have been struck down instantly.

Apophis sat down on his throne, a modest chair made from pine-wood. Through his ostentatious simplicity and austerity, he was building up a reputation as a careful administrator of the public good.

The procession of envoys began immediately. One after the other, they laid their countries' riches at Apophis's feet. There were soon heaps of precious stones, pots of priceless ointments, archers' wrist-protectors, breastplates, daggers . . . But Apophis showed not a glimmer of interest, such was his impatience to see the gifts from the Minoan envoy. The Great Island had signed a treaty of alliance with the Hyksos, but what did that signify? Only the splendour of its gifts would show whether its word was good.

The envoy approached, followed by ten of his countrymen, each of whom had the black hair and straight nose characteristic of their race. Two of them bore a low-cut embroidered kilt decorated with braid; there were diamonds stitched into the embroidery.

The envoy bowed. 'May our sovereign receive the homage of Minoa. She recognizes him as emperor of the most vast empire the world has ever known. May Apophis govern it with greatness.'

The other Minoans presented gold ingots and rings, swords, and silver goblets and vases, some of which were in the shape of the heads of lions or bulls. Admiring murmurs ran through the assembled throng. These were truly magnificent gifts.

'I accept this homage,' said Apophis. 'Henceforth, Minoa

shall have nothing to fear from the Hyksos army. Let tributes be brought to me regularly, and I shall be the best possible defender of my Minoan vassals.'

The pharaohs had kept for use at court only one-tenth of the tributes paid to them, and had put the remainder back in the trading cycle. Apophis did exactly the opposite, in order to enrich those who administered his government and thus to ensure their devotion to him. Of course, this was among the most closely guarded of all state secrets, and Khamudi constantly praised his master's generosity and unshakeable determination to ensure that even the humblest folk were free from want.

At the moment, Apophis was thinking not of the profits his position brought him but of the immense empire he had come to possess. He ruled Egypt, Nubia, Canaan, Phoenicia, Syria, Cyprus, the Cyclades, Minoa, Anatolia and part of Asia. In all these regions egg-shaped jars in the Canaanite style were found. Their presence marked the Hyksos's control of all aspects of trade: they were a sign that Apophis held power and would not tolerate any dissent.

'I shall govern without Ma'at, the goddess of the vanquished,' he announced, 'and I shall impose everywhere the power of Set, which I alone can control. The Hyksos have struck down the Egyptians and I, Apophis, am the new pharaoh, the founder of a line which will eclipse all those that have gone before. My coronation names shall be "Beloved of Set", "Great is the Power of Ra", and "Great is His Heroic Victory", for even the sun answers to my desires. Thus I shall become King of Upper and Lower Egypt, and each time my name is written or spoken it shall be followed by the triple vow of "Life, blossoming, unity".'*

Taking care not to raise his eyes to his lord, Khamudi

* 'Ankh, udja, seneb', often translated by the approximation 'Life, health, strength'.

presented him with an amulet in the shape of a looped cross. Apophis hooked the ankh on to a gold chain and placed it round his neck.

'This lapis-lazuli amulet reveals the secrets of heaven and earth to me,' declared the emperor, 'and confers upon me the right of life and death over my subjects.'

A stunned silence fell. No one would ever have dreamt that Apophis would proclaim himself Pharaoh, adopting the traditional names and titles and thus inflicting a death-blow on Egypt's soul. They all realized they were in the presence of a ruthless warlord, determined first to pillage the ancient culture and then to wipe it out. By all accounts it was better to submit than to arouse his anger, particularly since the Hyksos army was steadily gathering strength, in both men and weaponry. This was the dawn of a new era, one in which strength – whether military or financial – would have the upper hand. And, since Apophis was its absolute master, all that anyone could do was obey him.

Only the old Nubian envoy dared to voice a reservation. 'To be a true pharaoh, Majesty, it is not enough to choose coronation names. It is also necessary to have them recognized by the gods, by inscribing them upon the Tree of Knowledge, at Iunu.'

Khamudi would gladly have ripped out the insolent man's tongue, but the Nubians were easily provoked and for the time being it was in Apophis's interest to treat them with respect.

The emperor remained calm. 'You are right, my friend. That is indeed the custom.'

'But, Majesty, are you planning to follow the custom?'

'My reign shall begin dazzlingly and shall eclipse those which have gone before, because the gods protect me. My first task tomorrow will be to go to Iunu, where my name shall be rendered immortal.'

14

Now that the treacherous commander was dead, Khamudi himself commanded Pharaoh Apophis's impressive personal bodyguard. Well protected in his canopied chariot, the sovereign could not be hit by an arrow or by stones thrown by rebels.

At the entrance to the ancient and sacred city of Iunu, the Hyksos had herded several hundred Egyptian peasants together, and forced them to cheer the king. Those who did not shout loudly enough would be sent to the copper mines of Sinai.

It was here, in the city of the all-creating sun, that Egyptian spirituality had taken form. It was here that sages had written the texts engraved inside the pyramids at Saqqara, to ensure the resurrection and continual evolution of the royal soul.

Apophis had not had the library at Iunu destroyed, for he planned to profit from the knowledge of the vanquished race in order to dominate them more completely and to extend his conquests further each day. The Egyptians were too bound up in their search for wisdom and social harmony, and had forgotten the most important thing: that only strength could give victory.

On the flagstones before the main temple in Iunu, alone in the sun, stood the High Priest. His head was shaven, he wore a panther-skin decorated with dozens of gold stars, and in his right hand he held a consecration sceptre.

'What do we know of this insolent man?' Apophis asked Khamudi, stepping down from his chariot.

'He is a scholar, attached to the ancient beliefs and regarded by his fellow priests as the guardian of tradition.'

'Tell him to bow before his king.'

Khamudi passed on the order, but the old priest remained as unbending as a statue from the age of the pyramid-builders.

Fighting to contain his fury, Apophis stepped forward. 'Do you not know the punishment you are risking?'

'I bow only before a pharaoh,' replied the High Priest.

'Well I am one! And I have in fact come to inscribe my coronation names on the Tree of Knowledge.'

'If you are what you claim to be, that is indeed your duty. Follow me.'

'I and my men will accompany you,' cut in Khamudi.

'That is out of the question,' replied the High Priest. 'Only Pharaoh may approach the sacred tree.'

'How dare you!'

'Enough, Khamudi. I, Apophis, am willing to conform to tradition.'

'It's too dangerous, my lord.'

'The High Priest of Iunu knows that, if anyone were to kill me, all the temples would be razed to the ground and the priests executed.'

The old man nodded.

'I shall follow you, High Priest.'

Apophis felt no emotion as he entered the magnificent shrine that had greeted every pharaoh since the uniting of the Two Lands. Then suddenly, for a few moments, the calm atmosphere of the place, where Ma'at was still worshipped, made him slightly nervous. To banish the feeling, he avoided looking at the carved panels and the columns of hieroglyphs which, even in the absence of human presence, celebrated the sacred rites and declared the presence of the powers of the Creator.

The High Priest entered a vast open-air courtyard, in the centre of which stood a giant persea tree with lance-shaped leaves.

'This tree was planted at the beginning of the reign of Pharaoh Djoser, the creator of the step pyramid,' explained the High Priest, 'and its longevity defies time. On the leaves of one of its main branches are written the names of the pharaohs whose reigns have been approved by the gods.'

'That's enough talk. Give me something to write my name with.'

'The rite specifically states that you must wear the ancient headdress, place a gold uraeus on your forehead, wear a short kilt, prostrate yourself and—'

'Stop this nonsense, old man! The Hyksos emperor does not submit to outdated rituals. Just give me something to write my name with on the leaves.'

'For the Stem of Millions of Years to continue to grow, you must use the brush of the god Thoth. Do you accept?'

Apophis shrugged.

The High Priest began to walk away.

'Where are you going?'

'To fetch the brush from the temple treasury.'

'Do not try to trick me.'

Apophis wished he had some protection. In the High Priest's place, he would have organized an ambush. But the devotees of the old cults disapproved of crime. They continued to cower in their unreal world, deluded by the illusion of Ma'at.

The old man soon returned, carrying an acacia-wood box. In it were a scribe's materials: a palette with holes for ink, cakes of red and black ink, pots of water, and a brush.

'Dilute the cake of black ink with a little water, dip in your brush and write.'

'Those are menial tasks. Do them yourself.'

'I can prepare the brush, but you must wield it.'

Apophis seized it and tried to write one of his names, 'Beloved of Set', on a broad, long leaf. But nothing showed on the leaf.

'Your ink is of poor quality,' he snarled.

'I guarantee that it is not.'

'Dilute the red.'

The High Priest did so, but the result was the same.

'Are you mocking me, old man?'

'You must face the truth: the Tree of Knowledge refuses to receive your names, for the gods will not admit you to the line of pharaohs.'

'Go and fetch some new cakes of ink immediately.'

'As you wish.'

When the High Priest returned, Apophis saw that the new cake of black ink had never been used.

'Never insult me with inferior things again, old man. As this day is a glorious one for the Hyksos, I shall forgive your ill will, but you will get no further mercy from me.'

His new attempt at writing on the tree's leaves ended in another failure.

'The ink is not responsible,' said the High Priest. 'You are not a pharaoh and you never will be.'

Apophis regarded him with icy hatred. 'You are putting a curse on me. Your sceptre – that's what it is.' He tore it from the old man's hands and broke it in two. 'See what I have done with your pitiful magic,' he sneered. 'Now the tree will accept me.'

But the brush slid across the leaf, leaving not a mark. Apophis flung the brush down and ground it beneath his heel.

'Who is permitted to enter this courtyard and read the names of the pharaohs?' he demanded.

'Only the High Priest of Iunu.'

'Will you place my name in the temple records?'

'That is impossible.'

'Do you not value your life, old man?'

'It is better to die in righteousness than to live in falsehood.'

'You are the only witness to the tree's refusal – so you must die.'

Apophis unsheathed his dagger and plunged it into the heart of the High Priest, who made no attempt to defend himself.

'I was beginning to get anxious, my lord,' said Khamudi. 'Did all go well?'

'Extremely well. My names are written for all eternity upon the Tree of Knowledge, and in much larger letters than my predecessors'. The gods bowed down before me, and we have no more to fear from Egyptian spells. Festivities are to be held, so that the common people may acclaim their new pharaoh.'

'I shall see to it at once. Anything else, my lord?'

'Have all the priests in this temple killed, close its doors and ensure that no one enters. That will ensure that my coronation names remain beyond the reach of human eyes.'

15

Ahhotep put on a peasant-woman's clothing and tied up her dark hair in a green band, the colour of which matched her eyes. It was decorated with small lotus blossoms, and had been given to her by her mother when she had her first blood.

Once satisfied with her humble appearance, she set off for the landing-stage.

Seqen intercepted her there. 'Princess . . .'

'What is it?'

'If you are going on a journey, it would be better to avoid the Nile – it is angry at the moment. The best thing would be to take the country roads. I can provide the finest bearer in all the region to carry what you need.'

He pointed to a handsome grey donkey with a white muzzle and belly. Its nostrils flared wide, its ears were huge, and lively intelligence shone in its eyes.

'Long-Ears is a giant among donkeys. He weighs more than five men, can carry an immense load without tiring, and will live to forty. He can work out the best route to take, and always knows if danger is near. I have filled his two panniers with mats, blankets, sandals, bread, dried fish, onions and water-skins.'

'Are you lending me your donkey?'

Seqen looked embarrassed. 'He will obey no one but me, Princess.'

'I am going to Kebet, and then to Per-Hathor. It will be dangerous.'

'My lady, I told you that I want to fight the Hyksos and I haven't changed my mind – in fact, I'm more determined than ever. We will pass for a couple of peasants and we shall be a lot less noticeable than a young woman travelling alone. And if we meet trouble, I shall defend you.'

How on earth could this thin, shy boy manage that? wondered Ahhotep. But his suggestion of posing as a married couple made sense.

'Laughter will guard Queen Teti while we are away,' added Seqen. 'With him to protect her, she will have nothing to fear.'

'In that case,' said Ahhotep, 'let's start at once.'

Long-Ears listened intently, and halted in his tracks.

Some distance away on the right bank of the Nile, where the river described a broad westerly curve, lay the town of Kebet. It was under the protection of Min, the god who ensured the fertility of nature and protected those who ventured into the desert.

Kebet lay seven days' march from the Red Sea, the gateway to east Africa and the Arabian peninsula. It was Egypt's principal centre for buying and selling minerals: quartz, jasper, emeralds, obsidian, breccia and porphyry were all to be found there, as were malachite, herbs and spices, resins and even ivory.

'Why has Long-Ears stopped?' asked Ahhotep.

Seqen stroked the donkey's head, but it did not move. 'There's danger close by,' he said. 'We must take another path.'

'But I need to know if Kebet is in Hyksos hands.'

'Then wait for me here.'

'Aren't we supposed to be behaving like a married couple?' asked Ahhotep.

'I shall talk to Long-Ears.'

After a long discussion, the donkey agreed to move

forwards, but only very slowly.

As they rounded a thicket of tamarisks, they were confronted by a dozen armed Egyptian soldiers.

'This is Kebet guard-post,' declared their officer. 'Anyone who wants to travel north to trade must pay a fee: men, women, children and even their donkeys. Only the emperor's soldiers go free.'

'We only want to go into the town,' said Seqen, very humbly.

'Why?'

'To exchange mats for vegetables.'

'If you are planning to avoid paying the fee by going through the town, you can forget it. My colleagues are stationed at every exit. And they charge the same fee.'

'Yes, sir. Please, which is the right road for Kebet?'

'Go back the way you came and take the first path on your right. It will lead you to the main road, which ends at the town's main gate.'

Without undue haste, the peasant couple walked away, much to the disappointment of the officer, who would gladly have subjected the pretty brown-haired girl to a strict search.

Ahhotep had expected a city bustling with traders and mineral-hunters, a place with lively markets where people discussed business and caravans passed through on their way to the desert. But Kebet was almost empty and virtually all its famous inns were shut. In the narrow streets, the few passersby walked quickly and refused to be drawn into conversation.

Here and there Ahhotep and Seqen saw small groups of Egyptian soldiers; but not a single Hyksos.

'I have a bad feeling about this place, Princess. We should leave at once.'

'We haven't found out anything yet. There must be at least one inn or ale-house open.'

On the north side of Kebet stood the great Temple of Min

and Isis, surrounded by a wall of baked earthen brick, but this district was as dead as the others. Although the side doors of the temple were open, neither priests nor craftsmen entered or emerged.

'Over there,' said Ahhotep. 'A merchant delivering jars.'

The place was indeed an 'ale-house', and a rather sordid one at that, with dirty walls and smoke-blackened ceiling. In a corner, two very unalluring girls were tattooing lizards on their thighs.

A small, fat man with bad breath stepped in front of the pair. 'What do you want?'

'Some beers,' replied Seqen.

'Can you pay?'

'We'll give you a new mat.'

'Show me it.'

Seqen took it out of one of the panniers, all the time stroking Long-Ears, who did not like the innkeeper.

'It looks like a good-quality item, friend. And so does your donkey: a magnificent animal. You're not selling it, are you?'

'No. He's too useful.'

'A pity. And you're not looking for work for this pretty young girl, I suppose? I'd have some for her – and I can swear that the three of us would make a fortune. If her body's as good as her face, she'll have the best customers in Kebet.'

'We just want some beer to drink.'

'As you wish. But think about it.'

The pair sat down near the door. The prostitutes cast envious glances at Ahhotep, while the little fat man filled two cups with a murky liquid.

'I didn't know Kebet was such a quiet town,' said the princess with a smile.

'Everything's changed a lot. There used to be so many folk in here you couldn't hear yourself speak. Caravans left, caravans arrived – you didn't even have time to take a day off. But that was in the good old days, when people made a comfortable living. Now times are bad. There are only three ale-houses left and fewer and fewer customers . . . Where have you two come from?'

'From the countryside near Thebes.'

The innkeeper almost choked. 'Whatever you do, don't say the name "Thebes",' he whispered urgently. 'There are Hyksos spies everywhere.'

'Who's the mayor of this town?' asked Ahhotep.

'Lord Titi.'

'Is he in the pay of the Hyksos?'

The fat man scowled. 'Who might you be, asking questions like that? I don't know anything, and I shan't tell you anything. You're Theban rebels, aren't you? Get out of my ale-house, right now! There have never been any rebels in my place and there never will be, and you can shout that as loud as you like. Go on, get out!'

A loud braying made Seqen start. 'Long-Ears!'

As the young man leapt towards the door, someone hit him in the stomach with a stick. He doubled up, gasping for breath; Ahhotep ran to him and knelt down to help him.

A dozen angry soldiers came barging in.

'Whose is this donkey?' demanded one of them.

'Ours,' replied the princess.

'He's just broken an officer's arm. Follow me to the guard-post.'

The innkeeper pushed Ahhotep out of the way and bowed low before the soldier. 'These two are Theban rebels – they threatened me and they want to kill Lord Titi.'

Ahhotep and Seqen got to their feet.

'A fine prize,' said the soldier with a fierce smile. 'We'll take you to the palace.'

The innkeeper grabbed the sleeve of the soldier's tunic. 'What about my reward?'

The soldier knocked him out with a blow of his club. 'You overcharge for your filthy beer, you son of a pig.'

16

'Two Theban rebels, here in my fine town? That's very interesting.' Titi, the mayor of Kebet, was a bearded man, with a round paunch and an aggressive voice. He spent much of his time cursing the soldiers, guards and servants who lived at the former royal palace, which had been transformed into a barracks.

Hands clasped behind his back, he walked slowly round his prisoners, who had been shackled by the soldiers.

'Who are you really?'

'Only peasants, my lord,' replied Seqen.

'You may be, but she most certainly is not. With such a flawless face and well-cared-for hands, she's a girl of very good family.'

'I'll tell you,' said Ahhotep, 'but only if I can be alone with you, and on condition that my companion comes to no harm.'

'Interesting: a rebel who imposes conditions . . . very interesting. You amuse me, my little one. Leave, all of you, and throw that fellow into prison.'

The interrogation room was a sinister place. It had wooden beds stained with dried blood, and whips hung on the peeling walls. But Ahhotep overcame her fear. She had not stood face to face with Mut only to end up tortured in a place like this, and she had had enough of being a prisoner in her own country.

'Take these shackles off at once.'

Titi rubbed his chin. 'And why should I obey you, young lady?'

'Because I am Princess Ahhotep, daughter of Queen Teti the Small, your sovereign.'

Titi stared at the magnificent young woman in stunned silence. 'If you really are who you claim to be, describe the palace at Thebes and write out for me the beginning of *The Tale of Sinuhe*, which your tutor must have made you read.'

'Set me free, and I will.'

'First I must search you.'

'If you dare touch me, you will regret it.'

Impressed by her regal bearing, Titi heeded the warning. 'Then describe the palace to me.'

Ahhotep did so.

'What is the queen's steward's name?'

'Qaris.'

Titi removed her wooden shackles, then handed her a scrap of papyrus and a brush.

Swiftly and accurately, Ahhotep drew the hieroglyphs that formed the beginning of the famous *Sinuhe*. The adventure story told of the flight of an eminent man who feared he would be wrongly accused of taking part in a plot against his king.

'Let's go somewhere more pleasant,' proposed Titi when she had finished.

'Set my companion free at once.'

'My men will release him from the cell and give him something to eat.'

The former royal palace at Kebet was in a dilapidated state. It had been a long time since a pharaoh had stayed in the town, and the majority of its apartments lay empty and neglected.

The mayor confined himself to a small two-pillared audience chamber, an office and a bedchamber whose windows gave on to the courtyard where the soldiers of his personal guard were quartered. The furnishings dated from the happy and prosperous days of the great pharaoh Amenemhat III, and were quite magnificent: seats and arm-chairs of sober design, elegant low tables, and delicate lampstands.

'I am overwhelmed to meet our last princess,' declared Titi, pouring cool beer into two cups. 'To tell the truth, I had heard your name spoken, but I wondered if you really existed. Forgive me for the deplorable quality of this beer, but the best brewers in the town have been requisitioned by the emperor.'

'Is Kebet occupied by the Hyksos?'

'They confine themselves to tours of inspection, because I managed to convince them that I am a loyal ally. But they aren't stupid enough to trust me completely, so they organize their own expeditions into the desert and give me no rights at all over the minerals they collect. I fear that Kebet, like most of the important cities in the land, may soon become a garrison town. The markets are dying and the people have barely enough to eat. Thanks to my good relations with the empire, I can still obtain sufficient grain, but for how much longer?'

'Have you created a network of rebels?'

'It would be impossible, Princess. There are spies every-where – even in this palace. Last month, ten peasants suspected of being Theban sympathizers were beheaded. This barbarous behaviour has sown fear everywhere, and nobody wants to be a hero any more. All I can do is feign friendship with the Hyksos, so as to spare the people more suffering. Last year, I did manage to celebrate the great Festival of Min, but I had to do it secretly, inside the temple with a few priests who knew how to hold their tongues. For those few short hours, we felt renewed hope that in the distant future we might see our traditions flower again; but our hope was swiftly dispelled. Each day, the occupation grows harsher.'

84

The Empire of Darkness

'For that very reason, we must not stand idly by any longer,' declared Ahhotep.

'What are you planning to do, Princess?'

'Thebes will raise her head and the other cities will follow.'

'Thebes? But what military does she command?'

'They seem pitiful because our troops have no spirit of unity. But that will change, Lord Titi – I guarantee it. I am convinced that there are plenty of brave men and that all they need is to be given the will to fight.'

'Is that the queen's intention?'

'I shall persuade her.'

Titi shook his head. 'That is an audacious plan, Princess – I might even call it madness. The puny Theban forces will be wiped out by the Hyksos army.'

'I am not thinking of a frontal attack. First, we must spread the news that Thebes has not given up the fight; then resistance will grow. Will you help me?'

'I repeat: this is madness. But who could resist your enthusiasm? Listening to you, I feel as if I am growing young again.'

Ahhotep's smile would have won over even the most sceptical of men.

'Go on letting the Hyksos think you are their ally,' she advised, 'and meanwhile surround yourself with men who are ready to give their lives to save Egypt.'

'That won't be easy.'

'Until the tyrant falls, nothing will be easy. But we must go forward, whatever the cost. Can you not try to rally the villages around Kebet to our cause?'

'It would be extremely dangerous.'

'When I come back, we shall gather our supporters in the temple and prepare to advance northwards.'

'May the gods hear you, Princess.' Titi frowned worriedly. 'If you and your servant walked freely out of the palace,' he went on, 'a Hyksos spy would be bound to alert his masters. So I must have you expelled from the town by my soldiers, like undesirable persons. But, Princess, come back soon!'

There were four of them, tall, unshaven fellows, armed with short-swords, and they surrounded Ahhotep and Seqen, who were followed by Long-Ears. As they passed by, the inhabitants of Kebet shut their doors. A woman and her child ran away in terror.

'Where are you taking us?' asked Seqen.

'To the southern gate of the city. There will definitely be no Hyksos lookouts there. We'll set you on the right road for Thebes and you'll get home in peace – as long as you don't run into trouble.'

His three companions split their sides laughing.

'It's a good job we're with you, because this area isn't very safe. With all these cowardly Egyptians intent on robbing travellers.'

Seqen bristled. 'What did you just say?'

'Didn't you hear me properly, friend?'

'Where are you from, soldier?'

The soldier smiled sarcastically. 'Just like my comrades, from a barracks in Avaris, where we were told that the only good Egyptians were dead Egyptians.'

Lowering his head, Long-Ears butted a Hyksos soldier and hit him full in the back. Then, timing his attack carefully, he kicked one of the others and stove in his chest. Caught off guard, the other two swung round towards the donkey, giving Seqen enough time to seize a dagger and slit the throat of the loose-tongued man.

The last soldier tried to run away, but Seqen sprang at him. Despite being much the lighter man, he wrestled the soldier to the ground, face down, and drove the dagger-blade into the back of his neck.

17

Seqen got to his feet, looking perfectly calm.

Ahhotep flung her arms round his neck. 'You behaved like a true hero!'

'Without Long-Ears, we wouldn't have stood a chance.'

The princess stepped back and looked at him in an entirely new light. 'This is your first victory.'

'I was so furious at that rat Titi that I hadn't time to be afraid. He betrayed us to the Hyksos. Let's go back and kill him.'

'But suppose he's innocent?'

'You can't deny the facts, Princess.'

'I thought he seemed sincere, and determined to follow the plan we've formed. He might have been betrayed by some of his own men who he thought were loyal. The Hyksos have infiltrated everywhere, and Titi himself told me Kebet is full of spies.'

Seqen was shaken. 'Then you don't think he organized this ambush?'

'Perhaps not.'

'All the same, you're not sure.'

'I can't afford to be naïve.' Ahhotep gazed thoughtfully down at the four corpses. 'This is an extraordinary moment: we've won our first battle against the Hyksos. The soldiers took us for easy prey – lambs to be slaughtered – but they're the ones lying there, dead. May their god-cursed emperor make the same mistake!'

'So far,' Seqen reminded her, 'our army consists of precisely one princess, one donkey and one novice fighter.'

Ahhotep laid her hands gently on his shoulders. 'Don't you believe that the gods' magic has just changed sides? We aren't submitting any more, we're fighting – and we're winning.'

A strange feeling of anxiety washed over Seqen. 'Princess, I . . .'

'You're shivering, aren't you? Don't worry, it's reaction after the fighting. It will pass.'

'Princess, I wanted to say—'

'Let's not leave these bodies in plain sight. We'll drag them into the reeds on the riverbank. The vultures, crocodiles and rats will make short work of them.'

Walking behind Long-Ears, the pair travelled to the east of Thebes, where the desert met the fields, then took a diagonal route towards the river, in the hope of borrowing a boat to take them to Per-Hathor, a day's journey to the south.

Ahhotep was astonished to see how few peasants were at work. Most of the fields seemed to have been abandoned, and there was no sign of the flute-players whose music had once accompanied farming work. Evidently the farmers had lost the will to work and now did only the bare minimum.

The travellers encountered no soldiers or guards. The Theban region had been left to its own devices, without any protection. When the Hyksos eventually decided to attack the city of Amon, they would meet not the slightest resistance.

Dismayed and angry, Ahhotep now realized the full gravity of the situation. Waset, the last free province in Egypt, had bent the knee, defeated, even as it waited for the invaders to pour in.

Long-Ears decided to leave a path which was too exposed,

and forced his way through some papyrus thickets. He halted a few paces from the river, in a place well screened by foliage.

Ahhotep and Seqen soon saw the reason for his caution: a Hyksos warship was sailing down the middle of the Nile. At the bow and stern were several soldiers, keeping a close watch on the banks. So the Hyksos could sail towards the Great South and Nubia without fear of opposition, while Thebes looked on helplessly.

'Let's take one of the desert paths,' said Seqen. 'On the river we'd be spotted straight away.'

The carob-tree was taller than five men, with dense foliage which provided the two Thebans and the donkey with an ideal shelter from which to observe the Hyksos fortress of Per-Hathor.

Ahhotep and Seqen lay on their bellies, side by side, astounded by what they saw. They had never imagined that such a monstrosity existed, so close to Thebes. Thick walls of brick, a walkway round the battlements, square towers, ditches for defence: these were just some of the features of the most formidable fortifications Egypt had ever seen. Moreover, in front of them a troop of Asian spear-throwers were practising.

'And this is only Per-Hathor,' whispered Seqen. 'Just think what Avaris must be like, Princess.'

'At least we know what we are up against.'

'This fortress is impregnable. And there must be many others like it, right across the country.'

'We'll destroy them one by one.'

Two Asian soldiers stopped training and looked towards the carob-tree.

'They've seen us,' murmured Seqen.

Ahhotep shook her head. 'The leaves hide us completely. But don't move, whatever you do.'

The two Hyksos headed towards the tree.

'If we run away,' said Seqen, 'they'll strike us down from behind. And if we stay here, they'll kill us anyway.'

'You take the taller one, I'll deal with the other.'

'The sound of fighting will attract their comrades – we have no chance. But I'll defend you to the last, as I promised, because – because I love you.'

An orange-yellow butterfly with a black head spotted with white alighted on Ahhotep's forehead.

The Asians were no more than ten paces away.

Ahhotep took Seqen's hand tenderly, and suddenly he was transported into a dream-world. He forgot the imminent danger, and closed his eyes to savour a moment he had not dared hope for.

After exchanging a few words, the two Hyksos soldiers turned back.

'This butterfly is called the monarch,' said Ahhotep. 'The birds don't attack or eat it. By settling on me, it made me invisible.'

Since they had just escaped from great danger, the two young people followed the tradition of kissing each other four times on the back of the hand. They stayed lying close together until sundown, when the Hyksos soldiers withdrew inside the fortress.

Ahhotep smiled and asked, 'Do you know what you said, Seqen?'

Displaying a degree of courage he would never have believed he had, the young man took her hand again. 'What I feel for you is like all the suns that have ever existed. A feeling that is at once uplifting, like the life-giving dawn sun, scorching hot like the noonday sun, and gentle like the evening sun. I fell in love with you the moment I saw you.'

'Love,' sighed Ahhotep. 'Is it still possible to love while Egypt is suffering a thousand deaths?'

'Without love, will we have the strength to fight to the

death? I shall fight for my country, but also for you.'

His words brought Ahhotep back to present reality. 'We must leave here,' she said.

They went carefully in the darkness, all their senses fully alert in case they met a Hyksos patrol or Egyptian peasants who might think they were being threatened and attack without finding out who the strangers were. They also had to be wary of snakes.

Long-Ears seemed to understand the need for caution, for his hooves struck the ground so delicately that they made no sound. Several times, he halted and sniffed the air.

His nerves stretched to breaking point, Seqen felt capable of killing giants in order to save the princess's life. And he swore to himself that, if he reached Thebes safely, he would train with such intensity and dedication that he would become the finest soldier in Egypt.

At last, the outskirts of the city of Amon came in sight.

Despite his fears, Seqen wished that the journey could have lasted for ever. Bathed in moonlight, Ahhotep was as beautiful as a goddess. He had lived with her, close to her, and she would never again grant him such a privilege. How insane he had been, he, a man of the common people, to reveal his feelings like that to a princess! Shocked by his impertinence, she would send him away.

When they reached the palace, the guards hailed her.

'Feed Long-Ears, then go and rest,' she told Seqen. 'I need time to think.'

18

The Afghan and his right-hand man, Moustache, threw the bunches of grapes into the vat then climbed in to tread them. The juice began to flow out through a hole in the side and a wine-maker, who was a member of their rebel band, collected it in an earthenware jar.

The members of the little group had left Avaris, where the guards were so omnipresent that they could no longer meet without risking denunciation and arrest. The Afghan had, however, left a few informants in each district, people whom he would contact – at irregular intervals, so as not to attract the attention of the Hyksos.

In Avaris, under the iron fist of Khamudi's henchmen, almost all Egyptians had been reduced to slavery and despair. But there were still a few who were determined to fight to the end.

In the Delta countryside, the invaders' cruelty was no less severe; but the peasants had proved more difficult to control than the town-dwellers. The Afghan had been surprised by their refusal to accept tyranny and their unshakeable resolve to free themselves from it. Unfortunately, though, they were not soldiers and would form only a pitiful army compared to the Hyksos regiments.

As the Afghan often told his fellow rebels, the only sensible strategy was patience, backed by unfailing vigilance.

Little by little they must win over the village headmen, and the small landowners; sound out each person who wanted to join the rebels, to see if they had the required qualities and ensure that they were not Hyksos spies trying to infiltrate the group. For his part, the Afghan preferred a small, reliable, close-knit band to a larger number of supporters who would be difficult to control and easy to detect.

The main priority was to kill as many Hyksos informants as possible, so that the emperor would gradually lose his eyes and ears.

Moustache paused in his grape-treading and wiped his brow. 'This will be good wine,' he predicted. 'But almost all of it will go to the Hyksos or be sold to foreign countries. We Egyptians are forced to toil like this, forced to produce more food each day, and yet we are dying of hunger.'

'Don't complain, my friend,' said the Afghan.

'Apophis has just had himself crowned pharaoh, and he's more powerful than ever. His empire is getting bigger and bigger, and his army's getting stronger and stronger.'

'Yes, that's true.'

'How can you keep on being so firm and resolute?'

'If I want to regain my fortune and re-establish normal trade between my country and Egypt, the only solution is to defeat the Hyksos. And I'm more stubborn than a disobedient donkey.'

'Deep down, you know we have no chance, don't you?'

'That's a question I don't ask myself – and you shouldn't, either. Has our man arrived with the sacks yet?'

'Yes, just now.'

'A promising recruit, don't you think?'

'Very. He owns three boats, two hundred cows and a palm-grove, and he controls more than a hundred and fifty peasants, all unquestioningly loyal to him. He offers us a safe haven and a forge where we can make weapons.'

The Afghan and Moustache left the pressing-room and

went to clean themselves up – the Egyptian could not resist drinking some grape juice while his companion was washing. Then they went to a room containing a large vat which would receive the juice produced when the pulped grapes were put in sacks and pressed, using a technique handed down from one generation to the next.

The would-be rebel was waiting for them there. He was about sixty, with white hair and an air of authority. He asked, 'Are you the Afghan?'

'I am indeed.'

'And you, a foreigner, have become the leader of Egyptian rebels.'

'Does that displease you?'

'I bitterly regret the fact that none of us has the courage to do it. Do you know what you're risking?'

'There's nothing worse than poverty and dishonour. In my country I was a rich and respected man, but because of the Hyksos I have lost everything. They're going to pay dearly for that.'

'Aren't you exaggerating a bit?'

'It's plain to see that you don't know Afghans. No one has ever beaten them and no one ever will. However, we must go on with our work. This place seems peaceful enough, but I'm suspicious.'

Moustache fixed a sack of pulped grapes to either end of two poles.

'What happens next?' asked the Afghan.

'We lay our poles across each other, to form a cross, and then turn them above the vat.

'They must be kept well apart,' said the newcomer. 'It's a long time since I enjoyed this kind of exercise. Don't we look like three perfect wine-makers?'

Nimbly, he climbed on to the poles, which the other two were holding, and pushed them apart, bracing his feet and maintaining his balance by gripping one of them. 'Now turn them,' he said. 'The sacks will be pressed and will filter the juice.'

Although clumsy at first, the Afghan soon matched his companion's pace.

'And what about you?' he asked the recruit. 'Are you fully aware of the risks you're running? You are an eminent citizen, the Hyksos tolerate you, and yet you plan to throw yourself into an adventure which offers you far more chance of losing everything than of winning.'

'Up to now, I've collaborated. But I've had enough. In the end I realized that the occupation is going to bring Egypt to utter ruin and that, like everyone else, I'll eventually be ground beneath the Hyksos heel. Careful, don't turn too quickly! I almost lost my balance.'

'Can you really count on your peasants?'

'Their families have served mine for several generations, and they all hate the Hyksos. The Egyptians aren't warriors, I admit, but their appalling suffering will give them the strength they yet lack.'

'And what about your forge?' said the Afghan. 'Can we use it at any time?'

'We'll have to be careful. The Hyksos guards who inspect my lands use the forge to repair their weapons, but we'll still manage to make our own.'

'Have you got the metal we'll need?'

'Some – just a small stock.'

'How did you get it?'

The recruit hesitated.

'If we don't tell each other everything and trust each other completely,' said the Afghan, 'it isn't worth continuing. I'm willing to give you command of the rebels, but you must prove yourself worthy of it.'

Now the poles were turning at a regular pace, and the juice was flowing freely.

'I had a contact in Avaris,' said the recruit, 'a cousin who worked in the great forge there, and who managed to steal a little copper. But there was an unexpected search, and he was arrested.'

'How are we going to get more, then?' asked Moustache anxiously.

'We'll find a way,' promised his fellow countryman. 'For example, we can falsify Hyksos delivery notes.'

The Afghan cut in abruptly. 'Is it true that you were visited recently by a senior official?'

'Yes, but how do you know that?'

'When you are preparing to recruit someone new, you watch him carefully. It's a matter of our safety.'

'Of course. I understand.'

'What I don't understand,' said the Afghan, 'is why you had a conversation with Khamudi, Apophis's right-hand man.'

'It's very simple,' protested the Egyptian. 'Khamudi visited all the forges in the area, because he keeps a strict check on the production of weapons.'

'That isn't true. The only one he visited was yours, and he spent a long time talking to you.'

The Afghan suddenly let go of his pole, and the landowner fell heavily to the ground.

'My neck!' he moaned. 'It hurts, it really hurts. Why did you do that?'

'Because you're a traitor.'

'I'm not, I swear I'm not. You're making a mistake.'

'Oh no I'm not,' retorted the Afghan, picking up his pole and setting one end down on the man's throat. 'You were very careful not to reveal your friendship with Khamudi. And he ordered you to infiltrate my group, because you're one of the Hyksos's most loyal collaborators. You were a bit too clever for your own good, you scum. Your leader may think we're stupid, but he's wrong.'

'I swear that—'

96

'A traitor's oath is worth nothing – except this.' The Afghan rammed the pole with all his strength into the Hyksos spy's throat, crushing his larynx; he died in a few seconds.

'He was too good a candidate to be true,' said the Afghan. 'Still, at least our security system worked. We must improve it still further.'

19

Seqen felt something huge and wet on his face as he slept beside Long-Ears. 'Oh, Laughter, it's you.'

The dog stopped licking him and tried to sit down on the young man's belly, but Seqen, fearful of being crushed under the weight, rolled aside and stood up.

The sun was already high in the sky. Seqen felt lost. He didn't know whether to go up to the palace or leave the city to escape the royal family's anger. If he begged Ahhotep for forgiveness, she might perhaps grant it, but why humiliate himself like that? However insane it might be, there was nothing discreditable about his love. And he was not the kind of man to run away like a coward.

'Come on, Laughter,' he said. 'We're going to see your mistress.'

The princess was wearing a long, pale-green dress, her face was almost bare of face-paint. She was reading sacred songs composed by the sages to the glory of the royal crowns, which were regarded as living beings that radiated fire capable of vanquishing the forces of darkness.

His face sombre, Seqen bowed low. 'Princess, I have brought Laughter back to you,' he said. 'Have I your permission to remain in Thebes?'

Ahhotep did not lift her eyes from her papyrus. 'Have your feelings changed?'

'My feelings . . .'

'Has your long sleep made you forget your absurd declaration?'

'No, of course not.'

'You should have thought deeply and realized that you have fallen victim to a mirage.'

'You're no mirage, Princess. You're the woman I love.'

'Are you quite sure of that?'

'On the life of Pharaoh, I swear it.'

'There is no Pharaoh any more.'

'Those who live for ever in the sky bear witness to my sincerity.'

Ahhotep laid the papyrus on a low table and looked the young man straight in the eye. 'Last night I couldn't sleep, because I couldn't stop thinking about you,' she confessed. 'I missed you.'

Seqen's heart raced. 'But . . .'

'It is possible that I love you. But marriage is something much more serious. Have you ever lain with a girl?'

Seqen blushed. 'No, I haven't.'

'And I have never lain with a man. Can you offer the proper marriage-gifts to a princess – that is to say, beds, chairs, storage chests, boxes for jewellery and face-paint, bracelets and rings, precious vases and luxurious fabrics which on her death will become her winding-sheet?'

Seqen was devastated. 'You know I cannot.'

'Never mind, I shall do without. My mother will protest, but I'll win her round. Now, let us be quite clear about what I require from my future husband. He must be neither greedy nor vain; nor must he be stupid, dishonest, or mean-spirited. He must not cosset himself and he must not be deaf to the voices of the gods.'

'I promise to do my best, but I don't know if—'

'You promise, that's what matters. Now let us deal with the most important matter of all. I want to have two sons as

99

quickly as possible. The struggle against the Hyksos will be a long one, and I shall bring them up in the love of their country and the will to set it free. If you and I die, they will carry on our fight.'

Seqen smiled. 'I accept all your conditions.'

Their lips were almost touching.

'I'm not like other women, Seqen, and I am forbidden to become like them. Even if we're happy together, our life will be stormy.'

'You've already taught me not to be like other men. To live with you, I am willing to make any sacrifice at all.'

They shared their first kiss, at first hesitant then fevered.

Seqen's trembling hands slipped the gown from Ahhotep's perfect body, dared to touch her perfumed skin and ventured a first caress which made her whole being quiver. She, the conqueror and the fighter, abandoned herself to the arms of her lover as he discovered how to express his passion. And they gave themselves to each other, forgetting everything except their desire.

Although she was not feeling very well, Teti the Small received her daughter, with only Qaris in attendance.

'You have never looked so radiant, Ahhotep. Can it be that you bring good news from your expedition?'

'Unfortunately, Majesty, no. A seemingly impregnable fortress has been built at Per-Hathor, Hyksos boats travel up and down the Nile unhindered, and the Waset countryside has no military protection at all.'

'Did you reach Kebet?' asked Qaris.

'I met the mayor of the town, Lord Titi.'

'Titi?'

'Yes, that's right. I thought he was a strange man, somewhat disillusioned with the Hyksos. I hope I have given him back his taste for battle.'

'He is one of our most loyal allies,' said Qaris, 'but his

network of rebels has been destroyed, and he himself escaped death only by claiming to be the emperor's loyal vassal.'

'Do you think he'd give orders for me to be killed by soldiers in the Hyksos's pay?'

'Oh no, Princess! He'd never do that.'

'Kebet will soon be a dead town,' predicted Ahhotep, 'and the Hyksos will probably build a fortress there, as fearsome as the one at Per-Hathor. Titi's only remaining forces are a small personal bodyguard, and he can't even celebrate the Festival of Min except in great secrecy.'

Qaris was appalled. 'It's just as I thought: we're encircled. I'm sure the Theban enclave will soon fall.'

'I'm sure it won't,' retorted Ahhotep. 'We must win the people's hearts, organize resistance and loosen the Hyksos stranglehold little by little.'

'I have had news from Avaris,' said Qaris. 'Apophis has just proclaimed himself pharaoh, and his coronation names have been written on the Tree of Knowledge at Iunu.'

'How could he dare?' stammered Teti, her heart almost breaking.

'Before long, Majesty, we shall have to recognize his sovereignty and offer him allegiance. After all, Thebes, like the rest of the Two Lands, belongs to the King of Upper and Lower Egypt.'

The queen was on the verge of tears. 'Leave me, both of you.'

But Ahhotep took her arm and said, 'Come with me, Mother, I'm going to prove to you that there's still hope.'

She led her to her bedchamber and flung open the door.

Seqen, who was stretched out on the bed, gazing heavenwards, was so surprised that he only just had time to cover himself up.

'Ahhotep!' exclaimed Teti. 'Surely this doesn't mean that . . .?'

'Yes, it does, Mother. Seqen and I have made love for the

first time. From now on, we shall live together under the same roof, and we're therefore husband and wife. My husband himself will tell you how, with the aid of his donkey, he killed four Hyksos soldiers who wanted to kill us. We have won our first victory, Majesty!'

'Ahhotep, you . . .'

'Seqen doesn't belong to a great family, but what does that matter? Egyptian princesses marry the men they love, whatever their origin. He has no money, so he can't offer me a dowry, but that doesn't matter, either. We're living in a time of war. Our souls and our bodies are in harmony, and we're resolved to fight to the death. That's what matters, isn't it?'

Teti felt breathless. 'And do you want children?'

'We're going to have two sons, and they'll be as brave in war as their father.'

'Good, good.'

'Will you give us your blessing, Mother?'

'Well . . .'

Ahhotep threw her arms round her mother and kissed her on both cheeks.

20

In rage, the lady Tany hurled at the wall the mirror given her by her husband, the emperor. She hoped it would break, but the impact left the magnificent copper disc unharmed, so she stamped on it instead.

Born in the Delta, near Avaris, Tany had had the good fortune to catch the eye of Apophis, whose ugliness fascinated her. But she could not bear anyone to allude to her own ugliness, or mock her in the corridors of the palace. Small and fat, she had tried everything – slimming potions, beauty products, applications of mud – but the only result had been a succession of failures, each worse than the last. It was hardly surprising, because Tany loved oily food, rich sauces and cakes, all of which she refused to give up, and treated the palace doctors like charlatans.

Her mighty husband was too preoccupied with power to have much time for women. The cold blood that flowed in his veins did not arouse him to the games of love and if, from time to time, he violated some young Egyptian noblewoman who had been reduced to slavery, it was only to show that he exercised absolute power over his subjects.

Tany was of modest origins. She took great pleasure in humiliating the great ladies who were now her servants and whom, had it not been for the Hyksos invasions, she would have served. She never missed an opportunity to make them

suffer or show them that they were lower than the dust. None
could disobey her, still less dissent, for at one word from the
emperor's wife the rebel would be first whipped, then
beheaded. Not a week went by without the lady Tany taking
great pleasure in watching such executions.

There was only one shadow on the horizon: the arrival at
the palace of Khamudi's wife, Yima, an opulent blonde who
constantly flirted and bobbed her head like a goose,
especially when the emperor was around. But that pest of a
woman knew her husband would not tolerate even the
smallest misdemeanour: Khamudi had strangled his previous
wife with his own hands when he caught her in the arms of a
lover.

The lady Tany – Apophis had refused to bestow on her the
titles of Empress or Queen of Egypt – liked Khamudi. He was
brutal, ambitious and ruthless, with a calculating mind and a
real gift for lying. In short, he had all the qualities necessary
to become an important Hyksos dignitary. Of course, he
would never remotely equal his master, Apophis, and it was
in his own interest to remain second-in-command. If not,
Tany herself would put an end to his brilliant career.

Angrily, she ordered one of her serving-maids to retrieve
the mirror, and snapped at another, an Egyptian whose family
had once been one of the richest in Sais, 'Paint my face
properly.'

Though the girl was skilful, and did her very best to make
Tany look less ugly and less masculine, the result was
disastrous: the poor girl only made things worse.

'You're trying to mock me!' screeched Tany.

She lashed out with the mirror, and the servant collapsed,
blood pouring from her head.

'Get rid of that creature,' she ordered the others, who were
stupefied with horror, 'and wash my face. I must go and see
the emperor.'

*

'Be quick and brief,' Apophis told his wife. 'The Great Council is awaiting me.'

'I don't involve myself in politics, but I have an interesting piece of information.'

'Then stop mumbling and speak clearly.'

'One of my serving-women confessed under torture that the Egyptians are still giving each other gifts without declaring them to the tax-collectors. I've drawn up a list of the guilty parties.'

'You've done well, Tany.'

The emperor left his office, took his seat in his travelling-chair and, under the watchful eyes of his bodyguards, was carried by slaves to the Temple of Set. Here, where the storm-god's protection was strongest, he would address his senior officials, announcing new directives which they must enforce without fail.

Thanks to his wife, he knew that the old Egyptian ways remained alive and that it would take more time to wipe them out. The richer a man is, the more he gives: so said the pharaohs, who had applied the rule to everyone, even themselves. Generosity was a social obligation and profit must not be a man's goal. A great man who lacked generosity destroyed his reputation, left the domain of Ma'at and became irredeemably mediocre, doomed to lose all he had thought he had gained.

The quality of what was produced was considered more important than its price at market, and it was the job of temples to check it, at the same time ensuring the proper circulation of offerings so that one of the most important aims of the pharaonic state might be accomplished: social cohesion, linked to the well-being of each individual.

Traditionally, all Egyptians, so long as they had the necessary skills, had been free to make what they needed themselves, and could gain a small profit through the system of barter, which extended to services. For example, a scribe who wanted to have a house built could write letters for the stone-cutter in return for a certain number of hours of the latter's work.

In this way, in the Two Lands every individual was at once a debtor and creditor to several other people. The pharaoh kept watch over the reciprocity of gifts and the proper circulation of generosity. He who received must give, even if the quantity were very small, and even if there were a delay. And the king, who had received so much from the gods, must give his people spiritual and material prosperity.

Apophis detested this law of Ma'at, this solidarity linking earthly beings with those in the world beyond. The Hyksos had realized that it was an obstacle to the full exercise of power and the accumulation of wealth by the ruling elite.

On the pavement before the Temple of Set, Khamudi greeted his master. 'My lord, all the necessary measures have been taken to ensure your safety.'

A heavy silence reigned inside the building. Not one general, provincial governor or head of a government secretariat was missing. They waited anxiously to learn what fate the emperor had in store for them. Apophis took time to enjoy the fear he inspired, before revealing his decisions.

'The Law of Ma'at is abolished once and for all,' he announced. 'Therefore we no longer need a tjaty or magistrates. Justice will be handed down by myself and my ministers, the most important of whom shall bear the title of High Treasurer of Lower Egypt. This vital role I entrust to my faithful Khamudi, who will also be my spokesman. He will write out my decrees on papyrus and ensure they are sent to all parts of the empire, so that none may be ignorant of them.'

Khamudi smiled broadly. He had officially become the second most important person in the state and was already imagining the fabulous profits he would make through controlling the papyrus industry. Sending out his master's decrees in written form would be an exhilarating task.

Tomorrow, all the empire's subjects would think as they were told to think, and no one would have the right to speak a word in opposition.

'We have all shown too much forbearance to the people we have vanquished,' went on the emperor, 'and this softness must stop. The new law is simple: they collaborate, or else they will be condemned to slavery or to forced labour in the mines. As for rich landowners, craftsmen and merchants, they must declare to the High Treasurer everything they own – and I mean everything, including the smallest household object or scrap of fabric. We shall then tax them on their fortunes, and those who have lied will be severely punished. Khamudi's men will carry out frequent, detailed checks. Of course, the members of the ruling tribe will not have to pay this tax.'

All the dignitaries gave a sigh of relief.

'Furthermore, I do not wish the word "freedom" to be spoken ever again in my empire,' decreed Apophis. 'Laws will be enacted regulating all social and individual behaviour, and everyone must conform to the new code, whose guarantors you will be. I require detailed reports on every person exercising any responsibility, so that I can be informed without delay about anyone whose loyalty is suspect. So long as you obey me blindly, you, the senior officials of the Hyksos Empire, will be rich and powerful.'

A Canaanite asked to speak. 'Majesty, may we increase taxes in all the provinces?'

'Indeed, that is essential. I fix them at one-fifth of all income.'

'Forgive me, Majesty, but is that not enormously high?'

'We shall go much further, believe me. And the people will pay, under threat of reprisals. Know also that every ship will owe one-tenth of its cargo to the palace: that is the price of the right to sail upon the Nile or our canals.'

Khamudi was positively drooling.

'No more questions?'

'Yes, Majesty,' said a Syrian general. 'What about the rebel movement?'

'It has been almost wiped out. True, a few madmen still survive, but the necessary measures have been taken.'

'Why not raze Thebes to the ground?'

'Thebes is under control,' said Apophis. 'I am using it as bait to attract the last of the rebels and leave the Egyptians a false glimmer of hope. The desperate slave is less productive than the one who believes in a future, however far-off. I may add that large-scale immigration and forced marriages will fundamentally alter the population. In a few decades, the old civilization will have been extinguished and Egypt will be Hyksos for ever.'

21

The High Priest of Karnak could not sleep, so he decided to get up, leave his little house beside the sacred lake, and take a walk through Amon's domain.

How he would have loved to see great building-works undertaken, to see the temple grow and become more beautiful. But Thebes had been bled dry, and there was no longer a pharaoh. Karnak was lapsing into a deathlike slumber.

It was a beautiful evening. The fourteenth day of the rising moon, the left eye of Horus, was drawing to an end; once again, Set had tried in vain to cut it into pieces. Thoth, the god of knowledge, had caught his eye in his net in the ocean of energy, so that it could shine again and make minerals and plants blossom. Made whole again, the moon was the very image of life-giving vigour and the symbol of a happy Egypt, complete with all its provinces.

The High Priest rubbed his eyes. It must be a mirage. Yet he was wide awake and there was nothing wrong with his eyes. To be on the safe side, he gazed up at the full moon for several long minutes.

Then, sure of what he had seen, he headed for the palace as fast as his old legs could carry him.

'Forgive me for waking you, Steward, but this is very important,' said the High Priest.

'I was not sleeping,' said Qaris.

'Her Majesty must be told.'

'She is very tired, and she needs rest.'

'Look at the moon – look at it closely!'

From the palace window, Qaris looked out. Scarcely able to believe what he had seen, he ran to the queen's bedchamber and woke her as gently as he could.

'What is happening, Qaris?' she asked sleepily.

'Something absolutely extraordinary, Majesty. The High Priest and I have both witnessed it, but only you can decide if our eyes are deceiving us. All you need do is look at the full moon.'

In her turn, Teti the Small gazed up at the sky's message. Awestruck, she whispered, 'Ahhotep . . . It's Ahhotep's face.'

She threw on a robe, and she and Qaris joined the High Priest.

'The oracle has spoken, Majesty,' said the High Priest. 'The princess herself must also see it, and then we shall know how to interpret it.'

'Laughter is guarding her rooms,' Qaris reminded him. 'He will not let anyone in.'

'This is too important . . . I shall take the risk, stay behind me.'

As soon as the High Priest approached, the huge dog opened its eyes and raised its heavy head, which was resting on a comfortable cushion.

'The heavens have spoken,' said the old man, 'and your mistress must hear their voice.'

Laughter gave a whine, of a kind the princess recognized immediately. Kissing Seqen lovingly on the forehead, she put on a tunic and opened the door of her bedchamber.

'High Priest! What are you doing here?'

'You must look at the full moon, Princess.'

She obeyed and said, 'It is splendid. The eye is full again, and the sun of night is driving away the darkness.'

'Do you see nothing else?'

'Is it not the sign of hope, which must inspire us to carry on the struggle?'

Teti and Qaris appeared.

'Look more carefully,' urged the queen.

'But what am I supposed to see?'

'The oracle has spoken,' repeated the High Priest, 'and we now know the will of the heavens. It is for you to draw the consequences from it.'

'I refuse,' said Ahhotep firmly. 'You are the rightful queen and you must remain so.'

'Three of us saw your face in the full moon,' said Teti, 'and you yourself did not recognize it. The manifestation of such an extraordinary sign leaves no room for doubt: your role is to embody its regenerative power upon earth. The time has come for me to step down, Ahhotep; I feel old and tired. Only a young queen, endowed with the magic of this office, can perhaps restore to Thebes the vigour it has lost.'

'But I don't want to take your place, Mother.'

'That is not what this is about. The Invisible has been made visible, the High Priest has authenticated the oracle. Would you rebel against the word of heaven, the dwelling-place of the souls of the pharaohs you revere?'

'I want to consult Mut.'

Mut, the eye of the Divine Light, wearer of the double crown, wife of the Divine Principle, nourished by Ma'at, at once female and male, appeared to Ahhotep in the place of silence.

Ahhotep dared gaze upon the statue, which was dimly lit by a ray of light passing through a small opening in the ceiling of the shrine.

'You have permitted me to touch your sceptre and you have made me taste your power. Thanks to you, I have fought my first battles, and I feel ready to continue the fight, whatever the dangers. But the sun of night demands yet more: that I become Queen of Egypt. I do not want that burden – it seems too heavy for my shoulders. But to defy the oracle and refuse the will of the gods would increase Thebes's suffering still further, and the rebels would lose all hope. At this moment I am lost, and I need you to show me the way. I beg you to answer this question: must I accept the full moon's decision?'

The lioness's eyes grew red and her smile broadened. And the granite head nodded, three times.

From the palace terrace, Teti and Ahhotep gazed out at the west bank of Thebes, where the sun would soon set to confront the trial of death and prepare for its resurrection. Already risen, the moon shone with unusual brilliance.

Teti smiled gently at her daughter. 'What is a Queen of Egypt? She is the beautiful Lady of the Two Lands, full of grace and the sweetness of love which appeases the god. She is imbued with magic, she sings the rites with a loving voice, she shakes the sistra with pure hands. She is the enchantress who fills the palace with her perfume and her dew, and speaks only words of meaning. She alone can see Horus and Set at peace; she alone knows the secrets of the eternal conflict between two celestial brothers. Everyone lives for the queen's words, for she has the power to reconcile opposites and bring about the reign of Ma'at and Hathor, righteousness and love.'

'Those are impossible goals, Mother.'

'And yet they are those the sages entrusted to the Queen of Egypt in the time of the pyramids. Many of those who preceded me succeeded in fulfilling them; I failed. You, who are about to succeed me, must never lose sight of them. The higher one climbs, the greater are one's duties. You will stand at the very summit, and will have neither rest nor any excuse for failure.'

Ahhotep was afraid; filled with a fear deeper and more intense than any she had ever felt before. She would rather have faced a band of Hyksos soldiers than this small, fragile woman whose greatness had just been revealed to her.

'The House of the Queen is dying,' Teti went on. 'You must rebuild it, surround yourself with skilful, loyal people, lead without causing conflict, bring prosperity to whatever you touch. I wish that the heavens were not so ruthless in burdening you with such a heavy office at a time when our country seems on the point of death. You are our last chance, Ahhotep.'

Suddenly, the beautiful young woman wished she could become a child again, prolong her adolescence, enjoy her beauty, savour the pleasures of life before the murderous darkness covered Thebes.

Teti read her daughter's thoughts. 'Too late,' she said. 'The oracle has spoken, you have Mut's agreement, and your fate has been written in the stone of her statue. Only one thing can prevent you fulfilling it.'

'What thing, Mother?'

'Failure to survive your initiation.'

22

As Princess Ahhotep approached the sacred lake of Karnak, thousands of swallows danced in the blue sky. Among them were the souls of the reborn, who had come from the other side of life to hail the initiation of a Queen of Egypt.

The young woman was so deep in contemplation that each ritual word engraved itself upon her heart, and the High Priest was so moved that he stammered. Never had he imagined that the gods would decide to entrust such a perilous office to such a wild creature. But the depths he glimpsed in Ahhotep's eyes proved to him that they had chosen wisely.

'Make your offering, Princess,' he said.

Ahhotep knelt facing the east, where the sun had just fought a victorious battle in the isle of flame. Her lips uttered the ancient dawn prayer, a hymn to the miracle of life, which had once again overcome death and the dragon of darkness.

'Let the purification be carried out.'

Two chantresses of Amon took off Ahhotep's white robe. Naked, she walked slowly down the steps into the peaceful waters of the sacred lake, the earthly image of the celestial *Nun*, the ocean of energy where all forms of life were born.

'Evil and destruction depart from you,' intoned a ritualist. 'As the divine water purifies you, so you become a daughter of the Light and of the stars.'

Ahhotep would have liked time to stop in its tracks. She felt protected, sheltered from all danger, in perfect communion with the unseen power that was bringing her to rebirth.

'Your limbs have been purified in the field of offerings,' continued the ritualist. 'None of them is lacking or at fault. Your being has been made young again, your soul can soar in the sky. Now you must enter the hall of Ma'at, where your heart shall be acknowledged as righteous.'

Regretfully, and wondering anxiously how she could be sure she had never violated the law of Ma'at, she climbed out of the sacred lake. When the sun had dried her skin, the chantresses of Amon dressed her in a tunic of immaculately white ancient linen.

Unhesitatingly she followed the ritualist to the entrance to a shrine. He opened the door. On one wall was a depiction of the god Osiris, the supreme judge. Facing the princess was the queen, holding in her right hand a golden ostrich plume, symbol of heaven's justice.

Ahhotep sensed that she was addressing not her mother but the earthly representative of the goddess of righteousness.

'You who judge me, you know my heart,' she declared. 'I have never sought to do evil and I have only one desire: to liberate Egypt and her people so that Ma'at may direct our course once more.'

'Are you ready, Ahhotep, to confront injustice, violence, hatred, falsehood and ingratitude without filling the vase of your heart with them?'

'I am.'

'Do you know that on the day of judgment your heart will be weighed and that it must be as light as an ostrich plume?'

'I do.'

'May the stone of Ma'at be the plinth on which you build your reign. Feed on Ma'at, live through her and with her. Earth and heaven will not push you away, the gods will fashion your king. Go towards the light, Ahhotep.'

Although the stages of the ritual were carried out slowly,

115

the princess had the feeling that her initiation was taking place at almost breakneck pace. She crossed the star-strewn heavens, descended into the depths where Ptah, the divine craftsman, fashioned her limbs, climbed into the ship of Osiris, saw Ra at his rising and Atum at his dusk, drank the water of the flood and the milk of the celestial cow.

After she had been dressed in the ceremonial robe woven by the goddess Tayt, Ahhotep was perfumed and adorned with a great collar and bracelets.

'You have crossed space like the wind,' said the High Priest, 'and you have become one with the light on the horizon. May Horus, protector of royalty, and Thoth, master of knowledge, give you life as a queen.'

Ahhotep was summoned to stand on an offertory table. Two priests, one wearing the mask of a falcon and the other that of an ibis, raised vases above her head. Two rays emerged and bathed the young woman in an eerie light. Her heart swelled, and she saw into the far distance, like a bird of prey.

Priestesses covered her head with a headdress woven in imitation of a vulture's pelt, symbol of the heavenly mother; on top of this they placed the traditional crown of the queens of Egypt, in the shape of two tall feathers.

Teti the Small handed her a floral sceptre with a flexible shaft, the sign of female power.

Qaris had organized a modest banquet in one of the temple courtyards, away from prying eyes.

'Forgive the lack of elaborate ceremony, Majesty,' he said to Ahhotep, 'but your coronation must remain secret for as long as possible. In the palace there are too many curious ears. If the Hyksos were to find out that Thebes has chosen a young queen to govern her, their reaction might well be violent.'

'I also regret this secret coronation,' added Teti the Small. 'But we are rebels, and it had to be like this.'

The High Priest approached Ahhotep, carrying a bow and

four arrows. 'We are in a place of peace, Majesty, but our land is occupied and henceforth you alone will represent the hope of freedom. In presenting you with these weapons, I beg you to embody the goddess of the city of Thebes, so that she may at last take up the struggle again.'

Ahhotep had never handled the large bow. Yet the faith within her enabled her to know instantly what to do. She shot the first arrow north, the second south, the third east, and the fourth west.

'May you have conquered all four directions, Majesty,' said the High Priest. 'They know who you are and what you wish. May the space crossed by the moon, your protector, inspire all that you do.'

Accompanied by Laughter, Seqen was permitted to sit beside his wife. The few guests sensed the gravity of the moment, and it robbed them of their appetite for the dishes prepared by the High Priest's cook. Only the dog did justice to the roast pigeons and the Nile perch.

'Seqen, is everything as usual at the palace?' asked Teti.

'Yes, all is calm. Rumour has it that you and your daughter are praying to Amon, begging him to protect the town from the fury of the Hykos.'

One of the High Priest's assistants brought a jar of wine. 'Here is a fine vintage dating from the year before the invasion,' he said. 'It still has the taste of freedom. But before it is drunk, I would like to sing you an ancient poem, accompanying myself on the harp.'

His voice was cracked, but the words were very clear.

'When a form takes flesh, it is condemned to die. The spirits of life will make your name live, and you will have a fine place in the West. But the river never ceases to flow, and each man must go at his appointed time. The tombs of the nobles have vanished; their walls have crumbled to dust as though they had never existed. Have

117

one happy day, Queen of Egypt: rejoice in this moment. Follow your heart throughout your life, perfume your skin and wear lotus garlands at your throat; forget sadness while those you love are seated by your side. Remember this happiness until the moment when you step into the land of eternal silence.'

Everyone was plunged into gloom by these sombre words, which removed all gaiety from these poor festivities. Nevertheless, the wine was poured, and Seqen hoped that it would dispel the atmosphere of melancholy.

Laughter leapt up on his hind legs and, with one swipe of his paw, knocked away Ahhotep's cup as she put it to her lips. Then he turned towards the harpist, growling.

Ignoring him, the harpist ostentatiously drained his own cup.

Ahhotep stood up. 'You poisoned the wine, didn't you?'

'Yes, Majesty.'

'Are you in the service of the Hyksos?'

'No, Majesty, but I believe your enterprise to be utter folly, which will bring only misfortune and destruction. For that reason, I wanted us to die together, at the end of this banquet, in order to spare the country any more sufferings. But your dog decided otherwise . . .'

The harpist's lips turned white, he gasped for breath, his eyes bulged and his head fell to one side.

Ahhotep gazed up at the sky. 'Look at the moon. Its name, Ah, is masculine because the spirit that lives there is the god of battle. From now on, the silver disc in its ship shall be our rallying sign.'

On the palm of her left hand, the new queen drew what was both the beginning of her name and the programme for her reign.

23

Easily recognizable by his curly hair and by the mushroom-shaped headdress wound around his pointed head, Jannas the Asian was not displeased to be returning to Avaris on his flagship. As supreme commander of the Hyksos war-fleet, he maintained a discipline among his Anatolian pirates, Phoenicians and Cyprians at the point of a knife: these were men whose reputation for boldness and cruelty stood unchallenged.

Anyone who met Jannas for the first time would not have been afraid; quite the reverse. He was of average height, rather sickly in appearance, and moved and spoke slowly, giving the impression of a peaceable man in whom you could confide.

But those who had been taken in by that impression were all dead. Jannas had an aggressive nature which was all the more formidable because it found expression only in battle, and he was regarded as the greatest of all Hyksos heroes. He had triumphed in all four corners of the empire and had climbed to the highest rank in the army before being given command of the fleet by Apophis, who was obsessed with constantly improving his warships. Jannas knew every sailor, inspected every vessel himself, insisted on daily manoeuvres and punished ferociously even the slightest infringement of discipline.

Convinced that the empire would continue to grow because it was based on the army, the only worthy yardstick, Jannas was utterly loyal to Apophis. It was Apophis, after all, who had transformed the capital into a gigantic barracks where life was good.

The commander rarely rested, for he was ready to move at a moment's notice, wherever his informants indicated an attempt at sedition, however feeble. The mere sight of the Hyksos war-fleet was enough to put out the dwindling flames of rebellion. With the submission of Minoa, Apophis had achieved a decisive victory, a prelude to other conquests – which Jannas would spearhead.

Barring unexpected incidents, the commander planned to spend a week enjoying the quiet life of his official residence, and take the opportunity to enjoy regular massages. But he grew bored easily, and made sure to visit the port every single day; as he was doing now.

'My lord,' said a Cyprian captain as soon as Jannas stepped on to the quayside, 'something strange is going on.'

'Where?'

'In our disused warehouse. We've heard high-pitched cries, as if someone was torturing women. I have set men on guard all round it, and we await your orders.'

'Probably rebels who have taken Hyksos prisoners and are torturing them,' assumed Jannas, who was delighted by the thought of arresting them himself and making them pay for their crimes on the spot.

As they neared the warehouse, they caught the smell of burning flesh.

'Force the door,' ordered Jannas.

Ten soldiers ran at it with a beam and stove it in at the first attempt. The sight that met Jannas's eyes left him open-mouthed.

Four young girls lay naked and shackled on the ground. Sitting on a wooden chest was a fat, fair-haired woman, who laughed periodically as a man branded his victims with bronze tools heated in a fire. He was clearly enjoying his work.

And that man was not just anybody.

'Can it be you . . . the High Treasurer?' gasped Jannas.

Khamudi did not seem in the least troubled. 'It can indeed. And this is my wife, the lady Yima.'

The woman bobbed her head and smiled coyly at Jannas as if trying to seduce him.

'You are interrogating suspects, I suppose?' he asked.

'Suspects?' echoed Khamudi. 'Not at all, Commander. My wife and I are amusing ourselves with these slave-girls who have come up from the country. My steward found some old bronze branding-irons shaped like a goose, the sacred bird of Amon, and a lion's head. I wanted to see if they still worked and I'm trying them out on the skin of these idiot girls. They scream a lot, but that's the fun of the game.'

'Is the emperor aware of these practices?'

'Send your men away, Commander.'

At a sign from Jannas, they vanished.

'Our beloved Apophis knows everything I do,' sneered Khamudi.

'Torture is vital to make rebels talk,' conceded Jannas, 'but, as you said yourself, these girls—'

'I take my pleasure as I choose, Jannas. Is that clear?'

'Very clear, High Treasurer.'

'I don't care if you're shocked. But don't try to use this situation against me, or you will get your fingers burnt. Is that also clear?'

Jannas nodded.

'Yima, my darling, continue to amuse yourself. I am going to hear the commander's report.'

Yima applied the lioness-head brand to the buttocks of the youngest peasant-girl; her screams almost burst Jannas's eardrums.

Christian Jacq

'Let's go out on to the quayside,' he suggested.

Khamudi unhurriedly put on his robes. 'How are things with our rearward base in Canaan?'

'The city of Sharuhen is fully fortified. It stands at the mouth of the rivers and wadis, and controls the region, which has submitted completely to the emperor. The garrison consists of elite soldiers and I have had a vast port constructed for our warships, which are always ready to sail at a moment's notice. If you will give me the necessary authorization, the ship-building yard I am about to set up will build many more.'

'You have it,' said Khamudi. 'Are you on good terms with the garrison commander?'

'Very good. He's a Canaanite, a very able man, and his loyalty is absolute.'

'Whom have you appointed to command the local fleet?'

'One of my assistants. He'll do nothing without an explicit order from me – from you, too, of course.'

'Then you guarantee that Sharuhen will stand firm?'

'That town is one of the indestructible pillars of the empire,' Jannas assured him.

'Let us move on to Memphis.'

'Ah, there I have some reservations.'

'Why?'

'We built Sharuhen ourselves, and the Canaanites are ancestral enemies of the Egyptians. Memphis is the pharaohs' ancient capital, and' – Jannas hesitated – 'things are very different there.'

'Are you criticizing the measures I've taken?'

'Indeed not, High Treasurer. They are most effective. The government has been solidly established, guards patrol every district of the city, the workshops are producing first-rate weapons and my fleet controls the movements of even the smallest boat.'

'What more could one ask?'

'What worries me are the results obtained by our informants. Not a day passes without our making one or two arrests.'

'Rebels?' asked Khamudi.

'No, simple folk who refuse to accept the reality of the situation and still dare to protest against what they call "the occupation".'

'Why do these imbeciles refuse to understand?'

'Nothing can persuade them that their Egypt is dead and that from now on they are subjects of Pharaoh Apophis.'

'You have them executed, I hope?'

'The executions are held in public and the army forces the citizens to watch. Unfortunately, though, the fire has not yet been put out.'

Khamudi took Jannas's report very seriously. He had discussed the matter at length with the emperor, and was not entirely surprised. Memphis's capacity for resistance was proving greater than foreseen and – as he had suspected – they would have to resort to more radical action.

'Things cannot continue like that, Commander. In his wisdom, the emperor foresaw that certain Egyptians might be mad enough to go on believing in their past glory, so you are to return to Memphis immediately with the following instructions . . .'

Jannas showed no emotion as he listened to the orders. What the High Treasurer was demanding was monstrous, but a Hyksos – and the supreme commander of the navy, to boot – could not worry about that kind of thing.

With a spring in his step, Khamudi went back into the warehouse, from which screams were still issuing. Without a doubt his darling Yima would have kept a branding-iron on the fire for him so that he could put the finishing touches to their handiwork.

24

'I'm pregnant,' announced Ahhotep.

'Already? How can you be sure?' asked Teti. 'You must take the tests and—'

'The tests confirm it: I'm expecting a child, and it's a boy.'

'Good, good. Now, you must eat red meat, and take plenty of rest, and—'

'Red meat, yes; rest, no. You know the enormous task facing me, and my son must get used to hard work. Rebuilding the House of the Queen won't be easy – particularly as we must do it in secret.'

'You mustn't upset yourself, Ahhotep. You ought to—'

'Am I or am I not Queen of Egypt?'

Teti saw a new flame burn in her daughter's eyes.

'My first decision is that we must re-establish the link with our ancestors' traditions, and if I am to be a true queen I have an important duty to perform.'

Teti thought she had misheard. 'Surely you don't mean . . .?'

'Ah, but I do: exactly what you're thinking.'

Watched placidly by Long-Ears, Seqen was busy practising the military exercises that would transform him into an able soldier within a few weeks.

Although a tendency to excitability made Seqen a poor archer, his instructor was gradually teaching him to overcome it; moreover, Seqen had an instinctive feel for the axe and the club. He was nimble enough to dodge even the most vicious strokes and often caught his opponents unawares with swift counter-blows.

The young man was gaining strength at an astonishing rate. Lifting weights, running, swimming: nothing daunted him. And every evening he savoured the blissful moment when Ahhotep massaged his body with a truly magical ointment. Not only did it remove all traces of fatigue, but it gave him all the ardour he needed for new and passionate games. Seqen was madly in love with the young queen, and thanked the gods each morning for the happiness they had bestowed upon him.

'Could you make me a new weapon?' he asked his instructor.

'What sort of weapon?'

'A club with an oval head, longer than the average and with a knife-blade securely fixed to the handle.'

'That's not a bad idea. You could break heads and slit throats as well. I'll make you a wooden one, for you to try out against a peasant who wants to enrol in the Theban army. Don't damage him too much, though – new recruits are in short supply.'

When the new club was ready, Seqen tried it for balance. He liked it. He carried it down to the little barracks courtyard, where he found his opponent, a sturdy fellow with broad shoulders and a low forehead.

'Greetings, friend,' said Seqen. 'Do you want to learn to fight?'

'Yes, I do. Are you really Prince Seqen?'

'I am.'

'And you want to fight the Hyksos?'

'Don't you?'

'Not exactly, Prince.'

The man unsheathed a short-sword.

'During training,' Seqen reminded him, 'we use wooden weapons.'

'This isn't an exercise, Prince, this is your first and last battle.'

Seqen turned to ask his instructor for help, but he had vanished. Running away would mean climbing a high wall. Anyway, there was no time.

His opponent smiled grimly. 'Are you afraid, Prince? Quite right. It's no joke dying so young.' He came slowly closer.

Seqen took a step back. 'Who are you?'

'A good soldier paid to kill you.'

'If you spare my life and tell me who paid you, I'll make you a rich man.'

'The Hyksos wouldn't give me time to enjoy my riches – and in any case you've got no money to give me. You should have stayed a peasant, Prince, and not got mixed up in what doesn't concern you.'

Seqen stopped backing away. 'Kneel before your superior, soldier.'

The attacker was astounded. 'Have you lost your mind?'

'Since you belong to the Theban army and I am assuming command of it, you owe me respect and obedience. I will agree to forget this act of insubordination, but only if you hand over your weapon to me immediately.'

'I'm going to hand this sword into your belly!'

The attacker rushed at Seqen, but he dodged aside. As he did so, he brought his wooden club down on the back of the man's neck. Scarcely had the soldier turned round when the furious young man broke his nose with a well-placed punch, before slitting his throat with the knife on the handle of his club.

'You should have listened to your prince, you worthless scum.'

*

Seqen was fast on his feet, and succeeded in catching his instructor, who had been spotted running out of the barracks. With a well-timed sword-thrust, he wounded the man in the thigh, bringing him down.

Faced with Seqen's rage and threats of instant death, the instructor talked a great deal: yes, he had paid a soldier to kill him; no, he was not in the pay of the Hyksos, but several Theban nobles were advocating collaboration with the occupiers and were taking care to nip any sign of resistance in the bud.

With the queen's agreement, Seqen arrested the traitors himself, and a detachment of soldiers loyal to the royal family took them into the Western desert at nightfall. Without weapons or food, the miserable creatures would make fine prey for the bloodthirsty monsters that haunted those fearsome parts.

'Your second victory!' exclaimed Ahhotep. 'And you won it single-handed, with no help at all from anyone else.'

'There's a cancer in Thebes,' said Seqen. 'Before we do anything else, we must be sure of the people who surround us and those who want to fight at our side.'

'You're right. And that will be our second decision.'

'What's the first one?'

'We're going to the temple.'

'To the temple? Aren't you going to tell me why?'

'There's no time for that now.'

Intrigued, Seqen followed the queen to Karnak.

The only other people present in the shrine of Mut were Teti the Small and the High Priest of Amon. A lamp lit the shrine.

'As Queen of the Two Lands,' declared Ahhotep, 'I see Horus and Set made one again. For the reconciliation to take place, it must become flesh in the person of Pharaoh. That is why I recognize you as such: you, Seqen-en-Ra, "Valiant One of the Divine Light". Your second name shall be "Great

127

Bread", which also means "Great Earth", both of which you shall give back to us. You shall become at once "He Who Belongs to the Bee", who knows the mysteries of fire and air, and "He Who Belongs to the Reed", who knows the mysteries of water and earth.'

Ahhotep crowned her husband with the *names* headdress, one of the most ancient royal diadems. It enabled Pharaoh's thoughts to travel across the heavens and bring about the reunification of life and death, sunlight and moonlight, Ra and Osiris.

Seqen was so dumbfounded that he could not even find the words to protest. Clearly he was not really here in the shrine, and would soon emerge from this incredible dream.

'This ritual has been cut to its barest bones,' said Ahhotep, 'and your coronation will remain secret for as long as necessary, but that will not alter the great scope of your office, O King of Upper and Lower Egypt. Be at once builder, law-maker, and warrior. Render the earth fertile. Send forth the creative fire that gives us life, and the destructive fire that brings death to our enemies. Be the protecting dyke and the rampart, the hall that is cool in summer, warm in winter. Enable Ma'at to reign, and drive away injustice and tyranny.'

The High Priest unrolled the papyrus that, in accordance with the writings of the god Thoth, proclaimed the start of a new reign.

Teti the Small and Ahhotep then spoke the incantation that would give the young pharaoh the magical energy to carry out his programme of government – a programme contained in the name Seqen, meaning valour and the power to overcome.

'Pharaoh is reborn,' declared Teti, 'but the secret must be closely guarded until Thebes is safe again.'

'Everything is changed,' said the High Priest, moved almost to tears. 'Everything has changed, for Egypt once again has a royal couple. They will give us the strength to hold our heads high at last.'

25

It was not cause enough for celebration, but the events of recent weeks had encouraged even the most demoralized of the rebels.

. At Avaris, no more of them had been arrested. Those who had remained in the capital to glean information had to take endless precautions in order to pass it on safely, but the network established by the wily Moustache had proved sound. Untrustworthy people had been eliminated, and passwords and codes were changed frequently.

At Memphis, too, the prospects were improving. Several Hyksos spies had been identified, and the small groups of rebels were at last proving impenetrable. They still had no weapons, strategy or leader, but they talked about the future and had come to believe that freedom was not entirely dead.

The Afghan continued to use his favourite tactic: depriving the emperor of as many eyes and ears as possible. As soon as a Hyksos informant was identified, the Afghan organized an ambush with two or three comrades, and cut out the cancer. He was cautious, took as much time as he needed, and never hesitated to postpone an operation if there was the slightest element of doubt. At first Moustache had been impatient, but he had come to recognize the effectiveness of this meticulous work.

Thanks to the progress they had made, the rebels had been

able to set up their headquarters in the heart of the city, near the great Temple of Ptah. The Afghan, Moustache, and their men lived there, in an old, two-storey house surrounded by carpenters' workshops.

Whenever the Hyksos guards inspected the district, the rebels were immediately alerted by a lookout posted on the terrace of the house at the corner of the street, or by an old man sitting opposite, who raised his walking-stick. As a final security measure, a dog had been trained to bark in a particular way.

Despite the Hyksos's vigilance, the rebels were succeeding in weaving their web. Increasingly oppressed, the population of Memphis hated the Hyksos. The majority were too afraid to take action, but they were all ready to help those who were determined to win back freedom. People of all ages were putting themselves forward: but which of them would turn out to be reliable?

'Afghan, the priest of Ptah wants to see you,' said Moustache.

'Who sent him?'

'A temple baker, a very reliable contact.'

'Did you have the priest followed?'

'Of course.'

'Have the baker tell him to go to the first alleyway north of the temple. I will walk towards him, and you will be in hiding with two of our men. At the slightest sign of trouble, kill the priest. If there are too many Hyksos, run for it.'

'I won't leave you.'

'If this is an ambush, you must.'

Although he had not seen anything out of the ordinary, the Afghan was on his guard. He retraced his steps, pretended to walk away, then returned to the man sitting on a stool, with his eyes closed.

'Are you the priest of Ptah?' he asked.

'All three are gods. Do you know the desert?'

'I love only the black earth.'

130

The passwords had been correctly spoken. The Afghan sat down to the left of the Egyptian, who handed him some onions to munch.

'What have you to offer, priest?'

'An uprising in the northern district of Memphis, involving the majority of the dock-workers. We shall break into the weapons store, steal a lot of weapons, and then seize several Hyksos boats.'

'That's a very dangerous plan – even if you succeed it will be a bloodbath.'

'I know.'

'Who will be in command?'

'The High Priest of Ptah himself. He needs your men to kill the Hyksos sentries who guard the weapons store, and also to create diversions in the south of the city. The Hyksos will head there in force, and then we can attack the port.'

'We may well be slaughtered.'

'We shall be slaughtered anyway – if not tomorrow, some other day. We have only one chance in a thousand of retaking Memphis, but it's better to try than to do nothing.'

'You're right, priest,' said the Afghan. 'When do you intend to make your move?'

'In three days' time, at dusk.'

'This very evening, I shall call a meeting of the rebel leaders. You and I will meet here again at dawn tomorrow, and I'll tell you our plan in detail.'

In the rebels' house, the night was long and filled with enthusiasm. Despite warnings from the Afghan and Moustache, their comrades were eager to take on the Hyksos and inflict a stinging defeat upon them. The High Priest of Ptah's decision was of prime importance: the other Servants of God would follow suit, and the uprising would soon spread throughout the land.

Trying to keep a cool head, Moustache went in minute

detail over his diversionary tactics and his plan for killing the sentries. He had to calm a few hotheads who could already see themselves killing Apophis himself, but everyone eventually accepted strict orders. At dawn the meeting broke up, and they parted company with their hearts full of hope.

'Let's go and get some air on the terrace,' suggested the Afghan.

There was a pink glow in the eastern sky, and a few clouds were delaying the new triumph of the reborn sun.

'The watchman at the corner isn't at his post,' said the Afghan.

Moustache leant over the balustrade. 'Nor is the old man. They must have gone home to bed.'

'Both of them? That's strictly against the rules.'

The sound of barking disturbed the silence, and then came the agonized moans of a dog being beaten to death.

'They've killed the dog,' said the Afghan urgently, 'and the watchmen, too. We must get away from here – we've been betrayed. No, not the street. The only way is across the roofs.'

Jannas had decided to launch the attack at dawn, just as the priests were celebrating the first rites, calling upon the presence of a pharaoh who was not Apophis. Since the priests were entrenching themselves in this spiritual dissidence and providing material help to the rebels, the best solution was to break their back.

Jannas was of the opinion that arrests and the closure of the temples would suffice, but Khamudi had demanded a great deal more: that the priests be put to death and the sacred buildings of the old capital be destroyed.

Without understanding why, Jannas had been somewhat shocked by this order, even though he, a Hyksos warrior, was used to sowing terror and desolation. Perhaps, he thought, too many easy victories and too much comfortable Egyptian living had made him soft. And he should not have been bothered by

132

Khamudi's behaviour towards female slaves, either. Bringing proud Memphis to heel would put an end to these misgivings.

'Commander, how do we tell the high priests from the others?' asked an officer.

'You don't. You kill everyone you find in the temples and burn the bodies.'

'Is looting permitted?'

'Of course. I don't want to see a single temple left standing in Memphis.'

'And . . . what about the women?'

'The soldiers may use them. At sunset, all officers are to report to me.'

Moustache was covered in sweat and having difficulty getting his breath back.

Spotted by Hyksos soldiers, he and the Afghan had had to leap from roof to roof, at the risk of breaking their necks. An arrow had even grazed Moustache's temple, but the two rebels had proved more agile than their pursuers and had managed to throw them off.

'Down there,' panted Moustache. 'Afghan, look down there. Flames, huge flames!'

'It's the Temple of Ptah – they're burning it.'

The Egyptian had tears in his eyes. 'The Temple of Ptah? It can't be. They wouldn't dare.'

'A lot of Egyptians are going to die today, and Memphis will be broken. We shall have to find another base as soon as we've made contact with any others who escape.'

'Three days' time,' said Moustache. 'But how did that devil Apophis know he had to launch a preventive attack?'

'Precisely because he is a devil.'

'Then there's no point in going on.'

'Even devils have their weaknesses, my friend. In the mountains of my homeland, we're used to fighting them. Believe me, they don't always win.'

133

26

Sheltered from the sun by a canopy supported by two small pillars in the form of lotus-stems, King Apophis and High Treasurer Khamudi were feasting on dishes prepared by the emperor's personal cook, an Egyptian who was forced to taste every dish in the king's presence. Apophis had demanded antelope cooked in sauce, accompanied by lentils and split peas. Three slaves wielded fans with acacia-wood handles and ostrich feathers, so that the king and his guest would not be troubled by heat or flies.

'This red wine is excellent,' remarked Apophis, sprinkling cumin on his food to aid his digestion.

Khamudi preferred juniper, which was a combined stimulant, laxative and diuretic.

He said, 'This jar comes from the High Priest of Ptah's cellar, Majesty. His fine wines are now in your cellar instead.'

'A satisfactory expedition, wouldn't you say?'

'A total success,' agreed Khamudi. 'Memphis is on her knees at last. The temples have been burnt and destroyed, and the priests and their accomplices executed. Everyone knows what punishment the rebels suffered.'

'Jannas has done well. Have the stone blocks from the temples sent to Avaris; we'll use them to build quays. I want Memphis to be a dead city, whose trade and financial activities are transferred to my capital.'

The cook served the dessert, dates pounded in honey.

'Taste it,' ordered the emperor.

The Egyptian looked unwell.

'Is it sour?' asked Apophis sarcastically.

'Not at all, Majesty. I did not sleep well and I am tired. The dessert is excellent, I assure you.' His colour returned.

'The emperor must not run risks. Have this idiot executed, Khamudi, and replace him.'

At a sign from the High Treasurer, two Cyprian pirates dragged the unfortunate man away, ignoring his pleas for mercy.

'These Egyptians never stop whining,' said the emperor, 'which is why they are useless soldiers. But tell me, what news of our new Information secretariat?'

Khamudi ran a hand through his well-oiled black hair. 'I've made great progress, Majesty. The traditional methods of correspondence are under control, of course, but I have invented a new one which ought to please you. Before I describe it, permit me to give you this gift.'

Khamudi handed Apophis a magnificent amethyst scarab mounted on a gold ring. The emperor slipped it on to the little finger of his left hand.

'A pretty piece,' he said. 'Now tell me about your invention.'

'For the Egyptians, this scarab is a symbol of happiness. It embodies continual rebirth, both on earth and in the otherworld. It is also a hieroglyph meaning "to be born", "to become", or "to be transformed". The one you are wearing belonged to an illustrious pharaoh – though of course his glory was a mere illusion compared to yours. With this jewel, you will confirm yourself as the king who brings happiness to his subjects. At the very sight of this symbol, many prominent Egyptians will be persuaded that you are the sole embodiment of the future. Hence my idea: we shall produce thousands of scarabs and re-use old ones on which we shall write our official messages.'

135

Khamudi opened a small bag and took out five scarabs of different sizes and made of materials ranging from limestone to fine porcelain.

'On the flat side,' he continued, 'my scribes will write the texts I dictate. These little things are easy to transport, and will soon flood the empire with the information we wish to disseminate. And the Egyptians will regard the messages on our scarabs as signs of good fortune.'

'Brilliant, Khamudi, quite brilliant. But I want to read each and every one of these messages. Not one is to be sent out without my explicit agreement.'

'I understand entirely, Majesty.'

'Indoctrination is as effective a weapon as war-chariots, my friend. With war-chariots we kill bodies; with indoctrination we kill souls.' Apophis paused and scowled. 'Have the fan-bearers replaced. These good-for-nothings are weakening – I can scarcely breathe.'

Only too happy to have escaped with their lives, the slaves yielded their places to a new team.

Apophis stroked his wine-flask; it was the one on which a map of Egypt was drawn. 'Despite the destruction of the temples in Memphis a few small groups of rebels still exist, and they're all the more dangerous because they can move around easily. If they've been driven to despair, they may commit acts of terrorism which would annoy me exceedingly. They will not surrender and they are very difficult to identify, so we must put so much pressure on them that they have to leave their lairs and regroup.'

'How, Majesty?'

'By providing them with misleading information. We are going to make them believe that Thebes represents a real hope and that they must go there as soon as possible. You will therefore write a letter to this effect and entrust it to a special messenger who will go from tavern to tavern proclaiming – under the influence of drink – that he is the bearer of a very important message to the fortress at Per-Hathor.'

'Where shall I begin?'

Apophis gazed at the flask, deep in thought. 'The one to the south of Memphis – that's where they're hiding. And a little further south, around the old town of Henen-Nesut, elite soldiers will await the rebels as they travel to Thebes. I have the feeling that there is someone dangerous among them.'

Khamudi was astonished. 'But there's no one left capable of challenging us.'

'You must realize that sometimes one man can be more formidable than an entire army. This man must be killed as soon as possible.'

Seqen had been so shaken by his coronation, and the news that he was to become a father, that Ahhotep had granted him a few hours' rest in the Theban countryside. Protected by Laughter, the couple had enjoyed a long walk through the fields, ending by a canal bordered by tall willows.

'You shouldn't have done it, Ahhotep. You shouldn't have—'

'Of course I should. How could I have spent my life with a second-rate man? A queen's first duty is to give birth to a pharaoh, so that's what I did. And Pharaoh will be the father of my son.'

'But you know perfectly well that—'

'If you couldn't shoulder these responsibilities, I'd have given up the idea; but you can. However, I agree that you need a little time to develop your powers, so we shan't rush things – well, not too much.'

She kissed him passionately, and desire kindled within him.

'Let's lie down in the shade of the willows,' she said.

This quiet corner was a little paradise, well suited to the games of love. Seqen took off his kilt and laid it out on the riverbank. This improvised bed pleased Ahhotep, who received her eager lover's caresses with delight. Like her, Seqen was a creature of great enthusiasm, to whom tepid emotions were foreign. And a man like that had the qualities of a king.

'Why don't you catch some fish?' Ahhotep suggested later.

Seqen put together a rudimentary fishing-rod from reeds and used a nice fat earthworm as bait.

'According to my mother,' she said as she watched him, 'the only strong man left in Thebes is the minister for agriculture. He is the descendant of an old, rich family; he owns a great deal of land and the only thing he wants is to keep his wealth intact, so he orders his peasants to go on working for him instead of joining the army. My mother has tried several times to convince him that such lack of action is condemning Thebes to death, and him with it, but he doesn't believe a word of it and has become entrenched in his position. Almost all the nobles listen to him, so nothing changes; and we're behaving like faithful subjects of the emperor.'

'And what are you planning to do about him?'

'Either he obeys me or I shall dismiss him from his offices.'

'But this fellow seems as haughty as he is stubborn – he'll never obey a woman.'

'He's an obstacle which must be removed. As long as he's in office, we shall be powerless.'

Although Laughter seemed fast asleep, his head resting on his crossed front paws, he suddenly made a powerful leap at Seqen. Under the impact, the young man was knocked several paces away from where he had been standing. And the crocodile's jaws snapped shut on empty air instead of on the king's legs.

Thwarted, the creature prepared to attack again, but the giant dog's barking and the stones Ahhotep threw drove it away.

'You've caught the biggest fish of all,' commented Ahhotep.

'The scribes in charge of the canals aren't doing their job any more,' grumbled Seqen. 'In the old days, no crocodile would have been able to venture into them.'

'That's true, but there's something else, something much more serious. The crocodile's attack is a sign that someone has put the evil eye on us. We must fight back against it straight away.'

27

'You're right, Ahhotep,' said Teti. 'The evil eye is upon us, particularly upon our new king.'

'How can we save him?'

'You and he must acquire the *heka*, the magical power that deflects harmful influences. Without it success is impossible, but the evil eye is denying you access to it. Fortunately, the way it manifested itself betrays its origins. The willow is the sacred tree of the temple at Dendera. Probably the tree has been badly damaged, and the gods hold Pharaoh responsible.'

'We must repair the damage,' decided the young queen.

'But Dendera is in Hyksos territory!'

'A peasant couple and their donkey won't arouse the Hyksos's suspicions.'

The royal couple travelling without protection on roads controlled by the invader? Their plan was madness, but Teti had no power to oppose it.

Long-Ears did not slow his pace as he approached the guard-post outside Kebet, which meant that the officials would cause the travellers no problems.

In fact, the powerful noonday sun had made them lethargic. They simply made a cursory search of the bags the donkey was carrying, and took two pairs of brand-new sandals as a toll.

The temple at Dendera lay deep in remote countryside. It had been built during the time of the pyramids and was dedicated to Hathor. The overgrown gardens in front of the building were a sure sign that there were no longer enough priests and labourers to care for them.

Long-Ears halted and sniffed the air. Then, reassured, he set off again at a brisker pace.

'No Hyksos around here,' concluded Ahhotep.

An old woman came out on to the temple forecourt and confronted them. 'I am the High Priestess of this temple,' she said. 'It is too poor now to welcome and feed travellers, so I ask you to continue on your way.'

'We shan't trouble you,' replied Ahhotep. 'We've only come to see the sacred willow.'

'It is dying, as is the whole country. Neither you nor I can do anything.'

'I don't agree, High Priestess.'

'And who are you?'

'Ahhotep, Queen of the Two Lands.'

The priestess was taken aback. 'Is Teti the Small dead?'

'My mother is alive, but she has passed on her power to me.'

'Power, Majesty? What power?'

'Perhaps the power to regenerate the Willow of Dendera.'

'Alas, that is impossible! You cannot even get near it.'

'I must,' said Ahhotep firmly.

Wearily, the old woman led her two visitors to the rear of the temple, where there was a small lake. In the middle of it stood a tall willow with withered leaves; it was so bent that it looked as if it might collapse at any moment.

As Ahhotep climbed over the surrounding wall to examine the tree more closely, the water began to bubble and a crocodile's jaws snapped at her, forcing her to beat a hasty retreat.

'Our guardians spirit has turned against us,' explained the

High Priestess. 'When the willow falls, the evil eye will have
won.'

Seqen had a sudden overwhelming feeling of inner power.
'I shall make it stand straight again,' he vowed.

'Do not risk your life,' urged the High Priestess.

Ahhotep asked her, 'Do you remember the incantations
that were spoken when the willow was planted?'

'Of course, but it is a royal rite and has not been practised
for a long time.'

'Recite it to me. I shall endow Seqen with magical
abilities.'

Ahhotep stood as goddesses were depicted, their hands
radiating waves of energy to empower those they protected,
while the High Priestess spoke the words of the ancient ritual.
They celebrated the moment when the sun had reached its
zenith and the sacred tree had stretched up to the heavens, tall
and strong.

Banishing his fear, Seqen waded into the lake. If the
crocodile attacked, Ahhotep would come to his aid. But the
reptile* backed away, its tail thrashing the water in rage.
Then it began to grow quieter, and Seqen succeeded in
reaching the foot of the willow.

He bent down, plunged his hand into the water and
removed a small wooden crocodile. 'Look,' he said. 'Now the
monster is tamed.'

'And look at the tree!' exclaimed the High Priestess.

The willow was slowly straightening, turning its leaves so
that their silvery undersides faced the sun.

'The evil has been defeated,' said Ahhotep.

'How is that possible?' asked the High Priestess in
astonishment. 'Only a rightful pharaoh can do that.'

Calm and silent, Ahhotep and Seqen gazed back at her.

'You are Queen of Egypt . . . and you, her husband, are

* The Egyptians classed crocodiles as a kind of fish.

Pharaoh – that's the truth, isn't it? But you have no escort or servants, and you look like two peasants.'

'If we didn't, we wouldn't be able to move around the Hyksos-controlled areas,' explained Ahhotep. 'Now that the evil will has been broken, grant us the *heka*.'

'The most powerful one is in the sacred city of Iunu.'

'Iunu is much too close to Avaris,' replied Ahhotep. 'We'd be caught before we ever got there.'

'In that case, Majesty, you must be content with the *heka* of Hathor. Because of the evil eye and the sacred willow's weakness, the *heka*'s energy has not been reaching the temple. We must hope that straightening the willow has re-established harmony.'

The couple followed the High Priestess into the temple and then to the eastern shrine, which contained an inner shrine of pink granite. As soon as she opened the doors, a gentle light streamed forth from the gold statuette of Hathor the cow.

'Let the *heka* bathe you,' counselled the High Priestess. 'It is the power of the light that the Divine Principle created when it gave order to the universe. With the aid of its power, you shall do worthy deeds and fight off the attacks of destiny.'

Hand in hand, Ahhotep and Seqen forgot time and drank in the goddess's love.

The Afghan and ten of his men were eating dried fish and stale bread at their hiding-place, in the countryside south of Memphis. No Hyksos troop movements had been seen in the area since Jannas's devastating raid.

Moustache came over to them and reported, 'One of the lookouts says a friend is coming.'

They all picked up their weapons.

'It's all right,' said Moustache. 'It's the innkeeper's son.'

The lad was out of breath. 'There's a stranger drinking

beer at our inn,' he panted. 'He says he's carrying a special message from Avaris.'

'Well done, my boy,' said the Afghan. 'We'll deal with him.'

When the messenger left the inn, the rebels watched closely; he seemed to be alone. He set off down the track that led to the next village.

As soon as the man was far enough from the inn to be out of reach of help, Moustache sprang out and knocked him senseless with a single punch.

Quickly they searched him.

'The boy was right,' said Moustache. 'Here's a sealed letter from Avaris.' He broke the seal and unrolled the papyrus. 'This is most interesting. It's a message from Khamudi to the commander of the fortress at Per-Hathor, telling him that Thebes is still free and that rebels are assembling there. Wonderful! Now we know what we have to do. Let's gather all our men and go to Thebes. If we join forces, we'll be much stronger.'

'We're not moving from here,' said the Afghan firmly.

'But didn't you hear what I said?'

'I certainly did.'

'Then why don't you want to act on it?'

'Because it's a trap. A Hyksos messenger travelling alone, without military protection, and making himself known in a tavern: don't you find that surprising?'

'Well, if you put it that way . . .'

'We've had no news of Thebes, which has probably suffered the same fate as Memphis. The emperor wants to lure those of us who are left to Thebes so that he can ambush us on the way and wipe out every last man of us.'

In rage, Moustache ripped the papyrus into shreds.

28

The doctor examined the colour of Ahhotep's eyes, then her skin; finally, he checked that the blood-vessels in her breasts were firm, not flaccid.

'Your pregnancy is continuing perfectly,' he concluded, 'and the birth will be neither early nor late. But you must continue the daily massages.'

'And what about the results of the test?' she asked.

'Your urine made the barley germinate before the wheat, and the wheat before the spelt. So there is no doubt whatsoever: you will have a boy.'

Ahhotep left her bedchamber, ran into the antechamber, and flung herself into Seqen's arms. 'We're going to have a son,' she cried, 'a son who'll fight at your side!'

'I'd have preferred a girl as beautiful as her mother.'

'I decided we're going to have two sons, remember? Because at the moment Thebes needs warriors and leaders. Now, you must go back to the barracks, and I must go to the market.'

'Shouldn't you rest more? You're pregnant and—'

'I am making this child, and he'll be healthy and strong, believe me. Hurry away and train our men.'

The market in Thebes could have been that of a small provincial town. Out of habit people still haggled over prices, but all the cheerful chatter had long since vanished, and their main concern was the rumour of a Hyksos attack. Some people claimed that Memphis had been razed to the ground and that the same fate would soon befall Thebes.

Only a few men selling sacks of wheat and vegetables wore satisfied smiles. They had plenty to sell and, sooner or later, the customers would have to buy their wares, which were the most expensive in the market. They weighed them using a set of limestone cones of graded sizes, enabling them to weigh grain in any quantity from a handful to a whole sackful.

One of the traders, a red-faced man, sensed that Ahhotep was watching him and called to her, 'Come on over, young lady! What would you like?'

'To check your weights.'

The man almost choked. 'What! Who do you think you are?'

'Is it true that you and your colleagues work for the Agriculture secretariat?'

'What's that to you?'

'I have several copper ingots, each of equal weight, and I'm going to check your weights against them.'

'Get out of here this minute, you little hussy!'

A crowd had begun to gather, but it parted hastily as Laughter came thundering through to his mistress's side. Lips drawn back, he bared his teeth and gave a snarl that made the red-faced man's blood run cold.

'Let's . . . er . . . let's not do anything silly, eh?' he said. 'Surely a nice young lady like you wouldn't let that monster attack me.'

Ahhotep promptly laid three copper ingots on one side of the scales, and one of the trader's limestone cones on the other. To the onlookers' surprise, the scales promptly tipped in favour of the ingots.

'Your cone is underweight,' said Ahhotep, 'which means

you're stealing from every single one of your customers. Now I shall check all the other traders' weights.'

The men wanted to stop her, but in the face of the angry crowd's demands they had to comply. Not one of the cones was the correct weight.

'I know that girl,' exclaimed one of the onlookers. 'I work at the palace, and I tell you that's Princess Ahhotep. Thanks to her, we shan't be cheated any more.'

Everyone agreed and cheered her.

She turned to an old countrywoman who was selling leeks. 'From now on, you shall be in charge of checking the weights used here. Anyone caught trying to cheat must give his produce away free for one month. If he offends again, he will be expelled from the guild of merchants.'

Heray was regarded as the best baker in Thebes, and loved his work so much that until now he had managed to produce acceptable bread and cakes despite shortages of staff and increasingly erratic payment by his customers. Yet now even he was on the verge of giving up.

This morning had been the final straw. The flour delivered by the Agriculture secretariat was of such poor quality that it was unusable. In despair Heray had gone to see the palace steward, only to receive the usual answer: the agriculture minister had absolute power within his domain, and the palace had to accept the situation.

Heray lowered his considerable bulk on to a stool which was as tired as he was. Today, he would not bother lighting the oven.

As he sat brooding, he heard strange sounds outside in the street. He went to the door and looked out, to be greeted by a giant donkey accompanied by a beautiful brown-haired young woman.

'Are you Heray?' she asked.

'Yes, I am.'

147

'I am Ahhotep, daughter of Queen Teti, and here is the palace's answer to your complaint: Long-Ears has brought you flour of the finest quality.'

Heray gaped at her. 'Where . . . where did it come from?'

'From the minister for agriculture's granaries. Other donkeys will arrive shortly, and you will have enough for the palace and the barracks. Take on other bakers at once, and train them to take over from you.'

'Take over? But why?'

'Because you have been appointed Overseer of Granaries.'

In a large vat, the brewers mixed together barley loaves, date juice and water; the resulting brew was left to rest until it fermented. That done, they filtered it and then poured it into jars which were lined inside with sedimentary clay so as to keep the beer fresh and cool.

But the brewers were constantly complaining that it was impossible for them to produce good beer when the barley they were given was no good. Moreover, almost all the jars should have been replaced by now. The beer was virtually undrinkable, so nobody wanted to make it any more: after all, they were craftsmen and they had their pride.

The master-brewer was dozing in his brewery when a kick in the side jolted him awake.

'Ouch! What the . . .? A woman . . .?'

'I am Princess Ahhotep.'

Suitably impressed, the craftsman got to his feet. 'Forgive me. I was having a little rest, I—'

'There's a lot of work coming your way, so you'll need to employ twice as many brewers. The new Overseer of Granaries, Heray, is going to deliver you top-quality barley, and first thing tomorrow you will get new jars from the Agriculture secretariat. The palace expects to receive some very good beer.'

'It will be a pleasure, my lady!'

*

The minister for agriculture had a head shaped like a duck-egg. His cook pampered him, so he had been putting on weight. In future, he had decided, he would eat only one dish with a rich sauce in the evening.

In the mornings, he liked to sleep under a sun-shade beside his lotus-pond. In the afternoons, he listened to his stewards' reports. He was perfectly content, since nothing changed from one day to the next and he was still the richest official in Thebes. His policy had not altered since he was appointed: to cling on to all the privileges he had gained. Thanks to the queen's weak government, he had no trouble at all in doing so.

This morning his nap was interrupted: his personal scribe – most unusually – asked to see him before the noon meal.

'My lord, I have to inform you of some extremely serious matters.'

'Let us remain calm and collected.'

'Heray the baker has just been appointed Overseer of Granaries.'

'What does that matter? Honorary titles have to be handed out from time to time.'

'You don't understand,' said the scribe. 'He has become overseer of all the granaries in Thebes – including yours!'

'I trust this is some kind of joke.'

'I'm afraid not. On the palace's orders, large quantities of grain have been removed from your stores and delivered to the main bakery and brewery.'

The minister suddenly lost his taste for sleep. 'Is Teti daring to defy me?'

'No, it's her daughter, Princess Ahhotep.'

29

The minister for agriculture paced up and down in front of the door to the queen's audience chamber. Teti would pay dearly for this insult. Not only would she give him back his property, but he would force her to give him arable land as compensation. The fact that her daughter had gone mad was not his concern; but the queen ought to pay more attention to what her first-born was doing.

'Her Majesty will receive you,' announced Qaris very calmly.

'And not before time!'

As he went in, the minister saw that the little audience chamber had been repainted. Then he saw Ahhotep; dressed in white, and with gold bracelets gleaming at her wrists, she was sitting on a gilded wooden throne whose feet were shaped like a bulls' hooves.

'I do not want to see you,' he said. 'I want to see the queen.'

'She sits before you.'

'What is that supposed to mean?'

'Bow before the Queen of the Two Lands.'

The minister's jaw dropped. 'The Queen . . .?'

'Bow, or I shall have you arrested for insulting the crown.'

Her tone was so stern that the minister took fright. 'I did not know, Majesty, I—'

'Now you do know. Here are my first decisions. I have abolished several posts which have no place in a time of war. Heray, Overseer of Granaries, will take charge of Thebes's agriculture.'

'You mean . . . I am no longer minister?'

'That is correct.'

'But Heray is a nobody, Majesty. He's a simple baker – he'll never be able to manage our province's wealth.'

'Heray is an honest man,' said Ahhotep pointedly. 'In order to support the war effort, your lands and possessions have been requisitioned. I shall leave you just one house: the most modest one. You are to raise poultry there, to feed our soldiers. And try to put your heart into the work, unless you wish to sink lower.'

'Majesty . . .'

'This audience is at an end.'

The ex-minister had gathered together those close to him, with the intention of mounting a vigorous counter-attack. But no one wanted to fall in behind him.

'Why are you all so afraid?' he asked angrily. 'Ahhotep is alone and powerless.'

'Not as powerless as all that,' replied his personal scribe. 'She has the unconditional support of Teti the Small, who as you know is revered by all Thebans, and she is reinvigorating the army – in fact, many of the peasants who worked for you yesterday have just enlisted. True, the army's nothing but a rabble, but they are paid better than on your lands and they're loyal to Ahhotep.'

'I am sorry to leave you so early,' apologized the minister for finance, 'but I have been summoned to the palace before the noon meal, and Ahhotep does not like to be kept waiting.'

The other officials followed suit, each remembering an urgent task.

The ex-minister turned to his personal scribe and said with

a sneer, 'What a band of cowards! I'm glad you're still loyal. Together, we shall devise a way of countering these measures.'

'I am dreadfully sorry, but I'm a scribe and I have no taste for poultry-rearing. Heray has offered me a job more in keeping with my skills.'

'Get out of here, you traitor!'

How, the former minister wondered, had that slip of a girl managed to destroy his authority so quickly? And how had she turned against him so many experienced men who owed their careers to him? On the point of breaking down, he drank half a small jar of date wine, which helped him pull himself together. He came to a worrying conclusion: this young queen was really dangerous, and quite capable of going much further than she already had.

He must at once inform his Hyksos friends, whom he had long been supplying with information about everything that happened in Thebes. Thebes was no longer his motherland, and he would watch its destruction with the greatest pleasure.

The minister for finance received the news that his post had been abolished with obvious relief. The old man's only wish was for a peaceful retirement, and he thanked the queen for granting it to him.

In less than a week, Ahhotep had succeeded in dismantling a puppet government and concentrating its powers in the narrow circle made up of her mother, her husband, Qaris and Heray. She had not chosen Heray by chance: he had always protested against the Hyksos occupation, and Qaris had adopted him as a right-hand man.

She had still to resolve the problem posed by the commander-in-chief of the Theban army. He was much the oldest officer in the army, and was now as frail as the veils of mist on autumn mornings which were quickly dispersed by the sun.

Nevertheless, when she summoned him, he cut a fine figure. He bowed low, and said, 'I am at your service, Majesty.'

'How many men have we at our command?' asked Ahhotep.

'In theory, five hundred; in reality, no more than forty real soldiers. I have not recruited any more, since Thebes is not planning to resist the Hyksos.'

'That is no longer the case.'

'I'm delighted to hear it. Majesty, may I give you a piece of advice?'

'I'm listening.'

'Leave a group of incompetents in plain sight, men who will appear to be the official army. This decoy will keep the Hyksos smiling. Meanwhile, set up a secret camp where real soldiers are trained to handle every kind of weapon. It will take a long time, but it will work. And I can see no other means of preparing a true army of liberation.'

'Will you take on this task?' asked Ahhotep.

'I no longer have the strength, Majesty. Sickness has eaten me away. I fought it for as long as I could, in the insane hope that someone would give back Thebes her lost pride. Now that you are here, I can die in peace.'

That very evening, the old general died and Seqen was appointed commander of the army.

After hesitating for a long time, the former minister for agriculture had taken the only decision left to him: to go to Avaris himself and inform the emperor. The ridiculous Theban revolution would of course come to nothing, but Apophis would be pleased by this demonstration of his full and total allegiance.

Since his fall from power, the ex-minister had been abandoned by everyone and no longer trusted anyone. Entrusting his news to a messenger, however well paid, would be too dangerous. Having to leave Thebes, his lands and his possessions infuriated him, but he would soon return with the Hyksos army and exact his revenge with a cruelty beyond anything the arrogant Ahhotep could imagine.

'Guard-post in sight,' announced one of the bearers.

'Halt,' ordered the former minister. He got down from his carrying-chair and went alone towards the soldiers. This close to Kebet, they were probably pro-Hyksos forces; if they weren't, he would retrace his steps and take a different route.

'Emperor's men,' declared a sturdy fellow armed with a javelin.

'I am the Theban minister for agriculture and I must go as quickly as possible to Avaris to see our sovereign.'

'You, a Theban, recognize the authority of Apophis?'

'I have worked for him for a long time. I am his eyes and ears in Thebes. If you escort me to the capital, you will be well rewarded.'

Then he heard Seqen's grave voice behind him: 'So Ahhotep was right: you are indeed a traitor.'

30

The ex-minister almost fainted.

'We are not Hyksos,' said Seqen, 'but faithful servants of the queen. We have been following you since you left, to find out where you were going and intercept you before you reached the enemy.'

The traitor fell to his knees. 'Don't hurt me, I beg you! I am sorry, so very sorry—'

'Tell me who your accomplices are.'

'I . . . I haven't got any.'

'You're still lying.'

'No, I swear I'm not. I was the only one. I did inform the emperor – but only about small things, very small things, and it was in the interests of Thebes.'

Seqen and his men dragged him to the bank of the Nile, and the pharaoh threw a wax model of a crocodile into the water. Less than a minute later, the water began to bubble and swirl, and the gaping jaws of a huge, and very real, crocodile emerged.

'If you don't talk,' said Seqen, 'he will be your torturer.'

Trembling with fear, the traitor denounced all his accomplices, among them a washerman at the palace and an officer who had acted as a messenger.

'May the god Sobek decide your fate.'

The Thebans seized the traitor by the ankles and threw him into the river, which was soon red with his blood.

Seqen took Ahhotep in his arms. 'You were right,' he said. 'The Hyksos traitors in Thebes have all been arrested and executed. From now on, the emperor will be blind and deaf.'

'Only if he believes the minister is still alive and working for him. So we must send him regular messages informing him that Thebes is still declining and has lost the will to resist.'

Teti interrupted them. 'An official letter has come from Avaris. Apophis is demanding that Thebes send him a stele confirming that she recognizes him as pharaoh of Upper and Lower Egypt.'

'Never!' cried Seqen. 'We'll send him a declaration of war.'

'We can't,' said Ahhotep sadly. 'We are still far, far from ready. If he wants a stele, he shall have one. But the stone-cutter must alter most of the hieroglyphs – though with such skill that only someone who knows the secret will notice. He must break the wings of the birds, fix the serpents to the ground and prevent the suns from shining. No one will open the mouth of this stele, no one will bring it to life. The emperor will receive a dead stone.'

Apophis contemplated the stele with a disdainful sneer.

'The art of Senusret's day is indeed dead – Theban sculptors no longer have any talent at all. What do you think, Tany?'

She was munching a greasy cake. 'I loathe Egyptian art in all its forms. It really is the art of a race of slaves.'

'But you're Egyptian yourself,' pointed out Windswept, Apophis's younger sister. She was a magnificent creature, very tall and slim, and with something exotic about her appearance. Since Apophis's rise to power, she had busied herself furnishing the palace at Avaris with masterpieces from the towns of the Delta. Goblets of blue porcelain decorated with lotus-flowers, incense-burners, lamps shaped like lilies, beds decorated with the gods who protected sleep, matchlessly elegant chairs made from sycamore wood. Although he was indifferent to these marvels, Apophis could regard himself as a true pharaoh.

'I'm a Hyksos now,' protested Tany. 'Thanks to me, a lot of rich, arrogant Egyptian women have become slaves – those pretentious bitches have to prostrate themselves before me now.'

Windswept shrugged. She felt only contempt for Apophis's dreadful wife.

'Egyptian women were perverted by their freedom,' said Apophis. 'Our law requires all women to submit to men, for only men are capable of making rational decisions.'

'But,' said Windswept, 'it's the lioness who hunts and brings back the food.'

'Don't contradict me, my dear sister. Surely you aren't defending our slaves?'

'I'm not interested in politics. All I care about is beauty.'

'That's perfect. Continue that way.'

Casting a disdainful look at fat Tany, Windswept went out, leaving a scent of lotus-flowers behind her.

'Your sister hates me,' complained Tany. 'You ought to send her back to Asia.'

'She's useful,' said Apophis.

'Is she? How?'

'Windswept loves love, and no man can resist her. She enjoys being in Egypt, so I have set conditions she must comply with in order to stay. She must sleep with the most senior dignitaries of the empire and obtain their confidences in bed. In this way, I know all their vices and their ambitions. If anyone dares criticize me, he dies.'

'So she's going to stay in Avaris for a long time?'

'As long as she does as I wish.'

'My work is just as important.'

'I know, Tany, I know. Whatever you do, don't slacken your efforts.'

She gave a cruel smile. 'Yesterday my great friend Aberia arrested the widow of the mayor of Sais, who was disguised as a serving-woman. We'd been hunting that rebel for months – in the end she was denounced by one of her former maids.'

'Did she belong to an organized group?'

'No. Aberia tortured her with her own hands before strangling her, and the slut hid nothing from her, you can be sure. I have a list of Egyptian noblewomen who are still in hiding in the foolish belief that they can evade us. But Aberia will find them.'

The stele from Thebes had been set up in the Temple of Set, where the Great Council met. Today every council member brought good news. The Hyksos Empire was continuing to expand without its armies even having to fight; the new trading practices were making greedy men wealthy and keeping the common people in a state of submission from which they would never emerge. The Information secretariat was producing impressive numbers of scarabs, which would carry the emperor's thoughts into even the remotest places.

The world was becoming Hyksos.

And the conquerors owed this victory to Apophis, who inspired mortal fear in everyone who met him. Those who displeased him found their careers cut short; and sometimes their lives. Even the bravest men could not help trembling when they heard the emperor's harsh voice announcing his decisions which no one dared challenge.

As for Khamudi, he hung on his master's every word and did everything he could to turn Apophis's wishes into reality. The High Treasurer grew richer by the day, thanks to the papyrus and scarab-making industries, and he was delighted to discover the power of wealth. He could buy anyone he wanted, whenever he wanted.

'Did our ambush succeed?' Apophis asked him.

'A number of rebels were caught and beheaded at Henen-Nesut, Majesty. They were indeed trying to reach Thebes.'

'Keep the trap in place,' ordered the emperor. 'I am not entirely sure that the most dangerous man has yet been caught in our net.'

'The stele from Thebes shows that the will to rebel has been eradicated,' said Khamudi with relish. 'In addition, the latest letter from the minister for agriculture confirms that Teti the Small can do nothing to change that fact.'

'Let us go and check the tax revenues, High Treasurer. I have the feeling certain provinces are in arrears.'

31

It took Moustache and the Afghan several long weeks to regroup the few rebels who had escaped the massacre in Memphis. They had all lost heart, and most wanted to go home and submit to the Hyksos. Eventually, however, Moustache managed to convince them that if they did they would be signing their own death-warrants, because they were bound to be put to death after lengthy torture. Little by little, the old spirit of comradeship re-emerged. The Afghan gave them no rest, but subjected his band to intensive training, particularly in unarmed fighting.

The rebels were sheltered mainly by peasants, who, exploited and mistreated by the invaders, were happy to welcome men who still believed in freedom. So once again the Afghan began to weave the web that had been torn apart in Memphis, all the time making sure that every place they ate or slept was completely safe – and that they spent no more than a week at any one farm. He stressed the essential difference between sympathizers and true rebels. The former were growing in number by the minute, but there was no point counting on them if it came to a fight; and it would take several months to train the latter.

Moustache was just as wary as the Afghan. He subjected would-be recruits to exhaustive tests before accepting them into the group. He also took care to fence off the network to prevent it being wiped out if one of Apophis's spies managed to infiltrate it.

Then news arrived that the Hyksos had indeed organized an ambush near Henen-Nesut. All those rebels who had tried to reach Thebes had been caught and executed.

'And we are trapped between Hyksos in the north and Hyksos in the south,' complained Moustache. 'We are going to die like wild beasts, crouching in our den.'

'Not at all, my friend,' said the Afghan. 'We are making our den bigger. And if we do die, it will be in battle.'

'You still believe that?'

'So do you, deep in your heart. Today the enemy is a thousand times more powerful than we are, and it would be madness to face him openly. But it won't always be like this. Learn patience – that's the one virtue you lack.'

One of Moustache's men interrupted them. He said, 'There's something going on in a village not far away. Hyksos soldiers arrested a traveller and are preparing to torture him in the forge. Perhaps we ought to do something?'

'Too risky,' said the Afghan.

'But supposing the poor man's a member of a rebel group which is trying to contact us?'

'He's right,' said Moustache. 'I'm going to take a look.'

'Not without me,' retorted the Afghan.

The six Hyksos soldiers were specialists in interrogation. While keeping watch on the path that ran along the edge of the desert, they had spotted the stranger approaching from the south.

Although he looked rather frail, the fellow had proved to be made of sterner stuff than expected. Despite beating and flogging him cruelly, they had still got nothing out of him. However, the commanding officer knew a method which would make even a dumb man talk.

'See the furnace, you dirty spy? It has hot coals . . . If you

161

keep silent, you'll have a taste of them, and after that you won't have a face left.'

The prisoner lifted terrified eyes to his torturer. 'I know nothing – nothing at all!'

'Too bad for you.'

The smell of burning flesh was accompanied by such unbearable screams that a Hyksos smashed the tortured man's skull with a stone.

'You've killed him, you imbecile,' snarled the officer. 'How are you going to make him talk now?'

Before the torturer could reply, an arrow plunged into his chest.

The Afghan killed two more Hyksos, while Moustache sank his javelin into the back of a fourth, and then gave vent to his fury by strangling a fifth.

The only survivor, the officer found himself gazing into the Afghan's terrifying eyes.

'I am an officer in the emperor's service. If you lay a hand on me, you'll be condemned to death.'

'Leave him to me,' demanded Moustache.

The officer tried to run away, but the Egyptian was too swift for him. He caught him and dragged him by his hair to the forge.

'Now it's your turn to taste the fire.'

The officer struggled in vain. His face was plunged into the coals. He opened his mouth to scream, only for his tongue to be burned away.

Indifferent to his horrible death-throes, the Afghan examined the Egyptian's corpse. 'Come and see, Moustache. There's a piece of linen sewn inside his tunic, and someone has drawn a strange sign in red ink.'

'It looks like the moon-disc, in its ship.'

'It must be a message. This poor fellow can't tell us what it means, but it must be important – at any rate, he took enormous risks in order to pass it on.'

'Who was it meant for?'

'Certainly not the Hyksos.'

'Then he was looking for rebels,' ventured Moustache. 'He might even be a messenger from Thebes.'

'Don't raise your hopes too high,' said the Afghan. 'But we'll memorize the sign.'

He tore away the scrap of linen and burned it. If, by chance, it was indeed a coded message to rally the rebels, it must remain secret for as long as possible.

'What if there's another messenger?' said Moustache anxiously. 'Perhaps Thebes was sending out a last appeal for help.'

'Is the moon its symbol?'

'Not as far as I know.'

'Then we must forget Thebes and think in terms of a small band of rebels who'll try to make themselves known.'

'How can we join up with them?'

'There's only one solution,' said the Afghan. 'We must head further south.'

'But we'll walk straight into Hyksos patrols.'

'If we do, at least we'll know where they are.'

Although her belly was growing rounder by the day, Ahhotep was as active as ever. By reviving traditional trade practices in Thebes and driving out the fraudsters, she had re-established trust. The Thebans no longer spent their time spying on one another or withdrawing into themselves for fear of what tomorrow might bring. Bonds of friendship were being renewed and people sang the praise of Ahhotep, who visited the sick and found food for those in greatest need. Aware that the time for fine words had passed, the young queen had decided to attend to the basics of daily life.

Not that she neglected larger matters. 'Is there any news of our messengers?' she asked Qaris.

The steward's face darkened. 'I'm afraid not, Majesty.

163

They must all have been killed. I fear it may be impossible to get through all the barriers put in place by the Hyksos. And there are probably no rebels left north of Kebet.'

'I'm sure that is not so,' said Ahhotep. 'Cowards, collaborators and the timid may be in the majority, I grant you, but there are still some, even among the oppressed and the persecuted, who will never bend the knee. Those are the people we must contact.'

Qaris bowed, but said, 'I do not think we should send out more men to certain death, Majesty.'

'We must break out of our isolation and find out whom we can count on. If she has no contact with the outside world, Thebes will wither.'

Qaris wavered. 'One of our few remaining allies may perhaps be able to help us, if he is still alive – but I do not wish to raise your hopes too high.'

'Whom are you thinking of?'

'Babay, the old sage of Nekhen. He used to have excellent messengers at his disposal, and if they can still carry messages they would be very useful.'

'I shall go to Nekhen at once.'

'Majesty, in your condition—'

'There's only one condition which interests me,' said Ahhotep. 'The condition of my country.'

32

To reach Nekhen, which lay some four days' journey to the south of Thebes, Ahhotep and Seqen followed a track which ran along the edge of the fields. They were escorted by ten young soldiers ready to give their lives to save the queen. When she grew tired, she let herself be carried in a sycamore-wood travelling-chair.

Nothing untoward happened during the journey. The little group met only a few frightened peasants, who were careful not to ask questions and who hid in their miserable mud huts. It was clear that Waset was almost totally deserted, and that the Hyksos regarded it with such contempt that they had not left a single occupying unit there.

The outskirts of the old city of Nekhen, though, were an unpleasant surprise. Everywhere they saw fallen trees, abandoned pastures, dead cows. Happiness seemed to have abandoned the place for ever.

'Let's turn back,' said Seqen. 'The town will be nothing but ruins.'

'No. We must check,' insisted Ahhotep.

'Looters may have taken over the town, and there are only a few of us . . .'

'I want to know if Babay is still alive.'

Seqen was the first to step through the great open gate in the outer wall. The doors had been torn down, and the guard-

165

post laid waste. In the middle of the main street lay a dead dog.

'Two lookouts,' ordered Seqen, 'one to the left, the other to the right.'

Here and there were burnt-out houses. Everywhere lay broken pottery, fragments of furniture smashed by axe-blows, tattered remnants of clothing. But not a living soul. Even the age-old temple of the goddess Nekhbet had not been spared. Smashed statues and fallen pillars bore witness to its suffering.

'There's someone over there,' shouted one of the lookouts.

He pointed to a very old man who was sitting on the threshold of the roofed temple, reading a papyrus. He did not even look up when the visitors approached, so indifferent was he to the fate that awaited him.

'Are you Babay the sage?' asked Ahhotep.

He did not answer.

'Move further back,' she ordered the soldiers.

As soon as they were a good distance away, the young woman played her trump card.

'Pharaoh Seqen and Queen Ahhotep need your help in order to save Egypt.'

With almost unbearable slowness, the old man began rolling up his papyrus.

When he had finished, he looked at her for the first time, nodded, and said, 'The Divine Light placed the pharaoh upon the earth to bring harmony in place of disorder, to win the gods' favour, to enact justice and drive away injustice. He is not above Ma'at, but must be her servant and protect those who practise her way. It was so once, before the invasion. Today there is no pharaoh upon Egyptian soil.'

'You are wrong,' said Ahhotep. 'Seqen has been crowned at Karnak.'

The old sage looked at the young couple doubtfully. 'The Hyksos have destroyed Karnak.'

'I can assure you they have not,' said Ahhotep. 'Teti the Small has preserved Thebes's freedom and the temple is unharmed. The Hyksos believe us to be submissive and therefore no threat to them, but in fact we are working secretly to prepare for re-conquest.'

'Queen Ahhotep . . . The moon-god protects you and gives you an aptitude for battle. So you are the new royal couple – with neither army nor country.'

'We are training soldiers little by little,' promised Seqen.

The old man tore up the papyrus. 'Help me up.'

Despite his great age, Babay was stocky and heavy.

'Pharaoh Seqen and Queen Ahhotep,' he said when he was on his feet. 'Before I die, I shall have had the most beautiful dream imaginable.'

'What happened here?' asked Ahhotep.

'Three Hyksos warships dropped anchor here two months ago. The invaders ravaged the countryside and the town, killed those few who resisted, and forced the people to march to the North to be made into slaves. They spared me so that I might write an account of the punishment inflicted on any city or person who dares oppose the emperor. I have just destroyed that account. Come, let us go to my house.'

Babay led the royal couple to his home, a small, two-storey house near the temple. On the threshold, he paused and gazed out at his devastated city. 'If you are truly king and queen, never negotiate with the barbarians who destroyed this city and enslaved its citizens.'

Almost everything in the house had been looted; the only things left were a single mat and a worn-out scribe's palette.

Babay sat down. 'I'm tired, too tired to take up arms.'

'Qaris, our steward, thinks you may be able to help us,' ventured Ahhotep. 'He says you have excellent messengers at your command.'

Babay smiled. 'Excellent and very effective – that's true enough. But they have probably all been killed.'

167

'But you aren't certain?'

'I haven't seen them for a long time. Let us go on to the terrace, and I'll summon their leader.'

Once outside, Babay whistled a rhythmic tune, accentuating the high and low notes. Soon a handsome beige and white pigeon appeared, and alighted at his feet.

'Rascal, you are still alive! Bring me the others.'

The bird flew off. A little while later, he returned with six other pigeons.

'You're all safe!' exclaimed Babay, with tears in his eyes. 'So the gods haven't altogether abandoned us. I spent more than a year training them, Majesty, and I must teach you how to give them clear instructions. When your mind communicates with theirs, they will go where you tell them, and then return to the place from which they left.'

From the very first experiments, Ahhotep saw that the birds were exceptionally intelligent. They quickly grasped the fact that she was taking Babay's place and that from now on they must carry out her orders.

'Grant me one week, Majesty,' said Babay, 'and they will become faithful messengers who will never betray you.'

The birds could travel long distances in a single flight, flying at great speed and never losing sight of north, thanks to their innate sense of direction. The fact that there were so few of them was only a temporary handicap, for one female laid two eggs ten days after mating, and only a month after fledging, the young pigeons were ready to begin work.

'What splendid recruits!' exclaimed Seqen. 'They'll make a mockery of the Hyksos barriers.'

'You cannot stay here, Babay,' said Ahhotep. 'We'll take you to Thebes.'

'That's out of the question, Majesty. I was born here and have spent all my life here. For me, this is the most beautiful place in Egypt. One day, if you respect the law of Ma'at and if you are strong enough to overcome the obstacles, defeats and betrayals, you will return to Nekhen and give her back her past splendour.'

'We cannot simply abandon you,' insisted Seqen.

'Will you give me a little wine, Majesty?'

The old man drank deeply from the jar Seqen handed him, then lay down and rested his head on some cushions.

And then Babay serenely passed away.

33

Fat, Thin, Long-Beard, Jovial, Impatient and their colleagues had one thing in common: they all cursed Ahhotep, who had dragged them away from their routine and given them jobs as washermen. They had to soak clothes, lengths of cloth and assorted fabrics in large cauldrons, rinse them in clean water, wring them out, hit them with wooden beaters, hang them up to dry, fold them impeccably and sometimes even perfume them. Theban housewives had recovered their taste for cleanliness, and little by little the entire city was becoming spick and span again, including the districts where the humblest folk lived.

The work was so back-breaking that the washermen forgot all about the Hyksos threat and thought only of their own working conditions, which they planned to improve by complaining to their overseer.

'We're stopping work,' declared Jovial.

'I'm not taking a risk like that,' said Thin. 'The princess is quite capable of having us arrested.'

'We're stopping because we've run out of soap. So we can't do the washing properly, can we?'

'He has a point,' agreed Fat.

Impatient abandoned his pile of soiled women's linen, and they all went to see the overseer. As spokesman for the group, Impatient voiced their vehement protests.

The overseer listened carefully. 'Provision has been made for this,' he said when Impatient had finished.

'Provision? For our justifiable complaints?'

'No, for a shortage of soap.'

'Well, as we've run out, we aren't going back to work.'

'You may rest until the delivery,' said the overseer. 'Ah, here it is now.'

Long-Ears plodded serenely up, bearing a large consignment of soap cakes made from limestone and vegetable fats. He was not alone: just behind him was Ahhotep, resplendent in a pale-yellow dress.

At the sight of her, even Impatient was lost for words.

'By all the gods, she's beautiful!' whispered Jovial.

Ahhotep took a jar from the bags the donkey was carrying.

'Here is some good beer for you to have with your noon meal. The palace is pleased with your work, so you shall all receive an increase in your wages. Also, the overseer may take on apprentices, so that your burden of work becomes less heavy.'

Everyone lost the urge to protest.

'We shall drink to your health, Majesty,' promised Fat, 'and to the health of the child you are carrying.'

Ahhotep had re-established strict rules of cleanliness, which, as far as she was concerned, lay at very heart of the struggle for freedom. When dirt won, morale waned and fear and laziness invaded people's souls. From one day to the next, each Theban must win back his dignity, and he could only do so if his body, his clothes and his home were clean. Teams of street-cleaners complemented the work done by individuals, and the transformation was soon noticeable. Once again, Thebans were living in a charming and spotless city.

This modest victory over despair gave their lives new meaning. Instead of withdrawing into themselves, they started talking and encouraging one another.

171

'The women have started wearing face-paint again,' observed Teti.

'I am delighted to hear it,' said Ahhotep. 'Their beauty, too, will help rebuild our will to be free.'

'Unfortunately, we shall soon have run out of what they need. The palace reserves are almost exhausted, and the makers of face-paints have all moved to Edfu.'

Edfu, several days' travel to the south, was in the occupied lands.

'Governor Emheb,' said Qaris, 'was one of our most loyal supporters. How can we find out if he is still alive and, if he is, what freedom of action he has? We cannot use the pigeons without contacting him first.'

'There is only one solution: we must go there and see for ourselves.'

'Not you, Ahhotep,' protested Teti.

'No one will look twice at a poor fisherman and his pregnant wife.'

The boat was a humble one, with a patched sail and creaking oars, but the north wind blew steadily, enabling Seqen and Ahhotep to make good progress towards Edfu.

The young king had changed a great deal. Through training and intensive exercise, the thin lad had acquired the stature of an athlete.

'Do you feel ready to become a father?' asked Ahhotep.

'Thanks to you, I feel ready to win any and every battle.'

The young couple spent an enchanting night in the uncomfortable boat, hidden in a papyrus thicket. Alone in the world for a few hours, they knew that their love, fierce as a storm and tender as autumn sunlight, gave them a strength no ordeal could erode.

At daybreak, they set off again.

Near Edfu, a Hyksos war-boat ordered them to stop. Seqen lowered the sail and bowed like an obedient slave.

'Who are you and where are you from?' demanded an officer with hooded eyes.

'I'm a fisherman from Edfu and I'm on my way home.'

'Is this woman yours?'

'Yes, my lord, and she's expecting our child.'

'Show me your catch.'

Seqen opened a willow basket containing three average-sized perch.

'You must pay the toll,' said the officer.

'But, my lord—'

'Don't argue. Just give me those fish.'

'But we're going to have a child and I need to sell them to—'

'I said: don't argue. In future, stay closer to the town.'

The little boat berthed between two skiffs moored to wooden stakes with papyrus ropes, and Seqen helped Ahhotep step out on to dry land.

A rough-looking fellow hailed them. 'Who do you think you are?'

'A fisherman.'

'No you aren't. I'm one myself, and I know all the fishermen around here. You're not from these parts.'

Something she glimpsed in the man's eyes prompted Ahhotep to reveal part of the truth. 'We've come from Thebes.'

'Thebes? But it's been destroyed.'

'The Hyksos have lied about it. Thebes is unharmed, and is resisting the oppressors.'

'Thebes unharmed . . . then Egypt's still alive.'

'Is Edfu occupied?' asked Ahhotep.

'Jannas's army killed all our soldiers and stole all our money and goods, then went back to the North, leaving only guards here. But I'm so afraid of being arrested that it's three months since I dared set foot in the town.'

173

'Is Governor Emheb still alive?'

'I don't know. But whatever you do, don't try to enter Edfu. You'd never get out alive.'

'Which entrance is the least closely guarded?'

'The eastern gate. But don't do it – it's insane.'

Ahhotep merely smiled. 'Will you help us?'

'I can't myself. Life may not be happy, but I'm getting by. My brother might go with you, as if you're fisher-folk going to sell your fish in the market. He bribes the guards to let him work.'

The brother agreed.

As he watched the couple walking towards the town with his brother, the rough-looking man shook his head in disbelief. Why were this young fellow and his pretty, pregnant wife walking straight into the lion's jaws?

34

The outskirts of Edfu were almost silent. People exchanged goods with hardly any haggling, and kept a permanent eye on the Hyksos guards who patrolled the streets and squares at all times. People were often arrested for no apparent reason, and no one emerged unharmed from interrogations. At best, suspects had broken limbs; at worst, they were deported to the copper mines.

The fisherman's brother left Ahhotep and Seqen near the Temple of Horus. The entrance was sealed, for the emperor had forbidden anyone to celebrate the cult of the divine falcon, protector of Pharaoh. That role was now reserved for Set of Avaris.

An amulet-seller flourished his wares, which were as ugly as they were ineffective, at the couple. 'They aren't expensive,' he said, 'and they'll protect your child. I'll give you four for the price of two.'

'We're looking for Governor Emheb,' said Seqen.

The seller hurried away.

'Why do they all refuse to talk about the governor,' wondered Ahhotep, 'unless he has sold himself to the Hyksos?'

'We've got the answer we came for,' agreed Seqen. 'Let's leave.'

They walked along the southern wall of the temple, then set off towards the outskirts.

Christian Jacq

But this time the eastern gate was guarded by Hyksos armed with swords and clubs; it would have been pointless to try and run away.

Some peasants were leaving the town without being questioned. Seqen and Ahhotep fell into step behind them.

'You two,' said a guard, 'where are you going?'

'To our boat, sir,' replied Seqen. 'We're fisher-folk.'

'You've been heard asking questions about the governor.'

'We'd have liked to meet him,' agreed Ahhotep.

'Why?'

'To ask him to give us a new boat. Ours is rotting away.'

'That story doesn't hold water. Come with us.' The guard beckoned to two of his colleagues, and the three of them marched the young pair towards the centre of town.

Seqen thought he might be able to kill the guards, but he was afraid Ahhotep might be injured in the fight. So he decided on a different plan: once he was in Emheb's presence, he'd take him hostage. For the king had sworn that he and the queen would leave this town unharmed.

The governor's palace was similar in appearance to Titi's at Kebet. Scribes were writing away in their shabby offices, soldiers were apathetically cleaning their weapons, and stray cats were scavenging for the smallest scrap of food.

'Go in there,' said the guards' leader.

It was a dark, dirty outhouse.

'When will we see the governor, sir?' asked Seqen.

'You're a stubborn one! Don't worry, you'll see him.'

The door closed behind them.

The earthen floor was piled with worn-out sandals and dirty rags.

Seqen looked around and spotted a hole in the back wall. 'I can make it bigger, and we can escape through it.'

'No, we mustn't do that,' replied Ahhotep. 'We must see Emheb.'

'But what if they only let us out of here to execute us?'

'The governor will see us, I'm sure of it. I shall kneel before him, then I shall seize his sword and threaten to slit his throat if he doesn't give us a boat to take the three of us back to Thebes. That traitor doesn't know it yet, but he's already our prisoner.'

Seqen took his wife in his arms. Her soft, scented skin made him forget their foul-smelling prison.

When the door opened, they were still in each other's arms.

'Follow me, lovebirds,' ordered a palace guard.

'Are we going to see the governor at last, sir?' asked Seqen in a small, timid voice.

'Move! Quickly now!'

At the centre of the courtyard stood a wooden block, with an axe planted in it. Would Seqen have time to grab the axe and kill the headsman?

'This way.'

They moved away from the place of execution and were pushed into a pillared audience chamber with faded wall-paintings.

An astonishingly big man came forward to observe them. Everything about him was outsize: his eyes, his nose, his shoulders, even his ears. Judging by his huge belly, he was a man who enjoyed the good life, but this impression was belied by the hard glint in his eyes.

'Are you looking for me, young folk?' he asked.

'If you are Governor Emheb, yes indeed,' replied Seqen.

'You, girl, show me your hands.'

Ahhotep did so.

'They are delicate and pretty, and they don't smell of fish.'

'It's my husband who does the fishing.'

With surprising speed for a man of his bulk, Emheb tore off a piece of Seqen's tunic and sniffed it. 'This doesn't smell of fish, either. Who are you really?'

The governor was unarmed, and the guards were too far from Seqen for him to seize their weapons without a fight.

Christian Jacq

They would have time to warn their colleagues, and the king would be overwhelmed by force of numbers. Besides, from the look of Emheb's enormous neck, it would be impossible to strangle him.

'Why have you betrayed your country?' Ahhotep demanded, staring so intensely at the governor that he felt quite uneasy.

'You're Thebans, aren't you?' he said.

'This is your day of glory, Emheb. You and your Hyksos are about to murder Queen Ahhotep, Lady of the Two Lands. I ask only one favour. Spare this peasant: I forced him to accompany me.'

She hoped she could save Seqen; while Seqen swore a silent oath not to let the Hyksos soldiers lay a hand on his wife.

The governor of Edfu knelt. 'I am your servant, Majesty. Command, and I shall obey.'

The guards followed suit.

'These men aren't Hyksos,' Emheb explained, 'they are Egyptians. I had the Hyksos men killed one by one, and replaced them with my own men, while letting the emperor believe that the town had submitted completely to him. I declared myself his ally, and he has entrusted me with the task of bleeding the region dry with higher and higher taxes. My only hope has been to find a way of launching an attack. It would undoubtedly fail, but at least it would allow us to die with dignity.'

'You may rise, Governor.'

Emheb was visibly moved. 'Am I to understand, Majesty, that Thebes still lives and is ready to fight?'

'Forget about your attack. To create a real army, we shall need patience and the utmost secrecy.'

'I am your servant, Majesty.'

'Not only mine, Emheb. You are in the presence of my husband, Pharaoh Seqen.'

178

The Empire of Darkness

Ahhotep thought the governor was going to faint.

'A king? We have a king? Majesty, you are telling me of true wonders!'

'At the moment we are greatly in need of ointments, face-paints and skilled workers who can make them.'

Emheb's face lit up with a broad smile. 'In spite of all their searches, the Hyksos have never found my secret stores of incense and styrax. I also have plenty of ointments of different qualities, so you can supply both the temple and individuals. As for skilled workers, the finest in Egypt do indeed live in Edfu. Several of them will go with you when you leave for Thebes. But now, Majesty, come and see my treasures – all this time they have been waiting for a new royal couple.'

With infectious enthusiasm, the governor showed his guests the underground chambers below the temple, where censers, vases and pots of ointments had been kept hidden.

'We shall change nothing,' decided Ahhotep. 'The Hyksos must continue to believe that Nekhen is dead and Edfu is dying.'

35

Seqen paced up and down outside the room where his wife was in labour.

'Are the midwives really skilled enough?' he asked Qaris, who was almost as nervous as he was.

'Have no fear, Majesty. They are the best in Thebes.'

'But Ahhotep was in such pain! She ought to have been resting these last few weeks. The journey to Edfu exhausted her.'

'With respect, Majesty, it was crowned with such success that the future suddenly looks much brighter.'

'I know, Qaris, I know. But the queen ought to take more care of herself.'

'A Queen of Egypt is a Queen of Egypt,' Qaris reminded him fatalistically. 'And when her name is Ahhotep . . .'

'Surely having a baby shouldn't take this long?'

'Our specialists can deal with even the most difficult births.'

'In the time of the pyramids I'm sure they could, but can the specialists we have in Thebes today? If something serious happens, neither Ahhotep nor the child will survive.'

The steward did not have the courage to contradict him. Seqen took to pacing up and down again.

Just as the sun was reaching its zenith, Teti emerged from the delivery room, a baby in her arms.

tribes had just chosen a young king, Nedjeh, whose reputation for vanity and cruelty was almost the equal of Apophis's.

Taking this disagreeable news seriously, the emperor had summoned his envoy to Nubia, who sent him regular information about his black allies. The envoy was a first-rate spy and, despite having only one eye, knew everything that happened in the far-away South. A former army general, he had so much blood on his hands that no act of brutality repelled him.

It was not an enemy who had rendered him one-eyed, but a little bitch of a Nubian girl whom he had beaten to death for not pleasing him enough. Before she died, she had had just enough strength to drive a bone needle into his left eye.

Apophis found One-Eye awaiting him in the reception hall; the man was already finishing his second jar of white wine.

'Majesty, the harem is a wonderful idea,' said One-Eye. 'I didn't leave it for three days, and enjoyed I don't know how many magnificent Egyptian women – they were so refined I thought I was dreaming: it's a real change from the ordinary. Majesty, you are a genius.'

Apophis did not dislike flattery, but at present he was too worried to appreciate it. 'Don't you think Khamudi's report is too pessimistic?' he asked.

'It simply repeats what I have told you, Majesty. The High Treasurer is efficient and ruthless – we get on wonderfully well.'

'So much the better, One-Eye, so much the better. But you aren't usually nervous in the face of the Nubian tribes.'

'I have a principle: never attack unless you're sure of winning. To exterminate those wild beasts I would need a larger, more battle-hardened army than theirs. Today, that is not the case.'

'You have allowed the enemy to gain the upper hand?'

'In a way, yes, Majesty. I did not foresee the rise of this man Nedjeh, and in any case my informants told me he had no future – I ran one of them through in front of his colleagues, to demonstrate my extreme displeasure. When I came here, I knew that you would, quite rightly, condemn me to death, which is why I took my pleasure in the harem until I was utterly exhausted.'

Apophis thought for a moment. On one hand, his subordinates were not permitted to fail in any way. On the other, One-Eye would not be easy to replace; besides, he would be careful to make not one more mistake. So Apophis decided that the official account would be an adaptation of reality: if Nedjeh had been appointed leader of the Nubians, it was with the emperor's blessing.

'You will leave here alive,' he announced. 'As Hyksos envoy, you will deliver my personal congratulations to the man who has united the tribes.'

One-Eye could hardly believe his ears. 'Will you send me an army to annihilate him, Majesty?'

'Fighting the Nubians on their own ground would be extremely difficult – you know that better than I. And I still have no grounds for declaring war on my subjects in the Great South.'

'To the north of his territory, Nedjeh controls only Elephantine, but he will not stop there, Majesty.'

'Is he a fool?'

'I think not.'

'In that case, he knows that provoking the anger of the Hyksos would be disastrous. No doubt he will seek to strengthen his power in Nubia. One day, we shall use his talents. If he becomes inconvenient, we shall take action. Go back there, flatter him with words of friendship, and inform me of everything he says and does. And this time,' said Apophis menacingly, 'there are to be no mistakes.'

Astounded at having emerged from the interview unscathed, the envoy promised himself a night in the harem before departing for the South on his boat.

36

Pharaoh Seqen was close to despair. There would be no joyous celebrations of the new year, for the Hyksos were demanding even heavier taxes than the previous year. The emperor would not be content with another stele proclaiming his glory, and his tax-collectors would count every sack of grain with sadistic pleasure, knowing they were condemning the people of Thebes to starvation.

Fortunately, Seqen's agricultural reforms meant that Thebes would be able to meet the invader's demands. But all his efforts seemed doomed to failure, for the people of the last free city of Egypt were beginning to lose hope.

For more than two years, Queen Ahhotep had been slowly dying of a sickness which the Theban doctors could not cure. She slept for fifteen hours a day, and whenever she tried to stand up she felt so ill that she had to lie down again. She found it difficult to think clearly for more than a few minutes, and a deadly apathy was gradually taking hold of her exhausted body.

All that kept despair at bay was their cheerful little son, Kames, who brought a flicker of joy to the palace. Ahhotep had chosen his name carefully, for it meant 'He Who is Born of the Power of Life', and the child was growing stronger by the minute. Seqen sometimes thought that his wife's health had passed into the body of her son, but of course he could not reproach her for that. There had been such happiness at Kames's birth, such hopes for the future!

Qaris and Seqen were looking at the model of Egypt. Almost the entire country had become Hyksos, and the existence of small groups of rebels in the North remained no more than an unconfirmed rumour.

'My son probably won't celebrate his next birthday in this palace,' said Seqen. 'But where can we go? We can't go to the North, but neither can we go to the South, because Emheb says the Nubians are torturing and executing any Egyptians who refuse to collaborate. They have taken over our former fortresses, and their king, Nedjeh, is planning to expand his borders.'

'Apophis will stop him.'

'Now I understand why he has not razed our city to the ground: Thebes is the bait he has set for Nedjeh. If the Nubians attack the city, the Hyksos army will annihilate them.'

Teti hurried in, and said urgently, 'Come quickly, Seqen. Ahhotep is asking for you.'

Deathly pale, the pharaoh rushed to his wife's bed-chamber. He saw at once that Ahhotep was near death, and he squeezed her hand so tightly that a little light came back into her eyes.

'It is that demon who is stealing my life,' she whispered, 'Apophis, emperor of darkness.'

'I shall attack Avaris and kill him!'

'Take me to Karnak. Tomorrow is the new year, is it not?'

'Yes, but—'

'Draw the sign of the moon on my heart and entrust me to the One who has the power to save me.'

The Nile was turbulent, the annual flood was rising with alarming speed, and the merciless July sun had forced both men and beasts to take shelter.

At noon, Seqen carried his wife slowly up the stairs to the

roof of the Temple of Osiris, master of death and resurrection. He laid the Queen's naked body upon the flagstones, exposing her to the light of Ra, the only power that could defeat darkness.

Ahhotep had given so much of herself that every channel in her body had been completely drained of energy. The queen's hope was that she might be regenerated, like the ritual objects that priests recharged at the beginning of each new year. She, the daughter of the moon, was imploring the sun to create the impossible marriage from which new life could emerge.

Seqen felt a terrible anguish. Surely it was madness to expose his wife to such cruel, intense sunlight? And he was nothing: a king without a crown, who could not continue the fight without her. Ahhotep was the soul of that fight.

As the sun's energy entered the queen's body, it became radiant with light.

Fearing that his eyes would be burnt, Seqen turned away. Then, revolted by his own cowardice, he ran to Ahhotep to end her torment.

Her skin was burning hot.

'You must not stay here,' he told her.

'Have faith, Seqen.'

The implacable sun continued to beat down until every channel in the young woman's body was filled with its sap.

At last, Ahhotep got to her feet. 'The emperor of darkness has failed to kill me. This is the first wound I have inflicted upon him.'

Apophis let out a little cry of pain. His barber had just cut the emperor while shaving him.

In terror, the man fell to his knees. 'A thousand pardons, Majesty. It is not serious, I promise you.'

'Work done at the palace must be perfect.'

'This will never happen again, I swear!'

'Oaths are nothing but lies,' said the emperor. 'A dog which has bitten will bite again, and an incompetent fool will always be incompetent. My copper mines consume a great deal of labour. You shall end your days there.'

Two guards took away the barber, whose snivelling exasperated Apophis.

The unfortunate man's assistant dabbed the slight wound with linen and covered it with a honey compress. 'It will heal very quickly, Majesty.'

'Find me a new barber immediately.'

The day had started badly. Impatiently, the emperor awaited news of the army he had sent to Syria to burn down a village which had dared to protest against excessive taxes. As for his war-fleet, it was pursuing some Cyprian pirates who had been mad enough to attack Hyksos trading-ships.

Khamudi requested an audience. He, at least, was in high spirits. 'Total triumph, Majesty,' he announced. 'The Syrian rebels and Cyprian pirates have been wiped out – once again, Jannas has proved remarkably efficient. I have ordered the Syrians' bodies to be displayed in neighbouring villages to deter any future disturbance.'

The emperor was pleased with his High Treasurer. Rich, depraved and hated, Khamudi revered his all-powerful master and obeyed him unflinchingly. As long as he remained in power, Apophis would cover up his worst atrocities.

The empire was continuing to grow, but extreme vigilance was essential. Here and there madmen were setting up rebel movements, which Khamudi put down with extreme cruelty. In every land Apophis controlled, the funeral pyres of men, women, children and animals were growing more numerous every day. Even when a province seemed to have been pacified, Khamudi carried out preventive raids. The sight of local nobles being tortured and an entire town disappearing in flames cooled the fervour of any would-be dissidents.

'We must keep a strict watch on the Minoans, Majesty. I

188

have no proof, but they may have ordered the attacks on our boats. All my informants are on the alert.'

'Tell Jannas to make ready his fleet.'

Khamudi beamed. He was already picturing the destruction of the Great Island.

'Have you heard anything from One-Eye?' asked Apophis.

'Yes, Majesty. He says the Nubian princeling seems to be behaving himself, but I'm convinced that he will eventually attack Thebes. The lure is too tempting for him to resist.'

'First, he'll have to kill the soldiers who control Edfu.'

'That's precisely why I am sending them no reinforcements,' said Khamudi. 'Edfu is the last barrier before Thebes. If he destroys it, Nedjeh will think he's stronger than the Hyksos he has thereby declared war upon. We shall annihilate him during the battle of Thebes, which will be erased from the map; and we can then take control of Nubia at our leisure.'

37

'I'm afraid,' admitted Mouse-Face.

'So am I,' said Wry-Nose, 'but there's no danger. You know we have friends in high places. Queen Teti is weak, and her daughter is dying – and so is Thebes. We shall simply make ourselves rich and then leave. There's really nothing to fear.'

'If you say so, but all the same . . . robbing a tomb. I'm afraid.'

'I told you, there's nothing to worry about. Here, on the west bank of Thebes, there are only a few starving peasants left, and plenty of well-hidden tombs full of treasure. Just think what we could buy!'

'Yes, but what if we're caught?'

'We won't be. Come on, let's not waste time.'

Path-Finder was waiting for them at the bottom of the hill. 'The best tomb is over there,' he said, pointing. 'Have you got what you need?'

'Don't worry about that. Just show us.'

The first steps of the stairway leading down to a noble's tomb were easy to find.

'I uncovered them,' explained Path-Finder. 'My father knew where the tomb is. He promised the dead man he'd never reveal the location to anyone. But times are so hard . . .'

'The times are the way they are. Let's go to it.'

With copper crowbars, Mouse-Face and Wry-Nose demolished a protecting wall, entered a passageway and lit a torch. The door of the tomb did not resist for long, and they entered the burial chamber.

Beside the sarcophagus lay chairs and chests containing jewels, clothing, sandals and toilet items which Wry-Nose stuffed into bags.

'Let's get out of here quickly,' urged Mouse-Face. 'I'm sure the dead man's soul is watching us.'

'But,' protested Wry-Nose, 'we haven't yet even touched the most important thing: the sarcophagus.'

'No, not that!'

'There must be a gold collar and some beautiful amulets in there. We're going to be rich!' He smashed the lid of the sarcophagus.

The mummy was perfectly preserved. On its chest lay a garland of dried flowers.

Wry-Nose attacked the bandages. Horrified, his accomplice returned to the corridor, so as not to be present at this sacrilege. But, when he heard shouts of joy, his remorse evaporated.

'Gold amulets,' gloated Wry-Nose, 'a big lapis-lazuli scarab and rings! Help me fill these bags.'

Although he dared not look at the desecrated mummy, Mouse-Face nevertheless lent a hand.

When they emerged from the tomb, Path-Finder was waiting for them.

'There you are at last. A good haul?' he asked.

'Wonderful,' said Wry-Nose. 'Shall we share it out now?'

'Of course.'

As Wry-Nose was showing him an amulet shaped like a leg, Path-Finder plunged a dagger into his belly and tried to do the same to his companion. But Mouse-Face had dodged quickly aside and was only wounded on the hip.

Although he was bleeding profusely, he managed to run away, hoping that his attacker would not catch him.

'The man is dead,' said Qaris. 'He was called Mouse-Face and, despite the seriousness of his wound, he managed to cross the Nile and reach the palace to tell us everything.'

'Tomb-robbers!' exclaimed Ahhotep. 'How can people be so vile? Do these criminals not realize that the dead man's soul will punish them?'

'Their lust for gold is so strong that nothing stops them. And that isn't all.'

'The queen is still weak,' Seqen reminded him. 'We shouldn't give her any more shocks.'

'Don't hide anything from me,' ordered the queen.

'Then I must tell you that Mouse-Face gave me the name of the man who guaranteed them immunity. The criminal is none other than the officer in charge of the barracks, a man I trusted completely.'

This caused great consternation.

'Still more serious,' Qaris went on, 'is the fact that those who advocate collaboration with the Hyksos have not given up. In fact, the news of your impending death strengthened them.'

'In other words,' concluded Seqen, 'all my efforts to create a true Theban army have come to nothing. We shall never be able to fight the emperor.'

'Of course we shall!' protested Ahhotep. 'We simply need to change our strategy. The old general gave us the solution shortly before he died: we must set up a secret training-camp.'

'Here, in Thebes? In a population this size, it would not stay secret for long,' said Seqen.

'Now that the energy is flowing once more in my veins,' said Ahhotep, 'I shall pretend to busy myself with the citizens' well-being. The barracks will remain in place, but from now on it is to house only guards, who will ensure public order. The supporters of collaboration will think that our very modest ambitions are no threat to them. Meanwhile you, Seqen, will have your hands free to recruit and train our future soldiers.'

'Yes, but where?'

'On the west bank, of course. We shall make it known that thieves tried to loot the tombs of our ancestors, and that we have therefore posted guards around the burial-ground and forbidden anyone to go there. Only the souls of the dead, which are protected by magic, will have the right to dwell there.'

The queen bent over Qaris's model of Egypt. 'For caution's sake, we shall establish our secret camp here, in the desert to the north of Thebes. If any curious people venture into the area, our lookouts will kill them.'

'Majesty,' objected Qaris, 'this will be a long and arduous business.'

'It will take us several years, I am aware of that. But, if we succeed, we shall at last be in a position to fight.'

In half a day's time, the caravan from the oasis at Bahariya would emerge from the desert and reach the green outskirts of the Fayum oasis, a little paradise where men and beasts could rest before setting off again for Avaris.

The leader of the caravan, Adafi the Thief, had been in the Hyksos's pay for years. A sworn enemy of the Egyptians, who had humiliated his people since the dawn of time, he grew happier by the day as he enjoyed all the benefits of the occupation. Little by little, the land of the pharaohs was bleeding to death, to become merely one more of the emperor's provinces.

Adafi the Thief admired Apophis and, like him, believed solely in the use of force. After all, it was only by murdering three other caravan-owners that he had been able to seize

193

their donkeys, thus becoming one of the richest traders in Libya.

There was an additional source of pleasure. He had recently captured an Egyptian from the South, and had himself cut off his ears and tongue. Like a noble, he had made the wretch carry his sandals and his fan, which must be waved constantly to keep his master cool.

Adafi was delivering jars of good wine, salt and the finest dates to Avaris. The entire consignment was destined for Grand Treasurer Khamudi, who never paid for anything but had authorized the Libyan to take part of the production of the oases for himself.

Despite the early hour, the heat was already becoming uncomfortable.

'More air, you idle blockhead!' The Egyptian slave approached the donkey on which his master was sitting, so as to fan him more easily. He worked hard, in the hope that his heart would soon give out and death put an end to his torment.

Suddenly, the caravan halted. Angrily, Adafi the Thief dismounted.

His second in command soon came hurrying up. 'The lead donkey has stopped,' he explained. 'There's a corpse lying across the road.'

'What does that matter? We'll just trample it underfoot and go on our way.'

'But the corpse is wearing a necklace and bracelets, and the kilt and sandals look of good quality.'

'I'll see to this.'

Followed by his fan-bearer, the Libyan walked to the head of the caravan. Booty was a serious business, and he would help himself first.

The dead man lay on his back. He seemed young, and had a fine moustache and – more importantly – beautiful jewellery. Drooling with anticipation, Adafi the Thief bent down to tear off the necklace.

The Empire of Darkness

Coming abruptly back to life, Moustache seized the dagger
he had hidden in the sand and slit the corpse-robber's throat.
'Attack!' he yelled, leaping to his feet.

38

In accordance with their orders, the rebels gave no quarter.

For more than two years they had been attacking small caravans, sometimes in the Western desert, sometimes in the east. These operations were not easy to mount, for the group had first to obtain reliable information in order to minimize the risks. If the convoy turned out to be too large, or was protected by Hyksos soldiers, the Afghan and Moustache preferred to let it pass unmolested.

Nevertheless, they had won some fine plunder and had amassed large stores of food, together with clothes and various objects which they could barter if necessary. This caravan was their largest prize to date.

'The rebel movement is getting rich,' commented Moustache. 'Why are you pulling that face, Afghan?'

'Because we've hit too close to home. On the looter you killed, I found a scarab signed by Khamudi. This caravan was destined for him, and he will order an investigation.'

Moustache's joy evaporated. 'Whatever happens, he must not learn that we exist. But perhaps he'll think it was a raid by sand-travellers?'

'The sand-travellers are allies of the Hyksos, and they'd never dare attack an official caravan. In the case of a mistake, their first reaction would be to take their booty to Avaris to beg the authorities for forgiveness.'

'We've got ourselves into a fine mess,' said Moustache.

'There's only one thing to do,' decided the Afghan. 'We must make it look as though the merchants killed each other. So we shall leave most of the goods here, and just take a few donkeys.'

The rebels arranged the bodies to make it look as if there had been a general set-to.

'Look at that one,' said Moustache to the Afghan. 'They've cut off his ears and his tongue. But there is something more interesting: he is circumcised like an Egyptian, and under his left arm he bears a tattoo of the moon in its ship.'

'It's a secret sign – that much is becoming clear. This poor fellow was a prisoner. We should have spared him.'

'How were we to know?'

'There must be another group of rebels somewhere,' said the Afghan.

'Thebes is in its death-throes. Edfu is in the hands of the Hyksos, and Elephantine is under the Nubian yoke. Whether we like it or not, we're alone.'

'All the same, that sign exists, and this is the second time we've seen it.'

Moustache blinked. 'Do you mean you want to break through the blockade at Henen-Nesut and head south?'

'We aren't at that stage yet, although things don't look too bad. Our network is growing stronger by the month, we have several reliable bases, the peasants support us and supply us with information, we have a forge to make weapons, and we have enough to eat. Our domain may be a small one, but within it we're safe. When we're ready, we'll take care of Henen-Nesut, I promise you.'

'Come here, my darling,' begged the lady Yima, who had bleached her hair in order to look even more blonde. Bare-breasted and dressed only in a shawl, she lay simpering on her bed.

Khamudi slapped her. 'You are nothing but a bitch in heat. The emperor is waiting for me.'

Yima snivelled. She knew very well that her man was captivated by her charms and could not deprive himself of them for long. Tomorrow night, she would give him a young Canaanite girl, who would experience ecstasy and then become food for the crocodiles. Yima would take part in any kind of entertainment, so long as she was the one to organize it.

Khamudi walked heavily towards the small room in the fortress where he could speak with Apophis without anyone overhearing them. It was not this ridiculous matter of the caravan that was vexing him; those idiotic thieves had killed each other, no doubt because of Adafi's greed, but the goods had reached him in the end. Much more serious was the situation regarding Minoa.

According to one of his spies, the Minoans had indeed engaged the Cyprian pirates, with the firm intention of seizing several Hyksos trading-ships. Admittedly there was no hard proof, but nevertheless Apophis ought to act with all possible speed.

Jannas's war-fleet was within sight of the Great Island, ready to attack. Vessels carrying troops would join it before the assault.

Khamudi hated the Minoans. Arrogant, and steeped in their own past and culture, they did not behave like true vassals. On one occasion, he had thought of arranging for Jannas to be murdered, and attributing the blame to them, but the plan would have required the involvement of too many people, and the High Treasurer could not afford mistakes.

It was the Minoans themselves who had made the mistake this time. Knowing Apophis as he did, Khamudi was certain that the emperor's cold anger would be terrible and that only the destruction of the island would appease him.

Apophis was being shaved by his new barber, who had

difficulty in suppressing a slight tremor as he slid the blade of the razor across the master of the world's cheek.

'Good news, Khamudi?' asked the emperor.

'The situation is delicate, Majesty.'

'Hurry up and finish, barber.'

The barber hurried nervously, terrified of making a mistake. Fortunately he shaved the emperor perfectly, without cutting him, and then he vanished with his equipment.

'Jannas must attack Minoa,' said Khamudi. 'That arrogant island deserves to be punished.'

'So you are certain at the Minoans are a threat to our ships?'

'There's no doubt about it.'

'Then we must take action.'

'I shall pass on your orders to Jannas at once.'

'First wait to hear what they are. The Minoans are seasoned warriors, not easy to defeat.'

Khamudi was astonished. 'They will be crushed by sheer weight of numbers.'

'Of course, and they know it. So it is in their interests to satisfy my demands. They are to double their tributes and provide me with two thousand soldiers and fifty ships; and their finest painters are to come to Avaris to decorate my palace. If even one of these conditions is not satisfied, I shall consider myself insulted and Jannas will take action.'

Khamudi was delighted. The Minoans would never accept such humiliation.

Heray, the Overseer of Granaries, was a pleasant and affable man who knew everyone in Thebes and, on Ahhotep's instructions, provided free bread and beer to the poorest families. Thanks to his vigilance, no one went hungry. His officials loved him because he treated them with respect, so they did excellent work. The Theban granaries had never been better managed.

Who would ever suspect Heray of spying for the king and queen? He calmed people's worries, defused conflicts and had a fund of amusing stories to raise the lowest spirits. Affluent families were honoured to have him as a guest, and people went gladly to dine at his house. Consequently he had gained the trust of men and women, young and old, gullible and sceptical alike.

He and Ahhotep were walking in the palace gardens, watched by Laughter.

'I have the impression that this town no longer has any secrets from you,' said Ahhotep.

'Majesty, I have identified the main supporters of collaboration with the Hyksos. They are weak men, true, but I confess that I'm disappointed and worried, because there are many more of them than I thought. Thebes has been undermined by fear, selfishness and cowardice.'

'Anything else would have surprised me. Now, we know that the secret camp is essential if we are to build an army. I am relying on you to persuade the collaborators that we have given up all thought of dangerous ideas. Explain to them clearly that my only ambition is to have a second child and to live peacefully at the palace, enjoying the few privileges I have left.'

'I shall put them off their guard, Majesty.'

Laughter sniffed the air, fully alert, then flopped down on the ground, his front paws stretched out, ready to play. He gave yelps of joy when little Kames ran towards him.

When the dog licked his forehead, the child burst out laughing, then pretended to be afraid. 'Mother, Mother, save me!'

Ahhotep took the child in her arms and swung him up above her head. 'One day, my son, we shall be free.'

39

Ahhotep emerged from a byre where a cow was gently licking her new-born calf. The queen was inspecting land which had been abandoned by its owners for several years, but which was now being reclaimed. Encouraged first by the queen and then by Heray, farmers had started rearing stock again, while water-carriers came regularly to irrigate the gardens. Thanks to the fertile silt deposited by the Nile flood, the peasants reaped excellent harvests.

Ahhotep also ensured that dykes were properly maintained and new reservoirs created, so that even in the dry season Waset would not go short of water.

'All is ready, Majesty,' said Heray.

As the wine-growers had worked hard and the wine promised to be excellent, Ahhotep had decided to celebrate a festival in the heart of the countryside, in the presence of the city's leading citizens. Although the Hyksos threat was ever present, people were glad of the chance to forget their worries for a while, and everyone sampled the new wine with gusto. How exhilarating it was to give thanks to the god of the wine-press, to chatter about nothing in particular and to believe in the future, even if only for a moment.

Qaris called for silence. When all was quiet, he said, 'Many of you will be surprised not to see Her Majesty Teti the Small here. Our sovereign is with us in spirit, but her frail health does not permit her to leave the palace. She has instructed me to announce that she is officially abdicating and that henceforth her daughter, Ahhotep, will take on all the duties of the Queen of Egypt.'

The news was greeted with cheers.

A dignitary spoke up. 'We are delighted with Her Majesty's choice, but what will Pharaoh Apophis think of it?'

'In the official letter she has just sent him, his very respectful servant Ahhotep asks for his approval and begs him to continue to protect his obedient city of Thebes.'

The dignitary was one of those who advocated collaboration, and he smiled with pleasure at these words.

Many peasants, on the other hand, were not at all happy. The young queen wished she could tell them the truth, but the people of Thebes must be convinced that their new sovereign had given up all thought of fighting the Hyksos.

As for would-be rebels, they were contacted by Heray and his men. If they came through the rigorous selection procedure, they would be advised to announce loudly that they were leaving the miserable city of Thebes to try their luck elsewhere. And they would join the secret camp on the west bank, where they were put to the test by means of ruthless training.

It was with sadness that the revellers dispersed when the festivities were over.

Qaris could plainly see the Queen's frustration. 'Have patience, Majesty,' he urged.

'Has the other letter been sent?'

'It has been delivered to the guard-post at Kebet, which will ensure it reaches the emperor. As usual, I imitated the late minister for agriculture's writing and placed his seal upon the letter. The traitor informs Apophis that you, like your mother, are a mere figurehead, the representative of an outmoded tradition which amuses the common folk. Given your youth, your inexperience, your love of children and your lack of interest in public life, there is nothing to fear from you.'

Apophis would not have missed this for worlds. A woman . . . Thebes had chosen a woman as ruler and, what was more, a slip of a girl. But what was there to rule? A mere rabble, terrified at the thought that the Hyksos army might appear at any moment. How surprised they would be when Nubian warriors were unleashed upon them!

For the time being, Apophis would simply mock the ridiculous city of Thebes. The prospect of a confrontation with Minoa wholly occupied his thoughts. If he decided to strike, the blow must be decisive, demonstrating to all his present and future subjects that no one could challenge his authority. So he had encircled the Great Island with three concentric rings of ships: first, those containing elite archers and giant catapults; then ships transporting footsoldiers; and lastly cargo-vessels with supplies. According to Jannas's estimates, there were five times as many Hyksos soldiers as there were Minoans.

Yet the emperor was less sanguine than Khamudi. The battle would be fierce, and after the soldiers had disembarked they would have to capture the well-fortified Minoan capital. So Apophis was already preparing a second wave of attack, which he himself would command.

Nothing would be left of the rebel island. Not one human being, not one animal, not one tree.

'Here you are at last, Khamudi. What is the news?'

'Jannas has passed on your demands to the Minoans. They asked to negotiate, and he of course refused and gave them one day to respond.'

'Jannas is sometimes too conciliatory,' said the emperor. 'Is the second wave of attack ready to leave?'

'It is at your command, Majesty.'

*

The Afghan was still sceptical. 'According to a message from Avaris, almost the entire war-fleet is preparing to leave port.'

'Where is it going?' asked Moustache, intrigued.

'Rumour has it the Hyksos are planning to invade Minoa.'

'That doesn't make sense. The Great Island is their ally.'

'Our informant stated clearly that the emperor himself is to lead the expedition.'

'Is your man sure?'

'You know him better than I do: he works at the weapons store in Avaris, and you recruited him yourself. He risks his life and his messenger's to send us this kind of information.'

Moustache munched a fresh onion. 'Who's going to rule Egypt while the emperor's away?'

'Probably his faithful Khamudi.'

'Suppose we tried to kill him? With him out of the way, we could cause a peasants' uprising in the Delta.'

'It's a tempting thought, I grant you,' said the Afghan. 'But it's too good to be true, don't you think? Even if the emperor really is away, he won't have left his capital unprotected. A fine trap, no?'

Moustache could have wept, but he had to face facts. A handful of rebels was not going to seize control of Avaris.

Leaning on her daughter's arm, Teti the Small was delightedly exploring her city. She was astonished by the cleanliness of the streets and the large quantities of fine vegetables on display in the market. Everyone was happy to see their new queen's mother, who took great pleasure in talking to people and admiring the cooking-pots produced in the newly reopened workshops. After kneading and shaping clay soaked in water, the craftsmen left the pots to dry in the sun and then fired them at a low temperature. Besides pots, they made ladles, bowls and cups, which they glazed to make them impermeable.

Teti was also interested in the simple baskets woven from

flexible reeds and coloured red, blue or yellow. Those designed to carry heavy objects had their bases reinforced with two wooden battens and laid across each other.

'If you like this red basket, Majesty,' one of the craftsmen said to her, 'permit me to give it to you.'

'In exchange, you shall receive a pot of ointment.'

Teti did not open her gift until she reached the palace. Fortunately, the basket was empty. According to the code agreed with Seqen and Heray, that meant that the security of the secret camp was intact and that there was no immediate danger from collaborators. Otherwise, a small papyrus would have told Teti and Ahhotep what they must do.

'I shall drink a little white wine with my midday meal,' said Teti. 'That walk has made me feel young again.'

40

From his vantage-point high on the walls of the citadel, Apophis watched Jannas's flagship returning to port, followed by the rest of the war-fleet and a heavily laden cargo-ship.

Guards were stationed on the quayside, to prevent any popular demonstration; for the emperor had forbidden the revelry that used to accompany the sailors' return. Hyksos soldiers must be disciplined and ready for combat at all times.

Apophis received Jannas in the great audience chamber at the palace, in the presence of Khamudi and members of the ruling elite.

'Did the Minoans see reason, Commander?'

'To be certain of winning your favour, they have trebled their tributes and in a few weeks' time they will send you the ships and soldiers you demand. The king of the Great Island sends you his apologies, and promises that there will be no repetition of the unfortunate incident that obliged us to take action. He greatly regrets the fact that he was misled by incompetent advisers – who have since been thrown to the wild beasts.'

'And what about the artists?'

'The finest Minoan painters are at your disposal. They travelled here on the cargo-boat, which is the Great Island's first gift to you. Minoa is determined to prove that she is your loyal and devoted vassal.'

'Bring them in.'

There were ten of them. All had curly hair and wore brightly coloured tunics. The oldest was around fifty, the youngest twenty-five.

'Kneel before the emperor and lower your eyes,' ordered Khamudi.

With the aid of these men, Apophis intended to erase all traces of Egyptian culture from Avaris.

He told them, 'You are to decorate my palace in the Minoan style. I wish it to be even more beautiful than the palace at Knossos, and every painting must be breathtaking. If you succeed, your lives will be spared. If not, I shall consider your failure a personal insult.'

'As yet it is only the beginnings of an army,' Seqen told Ahhotep, 'but little by little my first soldiers are becoming true warriors, capable of defeating any enemy in hand-to-hand combat. Their living conditions are very harsh, but it is good that they are, for what awaits them is harsher still.'

Lying naked in the gentle shade of a sycamore tree, the two young people had made passionate love. And yet sadness clouded the queen's eyes.

'I don't understand,' she confessed. 'Although my mother gave me a sea-shell to ward off sterility and the evil eye, I have still not become pregnant. Are you eating enough celery?'

Seqen smiled. 'Do you think I need it to prove my desire for you? Even a single day away from you is too much to bear.'

'I want another son.'

'That would be a great blessing, but we must accept the will of the gods.'

'Kames will have a brother, I know he will.'

Seqen dared not raise the slightest objection. In any case,

his wife's caresses made him forget everything except her perfect body, so gifted in the ways of love.

Little Kames enjoyed learning the rudiments of wrestling from his father, walking with Laughter, and being cuddled by his mother while she told him fine stories in which justice always triumphed. But what he liked best was playing with his grandmother. When he played tricks on her, Teti did not scold him; she tried to catch him out in return, and the hilarious battle ended with peals of laughter and wonderful cakes which Teti had baked herself.

Spending time with this lively little rascal had given Teti a new lease of life. Her appetite astonished the palace cook, one of Heray's men, particularly since she never gained any weight at all but remained as slender and elegant as ever.

Teti visited the market without fail at least once a month, to the great pleasure of the people, who were at last beginning to think that their town might escape destruction.

The baskets she was given were always empty.

Heray's lookouts were extremely effective within Thebes itself, and Teti was careful to remind everyone that they must show respect towards the souls of the dead who rested in the burial-ground on the west bank. She and Qaris spread terrifying stories of ghosts and demons which devoured anyone foolish enough to venture into the realm of the dead.

Only the royal household knew about Seqen's frequent absences, and they were all members of the rebel movement. Teti and Qaris had firmly established Seqen's reputation as a hunter and fisherman who could not bear to stay in one place for long.

Those who advocated collaboration understood the situation perfectly: the ruling family had no appetite for war and accepted Hyksos control without question. Better still, since Ahhotep had taken power she had succeeded in improving the daily lives of all Thebans.

Despite this, Chomu the vase-seller was not happy. The son of an Egyptian father and a Canaanite mother, he had had great difficulty in gaining the respect of his fellow citizens, who were rather suspicious and reserved towards him. The death of his most influential enemy, the minister for agriculture, had enabled Chomu to forge links with other traders who believed, as he did, that the Theban dynasty had no future and the province ought to be governed far more directly by the emperor. For who but Apophis could make the city prosperous again?

Ahhotep's behaviour had surprised Chomu and his friends. He had been convinced that the headstrong girl would provoke the emperor's fury, but events had proved him wrong. Starting a family seemed to have given her a taste for the virtues of submission.

Consequently, those who refused to accept the all-powerful Hyksos preferred to leave Thebes, where no one had even been punished for favouring collaboration. And neither the ageing Teti nor the elusive Seqen would push Thebes into war. There was nothing to suggest that a fire still smouldered beneath the ashes.

Nevertheless, Chomu was uneasy. True, thanks to the small increase in trade he was not living quite so poorly; but why had the emperor not driven out Teti and her daughter? His friends said it was because Teti and Ahhotep were governing the enclave to the new pharaoh's satisfaction. After all, Thebes was only a provincial town, far from Avaris, and did not figure among the emperor's main interests. Everyone had enough to eat, so why, they asked, could Chomu not be content with the goodwill of the Hyksos, who seemed to have forgotten all about this small, moribund city?

Chomu rubbed his red beard. The emperor ought to be made aware of a man like him, so that he could entrust Chomu with responsibilities commensurate with his loyalty. But how was he to establish contact with Apophis? Leaving

Thebes would mean running grave risks, and Chomu had no taste for danger.

For the time being, he must simply persuade more Thebans to join the side of the collaborators.

'Are you absolutely sure?' Emheb asked the lookout.

'Absolutely. There were definitely two Nubian warriors. They shifted their positions several times, so as to study Edfu from many angles.'

So it was about to happen: the event Emheb had most feared. The Nubians had decided to push northwards and extend their boundaries beyond Elephantine.

Edfu, Nekhen, Thebes . . . so many easy targets.

Easy, but poisoned. Taking Edfu meant attacking the Hyksos. As soon as Apophis heard that the town had fallen, he would send Jannas south with orders to crush the Nubians and lay waste their whole country.

To prevent the Nubians attacking, Emheb would have to ask the emperor for help. But that would also result in Jannas's arrival, and the commander would be bound to unmask Emheb and the rebels, slaughter the inhabitants of Edfu and put to fire and sword the entire region, including Thebes.

Whether to be massacred by the Nubians or by the Hyksos: that was Emheb's only choice.

41

'Look, Mother, Look! It's Rascal.' Kames had made friends with the pigeon, which often carried messages between Edfu and Thebes.

Its errand accomplished, the bird fluttered down into the palace garden and allowed him to stroke it. The little boy had learnt how to untie the thread that bound a roll of papyrus to the pigeon's right leg. If it were ever on the left leg, Ahhotep would know instantly that the message had not been written by Governor Emheb.

Of course, the text was written in code and included the sign by which the rebels recognized each other, written three times and hidden among a jumble of meaningless words.

What the queen read turned her blood to ice.

Seqen, Teti, Qaris and Heray listened attentively as Ahhotep read them the terrible message from Emheb.

'We were right,' said Seqen. 'The emperor was sparing Thebes only so that he could use it as bait.'

'Can we withstand the Nubians?' asked Heray, without much hope.

'I have only a hundred fully trained soldiers at my disposal. Even if we joined forces with Emheb's men, we would be destroyed in the first attack.'

'The Nubians' reputation for cruelty is justified,' said Qaris. 'We must prepare the royal family's escape.'

'And what about the people of Thebes?' asked Ahhotep indignantly.

'Even if we tried to move them, they would be spotted and killed, by the Hyksos or the Nubians or both.'

'Then they must take up arms and fight under our command.'

'The civilians cannot do that,' argued Heray. 'Do not forget, Majesty, that the Hyksos's supporters will refuse to fight and will try to persuade their fellow citizens to do the same by promising their lives will be spared.'

'Qaris is right,' agreed Seqen. 'Ahhotep, Teti and Kames must leave Thebes. I and my soldiers will go to Edfu and fight at Emheb's side.'

'I am too old and tired to leave the town of my birth,' declared Teti. 'I shall stay here and try to negotiate with the attackers.'

'I will not leave my husband,' said Ahhotep.

'You and Kames are the future. With an escort, you will hide in the desert and—'

'And die like cowards, far from those we love? Never! Go back to the training-camp, Seqen, and prepare your soldiers to die like warriors. I shall write to Governor Emheb, informing him that we shall join him as soon as he needs us.'

Beautiful Windswept had set her sights on Minos, the most talented of the Minoan painters and the leader of the artists who had been forced to adorn Apophis's palace.

'May I watch you working, Minos?' she asked.

'I hate that.'

The tall, slender woman slid a delicate finger over her sensual lips. 'You know you have to obey the emperor, and the emperor is my brother. He won't refuse me anything – not even the head of a Minoan painter.'

212

'Without me, this palace will remain what it is: a hideous prison.'

'Do you think you are irreplaceable?'

'I know I am. And as soon as I've finished, I'm going home with my companions.'

'How naïve you are!'

The artist turned to look at the magnificent princess with a teasing voice. 'Why do you say that?'

'Because you will never return to Minoa. Don't you understand that you have become the emperor's property?'

Minos dropped his brush.

Windswept ran her fingers gently through the painter's curly hair and kissed him on the neck. 'It isn't so terrible, if you know how to behave. Egypt is a pleasant country, and you can make this palace more attractive. Besides, you dare not fail, remember?'

Minos did not move.

'I hope you aren't a lover of boys,' said Windswept anxiously as she untied his kilt; when she saw the effect of her caresses, she was reassured.

Unable to resist any longer, Minos took her hungrily in his arms and they lay down on the stone floor.

'There are more comfortable places to get to know each other,' she suggested.

'You seem to doubt my abilities as a lover, so I want to prove you wrong right now.'

The tribal ceremonies consecrated Emperor-Pharaoh Apophis's absolute power for a second time. His vassals bowed low before him, presenting him with the wealth of their respective countries, in even larger quantities than the previous year.

Particularly noteworthy was the Minoan envoy's speech. In well-chosen words, he hailed Apophis's greatness and emphasized how proud the Great Island was that its finest artists were decorating the palace at Avaris. Henceforth, Apophis's palace would be considered the centre of the world.

Commander Jannas had been summoned to represent the Hyksos armed forces of both land and sea, and to make it very clear to any aspiring rebels that they were heading for certain death. During Jannas's speech, the emperor watched the Nubian envoy closely, but his face remained untroubled.

Finally, High Treasurer Khamudi announced, as he did each year, that there was to be an increase in levies and taxes. This was vital if the Hyksos state was to ensure the well-being and safety of its subjects. Any delays or attempts at fraud would carry heavy penalties. If a vassal failed to honour his obligations, the army would swiftly remind him of them.

No envoy liked spending time in Avaris, where there were guards everywhere and the atmosphere was suffocating. And everyone knew that the emperor could make anyone disappear if the fancy took him.

The most relieved person at the ceremony was the Minoan envoy, who, despite his country's total submission, still feared reprisals. Knowing Apophis, Khamudi and Jannas, he had persuaded his king never again to attempt any kind of attack on the Hyksos, and to satisfy all the conditions the emperor had imposed upon the Great Island.

As his ship sailed away from Avaris, he spared a sympathetic thought for his Nubian colleague, who had just been summoned by Apophis. He would probably never see him again.

'You were very quiet,' remarked Apophis.

Despite his long experience, the Nubian envoy felt a lump in his throat and butterflies in his stomach.

'The ceremony was perfect, Majesty, and everything was made absolutely clear.'

'As the empire is at peace, I have decided to pay a little

more attention to Egypt and Nubia. So I am entrusting Commander Jannas and High Treasurer Khamudi with a new mission.'

The envoy quailed, convinced that the emperor's harsh voice had just announced the extermination of the Nubian people.

'Do not misunderstand me,' Apophis went on. 'My friend and faithful subject Nedjeh is conducting himself loyally and has committed no serious mistakes, so why should I punish him?'

By now the envoy was sweating profusely. In less than one month, Nedjeh intended to attack Edfu, then seize Thebes and present the emperor with a given situation. Apophis would rule the North, and the Nubians the South.

'Public finance is a difficult art,' went on Apophis. 'Despite the local rulers' goodwill, there are still areas of uncertainty, even annoying omissions. Khamudi is so devoted to the good of the state that he can no longer bear these imperfections. So a census must be carried out.'

'A census . . .?' stammered the envoy.

'Commander Jannas's troops will leave tomorrow for Elephantine, where they will count men and animals, head by head. Then they will carry out the same process in Nubia, while other soldiers will attend to the Southern provinces. Of course, I am counting on the full and active collaboration of my servant Nedjeh.'

'Of course,' repeated the envoy.

42

'A Hyksos boat is coming, Governor,' said the guard.

Emheb was astonished. 'Only one?'

'Yes, and not even a very big one. One officer and a dozen men have disembarked and are heading this way. When shall we kill them?'

'We shan't touch them until we know what they want. If a boat is reported missing, Jannas will react violently.'

Emheb was puzzled. Evidently the Hyksos had been alerted to the Nubians' intentions. Why had they sent only modest reinforcements? But perhaps this was just an advance detachment.

He might perhaps manage to convince them that Edfu was completely under control and could serve as a Hyksos base to bar the way to the Nubians, but that would be only a temporary measure. These emissaries undoubtedly heralded the arrival of Jannas.

'The officer wants to see you, Governor.'

'Bring him to me.'

More than twenty warships laden with Hyksos had sailed up the Nile past Thebes.

The streets of the city were deserted. At the palace, no one could hide their anxiety. Teti still played with Kames, but without her usual gaiety. Even Laughter was nervous.

'The emperor always strikes the first blow,' said Qaris. 'The Nubians were wrong to defy him.'

'And Thebes will pay the price for their folly,' said Ahhotep angrily.

'Take shelter, Majesty,' begged the steward. 'Join the king on the west bank.'

'As soon as Seqen and his men can cross the Nile, they will come to defend us.'

Heray rushed breathlessly into the audience chamber. 'Hyksos are disembarking. They'll soon be here.'

'I shall receive them,' announced Teti, holding Kames in her arms. 'They will not dare touch a grandmother and her grandson.'

'No, Mother,' said Ahhotep. 'Confronting them is my responsibility.'

The young queen left the palace to meet the Hyksos.

She would ask their leader to spare Thebes. What could she offer in return, except herself? No doubt the emperor would be delighted to make a slave of her. Once she was in his presence, she would find the right words to tell him what a monster and a coward he was. That would be her last battle.

The soldiers advanced inexorably. Ahhotep stood stock still in the sunshine, refusing to let herself be afraid.

Suddenly, she wondered if her eyes were deceiving her. No, it really was him.

'Governor Emheb!' she said.

'You have nothing to fear, Majesty,' he whispered. 'Neither the Nubians nor the Hyksos will attack you. The emperor has decided to carry out a census of the whole country, even Nubia. Jannas himself is in charge there, at the head of his troops, so it is impossible for Nedjeh to disobey. He is pinned down in his capital and must conduct himself like a loyal subject of the emperor. There is no question now of him seizing Edfu and Thebes, because his plans for conquest have been nipped in the bud. Apophis will know the

217

exact number of Nubian warriors and will tax their king accordingly. As for the small, unimportant town of Thebes, I, the perfect collaborator, am to deal with her most severely.'

Ahhotep would gladly have flung her arms round Emheb's neck, but dozens of eyes must be watching them.

'My city is independent!' she shouted. 'How can you, an Egyptian, betray your country by becoming a tool of the emperor?'

'Apophis is our pharaoh, Majesty, and we all owe him obedience,' replied Emheb loudly. 'I am here with only a few soldiers, who will undertake a census of the inhabitants of Thebes. If you do not cooperate, an entire regiment will undertake this task, after arresting and deporting those who refuse to comply.'

Ahhotep turned her back on him. 'The royal family consists of four people,' she said disdainfully, 'my mother, Teti the Small, my husband, Seqen, my son, Kames, and myself. As to the palace staff, see Qaris, the steward. And you can take care of the rest of the population yourself.'

Hidden behind a half-closed shutter, Chomu had missed nothing of the altercation. As soon as the queen had disappeared, he ran to the governoor.

'Welcome, O glorious Hyksos! My name is Chomu. I'm a trader and I represent the many Thebans who revere the emperor. We are ready to assist your soldiers in their task.'

Overcoming his nausea, Emheb managed a faint smile. 'I hereby appoint you local census enumerator. You are to set up an office with two Hyksos scribes, collect the declarations and file them. Be sure to inform me if you find any cases of fraud.'

'You shall have the exact number of inhabitants, Governor.' His lips wet with excitement, Chomu dared to ask the all-important question: 'Have I your permission to sign the final report, stressing my utter devotion to the emperor?'

'If I am satisfied with your work, why not?'

Never had Chomu tasted such a moment of ecstasy. He was the official census enumerator, working on behalf of the emperor! At last he was on the first rung of the ladder that led to the mayor's office. From there he would drive out the royal family and turn Thebes into a real Hyksos city.

The peasants of the Delta barely recognized their region any more. Military posts had sprung up everywhere, replacing shepherds' huts, and breeds of sheep unknown to the Egyptians had been widely introduced for their wool. The Hyksos required large flocks of sheep, for they refused to eat the pork so prized by Egyptians, and, unlike them, preferred woollen clothing to linen.

Each day, noted Moustache, the gulf between occupier and occupied was deepening. Although the number of collaborators might be growing, few of them truly believed in the virtues of the Hyksos order. The majority were trying to save their own lives by pretending to revere a tyrant whose might could not be challenged by any power on earth.

In this climate of desperation, it was not easy to recruit new rebels. On the other hand, those who chose to fight Apophis were ready to sacrifice themselves and would not balk at any danger.

Today Moustache had to admit failure. After working for a month with a group of pig-farmers, without any payment save a little food, he had revealed himself in the hope of signing up at least one. But although the five men were sympathetic, they did not feel able to embark on such a mad venture.

As they were passing the abandoned store-shed where the Afghan was hiding, waiting for the results of his friend's efforts, one of the farmers stopped in his tracks.

'There are Hyksos in our home!'

Ten footsoldiers clad in black breastplates emerged from the farm where the pig-farmers and their families lived.

Moustache could neither run away nor warn the Afghan.

The soldiers had spotted the peasants and were coming towards them. His only hope was that the pig-farmers would not betray him.

'Official census,' announced the officer, a sturdy Anatolian. 'Your names and the exact number of your animals. Ah yes, and I must inform you that the selling price of your pigs has been halved and taxes increased by the same amount.'

'You're ruining us!' protested a young farmer.

'That's not my problem, my lad. All you have to do is be like us and not eat pigs. So . . . I don't suppose you've hidden a few in that old shed over there?'

'No, it's abandoned.'

'All the same, we'll take a look, if only to check that you're not lying. And if you are, my lad, you'll be in serious trouble.'

'Defend yourselves – they want to kill you!' roared Moustache, breaking the neck of one of the soldiers, then seizing his sword and plunging it into the chest of the solder next to him.

Enraged, the Anatolian sank his spear into the belly of a pig-farmer who was trying to calm him. With no weapons but their fists, the peasants were no match for the Hyksos, but they held them off just long enough for a wild beast to leap out of the store-shed brandishing a pitchfork which he drove into the Anatolian's back.

The soldiers were too stunned to fight. The two rebels, highly skilled in close combat, left them no chance.

Moustache's blood-stained hands were shaking. The Afghan was trying to get his breath back. Not one of the pig-farmers was left alive.

The Afghan finished off the wounded Hyksos. In fury, Moustache trampled on their corpses until not a single face was recognizable.

43

High Treasurer Khamudi was sitting in his luxurious office in Avaris, receiving reports from the census enumerators. The man his underlings secretly nicknamed 'His Royal Self-Importance' and 'Lord Greed' had become exceedingly rich. Controlling the production of scarabs and papyrus, and creaming off a portion of the tax revenues with Apophis's agreement, gave free rein to his greed – he had put on a lot of weight – not to mention his rapacity.

After three years' work, the census was drawing to an end. In accordance with Khamudi's instructions, Hyksos soldiers had explored every far-flung corner of Egypt and Nubia, returning several times to the most densely populated areas, so that not a single human being or head of livestock should escape them. And the result was remarkable: not one person would avoid paying the many taxes decreed by the emperor.

Although somewhat disappointed during the early days of the enterprise, Khamudi had had an amusing idea: to entrust the first declaration to local scribes. If there were any mistakes when the Hyksos officials checked their work, they were burnt alive in a public place. The measure had had the desired effect: the Egyptian scribes had proved excellent collaborators, tracking down the very last peasant lurking on his tiny patch of land in the remotest province.

Khamudi therefore felt justifiably proud when he appeared

before his master, who was busy calculating new rates of pay for Hyksos soldiers and state officials. The procedure was as simple as it was effective: their increases in their pay were paid for by taking more from his subjects, who were in no position to protest.

'Majesty, the census is a dazzling success.'

'How much have our revenues increased?'

'By nearly a third. Even the Nubians have been brought to heel. I cannot say for sure that Nedjeh is not hiding one or two family treasures which he forgot to declare, but can we not pardon him that small error?'

'In return, you are to increase the price of the wheat we sell him. Any incidents worth noting?'

'We lost one patrol, which was foolish enough to go swimming at a place where the Nile is infested with crocodiles – all we found were a few fragments of flesh stuck to their uniforms. There's nothing else to report, for who would dare rebel against our army? Even the wild Nubians have realized that it's as well to obey Commander Jannas without question. And there is another reason to be pleased: we have completely destroyed the rebel movement, and the number of our Egyptian collaborators is on the increase. Emheb, the governor of Edfu, has been an active census enumerator. The Waset countryside had twice as many animals as we thought, and he even unmasked the owners of a single pig.'

'Did he do nothing to protect his own town?'

'Nothing at all, Majesty. Giving him an official mission has turned him into a true predator. With his help, we shall bleed Edfu dry.'

'Appoint him Overseer of Taxes for Waset, and ensure that his tax revenues continue to rise. His attitude is sure to inspire other leading Egyptian citizens, and speed up their people's decline.'

*

Even the Afghan was exhausted. Since the start of the census, the small group of rebels had had to keep constantly on the move, for fear of being intercepted by one of the many Hyksos patrols that criss-crossed Middle Egypt, not to mention the isolated farms.

Several times, the desert had provided them with temporary shelter, but lack of provisions meant they had to return to the countryside, where the peasants had proved hostile. Their concern was no longer recruitment but survival.

'We can't hold out much longer,' confessed Moustache. 'Our men's nerves are stretched to breaking-point. Having to live like hunted animals is tearing them apart with fear. Some of them even want to go home.'

'If they do, they'll be executed,' said the Afghan.

'They'd prefer that to being on the run all the time.'

'I'll try to make them change their minds. But if I can't . . .'

'Surely you won't kill them if they've lost faith?'

'Can you suggest a better solution?'

Moustache knew the Afghan was right; but how could this terrible situation be resolved?

'If we let them leave,' pointed out the Afghan, 'they'll betray us, and everything we've gone through in the past few years will have been for nothing.'

'But they're our comrades, not our enemies.'

'If they lose faith, they become enemies.'

One of the rebels warned them, 'There's a farmer coming this way.'

'Do we know him?'

'He's given us shelter before now.'

'See if he's being followed by any Hyksos.'

The peasant was alone. Protected by the Afghan, who hid behind a tamarisk-tree, Moustache agreed to talk to him.

'What do you want, farmer?' he asked.

'It's over – the census is over! The special patrols have left for Avaris, and so has the war-fleet. There are only the usual

223

occupation troops left. This very night, you can sleep at my house.'

Thebes had been bled dry. Ahhotep did not regret approving Emheb's strategy, but it had brought the inhabitants of the little city close to ruin. The new taxes on harvests would leave them scarcely enough to eat, and it took all Ahhotep's powers of persuasion to preserve their will to live.

Teti assisted her ably. On her frequent visits to the market, she explained to the housewives that the royal family ate neither more nor better than they did. And little Kames declared loud and long that Thebes would overcome all her enemies.

Chomu the vase-seller was deeply depressed. He had hoped the Hyksos soldiers would stay in Thebes and grant him the post of mayor as a reward for denouncing people who owned goods they had not declared to the tax-collectors. But, although he had congratulated Chomu warmly, Emheb had returned to Edfu without dethroning Queen Ahhotep.

How could the popularity of the young queen and her mother be combated? Bogged down in his disappointment, Chomu had hardly any arguments to offer the supporters of occupation, for Ahhotep was meeting all the emperor's demands.

Heray had comforted him a little by promising that he would certainly have an important part to play in the future. Chomu's devotion towards the new master of the country would not pass unnoticed, particularly since Governor Emheb had given glowing reports of this exceedingly diligent collaborator.

In fact, Emheb had been careful to make no mention at all of the little rat. Heray was watching Chomu like a hawk, because sooner or later he would recover from his depression and start doing more harm.

In Waset, the census was by no means at an end. Wary of

attracting suspicion, Emheb had not been able to prevent a Hyksos detachment from going to the west bank of Thebes, to inspect the burial-ground and the surrounding areas.

These were reputed to be uninhabited, but not even the tenth part of a cubit of ground must escape the census officials. And if they did their work properly, they would find the secret training-camp.

44

Rascal landed on Seqen's shoulder. He stroked the pigeon, then read the message it had brought.

'The Hyksos are inspecting the burial-ground,' he told his men. 'After that, they'll have only the Northern desert left to check.'

'We'll fight them and kill them,' vowed a young soldier.

'That would be a pointless victory,' said Seqen. 'Their disappearance would be reported to headquarters, which would send out an entire army, and we would be powerless against it.'

'But we can't just let ourselves be slaughtered without a fight.'

'We must face up to the urgency of the situation – and quickly.'

At the entrance to the burial-ground, the Hyksos commander recoiled. Governor Emheb had confided to him that no Egyptian would dare venture into this place, which was haunted by vulture-headed monsters with lions' claws. They attacked their victims from behind, put out their eyes, pierced their skulls, drank their blood and ate the marrow of the their bones.

The officer was a former pirate, who had killed enough enemies not to fear that kind of creature. But his soldiers, although well armed, did not share his views. And, despite his determination, the eerie atmosphere and heavy silence of the place made even the commander uneasy.

A dog barked, making the soldiers jump. Straight away, one of the soldiers fired an arrow. It hit a stele cursing unbelievers, and the burial-ground's last guard took to its heels.

'Surely we're not going to count the dead?' said a soldier.

'Why don't we see if there are any valuables in the tombs?' suggested one of his comrades.

'All right – but you go first.'

'Surely you don't believe those stories about monsters?'

'Of course not. But go first anyway.'

The Hyksos commander had a keen eye for booty, but all he could see was small tombs, some of them abandoned, some of them gutted. No, they didn't look at all promising.

'No one to count around here,' he said. 'We'll go and check the last white area on the map.'

'But, sir, that way's the desert.'

'Are you afraid, soldier?'

'Some people say it's dangerous, what with all the monsters out there.'

'No monster can resist three hundred Hyksos soldiers. Forward march.'

Seqen had removed all visible traces of the camp. His men were well hidden, some behind hills deeper in the desert, others in underground tunnels close to the camp. The king and two of his best soldiers had taken refuge in a cave, from where they could watch the area unseen.

Seqen saw the Hyksos scouts arrive. Soon they were followed by the advance guard, then the main body of the troops. They marched along briskly, as though eager to leave hostile territory.

Suddenly their leader halted and gazed down at the ground.

'I hope he hasn't found the entrance to a tunnel,' said one of Seqen's men worriedly.

'There aren't any there,' the king assured him.

The officer picked something up and held it high.

'It's one of the wooden swords we use during exercises,' Seqen cursed under his breath, furious at such carelessness – it might cost them their lives.

'It's a toy,' said a junior officer.

'Maybe. It's seen a lot of use.'

'Those are probably the only weapons the Egyptians have to fight us with,' said a soldier, and everyone laughed.

Turning slowly round, the commander scrutinized his surroundings. 'Search the whole area,' he ordered.

For more than three hours, the Hyksos searched for other objects which would indicate that the place had been or still was inhabited. They found nothing. The toy sword must have been carried there by a sandstorm, or else a brat belonging to a nomadic tribe had left it behind.

'We've covered the whole area, sir,' said a scout. 'Not a living soul.'

'There's still that cave over there, and it interests me. Let's take a look at it.'

'They're coming this way, Majesty!' whispered one of Seqen's men.

'Keep calm, soldier.'

'If they come into the cave, we're done for.'

'Have a little faith.'

'We ought to run away,' said the other soldier.

'Too late,' said Seqen. 'Go right to the back, flatten yourselves to the ground, and don't make another sound.'

At the entrance to the cave, Seqen had arranged some animal bones, some still bearing tatters of flesh.

'There's a monster in there,' said a Hyksos.

'Not a monster,' disagreed the commander, 'but certainly a meat-eater.'

'If it's still in there, it'll attack us.'

'There's a simple way of finding out. Archers, take up position.'

A dozen arrows flew to the back of the cave. One hit one of Seqen's soldiers in the arm, but Seqen immediately clamped his right hand over the man's mouth to stop him crying out. The other arrows flew over their heads and broke against the back wall.

'The creature isn't in its lair,' said one of the archers. 'Shall we wait until it comes back?'

'It would smell us and keep away. Besides, we aren't here to count the wild animals of the desert. We'll go back to camp.'

Much relieved, the Hyksos detachment left the forbidding place. Not even the most determined of rebels would want to live there.

Arm in arm, Ahhotep and Seqen watched the soldiers of the new Egyptian army putting up their tents and setting up camp again.

The queen herself had treated the wounded man. All his comrades had cheered her short speech praising their courage, which promised victories to come.

'The desert gives us the strength of Set,' said Ahhotep. 'There could be no better place for our secret camp. Now we must develop it.'

'How?' asked Seqen.

'Our soldiers deserve better than mere tents. We are going to build a fortress, barracks, houses and even a palace.'

'Ahhotep, you—'

'The Hyksos won't check these isolated places again. As we build, we shall have a single watchword: freedom. In

229

Christian Jacq

Thebes, there are too many collaborators. We must go on deceiving them until we're ready to act. Then we'll kill them to ensure our unity.'

Seqen could not argue with what she had said. This was exactly the mad plan he had been going to suggest.

'Why did you take the risk of hiding in that cave, instead of in one of the tunnels?'

'Because I wanted to see the Hyksos arrive and leave, so that my men wouldn't be in danger.'

Ahhotep led her husband to the cave where death had come so close to him. 'You have become a true leader,' she said, 'and I'm proud of you.'

She took off her dress, dropped it to the ground, and lay down on this improvised bed. 'Give me another son, my love.'

230

45

There were only three scribes in the secret camp. Once they had settled in, they worked hard all day long and a good part of the night administering the small settlement, which now consisted of a fort, a barracks, several houses and a modest palace.

The rebels' enthusiasm increased their strength tenfold. They had absolute faith in the royal couple, whose unfailing resolution was the best encouragement they could have had to continue their impossible task.

Bricks were made at the camp, and water-carriers continually went back and forth between the river and the desert. With the aid of the water, gardeners had managed to create fertile plots around the camp dwellings. Fishermen provided the soldiers with fresh fish, while the brewery and bakery produced basic food and drink. On moonless nights, a detachment crossed the Nile to collect consignments of dried meat from the east bank.

But filling bellies was not enough, Ahhotep knew. So she had ordered the scribes to set up a school where the rebels could learn to read and write. In the future, when Egypt was free, some of them would occupy positions of responsibility.

The queen had only one bodyguard, Laughter, who was not only strong but as fast as a hunting-dog. He had a sense of humour, and loved to sneak up behind the carpenters and put

Christian Jacq

an enormous paw on their shoulders. Most of them sweated profusely until the sound of Ahhotep's voice rescued them.

Craftsmen played a vital part in the preparations for war. While the soldiers trained under Seqen's command, they made arrows, bows, spears, swords and breastplates. But all this would be useless without a means of transport: they must have boats.

So the queen had engaged carpenters one by one, and they had been sworn to secrecy like all the other inhabitants of the camp. Emheb had sent highly skilled men to her from Edfu, which the Hyksos still regarded as a dependable town led by a devoted collaborator, a ruthless collector of taxes. Emheb, too, was secretly rearming, and his recruits had their base on the devastated site of Nekhen, which he was bringing back to life.

Thebes, Edfu and Nekhen: Qaris's model of Egypt now showed three cities free of Hyksos domination.

Promoted to head donkey, Long-Ears proudly led his fellow beasts of burden as they brought boat-building materials to the rebels' boatyard. They carried wood, papyrus and tools and never failed in their task, as if they knew they were taking part in something vitally important.

Everything was going too slowly for Ahhotep's taste, but she bore the waiting patiently. The creation of the boatyard was an all-important step: when the rebels at last had a war-fleet, they would be mobile and could launch their first attack.

The craftsmen worked in the open air, to the rhythm of songs whose words were not always fit for refined ears. The queen did not mind; she loved to linger and watch the crafts-men building the first boat, the bearer of so much hope.

The trunks of acacia trees were sawn into small planks, which the boat-builders fitted together like bricks to form the hull of the boat. They were fixed in place with long nails, or bound together with stout ropes passed through holes made

232

with a drill. With an adze, the head boat-builder shaped the sternpost, which served as a support for the tiller, while his assistants took charge of the stern and the keel.

The queen herself inspected the hull, both inside and out. The work was far from finished, for the planks had still to be smoothed, then caulked to make them watertight.

'Are you satisfied, Majesty?' asked the head boat-builder.

'Can't you go any faster?'

'We are going as fast as we can. If we hurried we'd spoil the materials, and we need strong boats to transport our troops. Unfortunately I haven't enough skilled workers, and training apprentices takes time – a lot of time.'

'We shall succeed,' promised the queen.

Ahhotep's smile was the most beautiful reward the boat-builders could have wished for. It made them happy to be alive and determined to see this through.

One of the craftsmen, however, did not share these sentiments. When he was recruited, he had simply wanted to earn more, and he had never imagined that a camp like this could exist. By creating it, Ahhotep had proved that she had gone mad and was leading Thebes to its downfall. Sooner or later, the Hyksos would discover this rebel band, and the reprisals would be terrible.

He was an apprentice boat-builder only twenty years old, and he had no wish to be killed in a fight which was lost before it began. For some time, he had been trying to persuade himself that Ahhotep's idealism would simply wear itself out. But the camp was working for good or ill, weapons were being made there, soldiers were being trained, and they were even building a warship.

It was pointless to talk to his superiors, because they all supported the queen's cause. It was up to him to act on his own, and to do something radical in order to prevent a catastrophe.

The heart and soul of this crazy plan was Ahhotep. Once

she was dead, even Seqen – although undoubtedly a fine leader – would be a broken man. The rebels would leave their base, return to Thebes and recognize the Hyksos's sovereignty.

So he would have to kill her.

Next time she visited the boatyard, he went over to her when there was no one else near, bowed and said, 'Majesty, may I show you something unusual?'

The queen was intrigued.

'It's at the far end of the site,' he went on. 'I think you will be surprised.'

Ahhotep followed him. They walked between rows of carefully stacked planks and entered a narrow space between trunks which had not yet been squared off.

'What is this surprising thing?' she asked.

The apprentice brandished a heavy wooden mallet and a well-honed chisel. 'You are a danger to all Thebans. Only your death will save them from chaos.' His eyes were filled with a murderous resolve.

'You're wrong,' said Ahhotep. 'Fighting is our only chance of survival.'

'You cannot fight the Hyksos – everyone knows that.'

'Are you a coward?'

The apprentice's eyes narrowed. 'We have no choice but to submit to the emperor. The power you seek is only an illusion.'

'If we truly want our freedom, we shall win it back.'

'That isn't true.'

'You're afraid, and I can understand that. But one day fear will change sides.'

'The Hyksos have won. Why won't you admit it?'

'Because the love of freedom must remain stronger than anything else, whatever the circumstances.'

'So much the worse for you, Majesty. You shall die with your illusions.'

234

He planned to smash the queen's skull with his mallet and stab her through the heart with his chisel; she would have no time to feel pain. Then he would flee and make for Kebet, where he would enlist in the Hyksos militia.

Just as he was raising his arm to strike, a heavy paw came down upon his shoulder.

He spun round. Laughter was crouching on the top of a pile of tree-trunks, just above his head. Enraged to see Ahhotep threatened, the massive dog turned his head and sank his teeth into the attacker's throat. Then he lifted him off the ground, paying no heed to his screams, which were soon lost in the rattle of his dying breath.

46

The report from the small group of rebels in Avaris, who risked their lives every time they passed on information, gave no cause for joy. The emperor's power was absolute. The Hyksos had the whole area in thrall, and the slightest attempt at sedition was repressed with extreme ferocity. The capital was like a gigantic barracks; the Egypt of the gods and the pharaohs was nearing its last gasp.

With the aid of the census, Khamudi had managed to tax even the poorest peasants, and the ruling elite continued to grow wealthier, as well as acquiring more and more Egyptian slaves.

'All we can do is attack the garrison at Henen-Nesut, kill as many Hyksos as possible and then die a worthy death,' said Moustache.

'At least read the message through to the end,' advised the Afghan. 'It mentions Thebes.'

'Thebes no longer exists.'

'It certainly does. Look: Queen Ahhotep has succeeded her mother, with the agreement of the Hyksos and under their control.'

'What does that matter? It's just a puppet dynasty. I'm going to speak to our men.' Suddenly, Moustache had a mad idea. 'Did you say Ahhotep?'

'That's her name, yes,' agreed the Afghan.

'Ahhotep . . . That means "the Moon is Full", and the moon is the secret sign we've been trying to decipher all the time.'

'You think Queen Ahhotep heads a band of Theban rebels? She's only a woman, my friend. How could she even begin to think of fighting the mighty Hyksos army?'

'Thebes may not be dead,' argued Moustache. 'Perhaps Ahhotep has gathered around her a few supporters who are as determined as we are. We must forget about attacking here, and leave for the South.'

'Cross the Hyksos lines? That's impossible.'

'It would be for our whole force, yes; but not for the two of us. And if I'm not mistaken, we'll establish a link with our Theban allies.'

First an inadequate Nile flood, and now the negligence of the Hyksos government, which had neither attended to the upkeep of the reservoirs nor filled the emergency grain-stores to feed the inhabitants of Upper Egypt.

Thanks to the measures Ahhotep had taken, Thebes would just escape the famine. But if fate continued hostile and brought another poor flood, many would die of hunger.

In mid-July, many wheat-fields had been stricken by crop disease and the harvest spoiled by unusually wet weather. Only the late November plantings had been spared this fresh misfortune. On the queen's orders, the soldiers and craftsmen at the secret camp were given the largest rations, so that they could continue training and working almost normally.

Now recovered from his depression, Chomu arrived at the palace, and asked to see Heray.

'You've demanded another milch-cow from me,' complained Chomu. 'I shall soon be ruined.'

'It was not my demand, but Governor Emheb's. He collects the Hyksos taxes from all of us, and everyone, even the royal family, is in the same plight.'

'The emperor wants us to be prosperous, not poverty-stricken.'

'Indeed he does, but the law is the law. Thebes cannot disobey it.'

'You must write to Apophis and explain our difficulties.'

'The queen is doing so, rest assured. The main thing is to obey his orders.'

And Chomu could only agree. But, although disarmed, he simply could not understand why the emperor was plunging his faithful Theban subjects into poverty.

He said, 'I hope the queen won't write in insolent terms.'

'On the contrary, Chomu, on the contrary. She has long since given up that attitude, which was as futile as it was childish. We are going through a difficult period, no doubt because we are a distant province, far from Avaris and the centre of the empire. But I'm sure our submission will eventually be rewarded.'

'So am I, Heray,' said the vase-seller. Then, after a pause, he went on, 'We haven't seen much of Seqen lately.'

'He spends his time hunting and running about the countryside. He's restless, and can't stay in one place for long. We don't complain at the palace, because he brings back game. Now, what about that milch-cow?'

'I'm happy to pay my taxes to the emperor and thus contribute to the greatness of the Hyksos,' declared Chomu proudly. 'It's a sacrifice, but it's necessary.'

Heray laid a hand on the Canaanite's shoulder. 'You are an example to all Thebans.'

The trader blushed.

As he left the palace, he was thinking about Seqen. True, Heray's explanations were plausible, but all the same . . . When the occasion arose, he would have that restless fellow followed. So as to be sure he was not fomenting some laughable plot with a few peasants.

*

Ahhotep, Heray and Qaris were in council in Qaris's model-room.

'Majesty. I have the feeling Chomu's becoming dangerous again,' warned Heray.

'Have you any specific evidence?'

'No, but he seems himself again, and once again determined to do you harm.'

'Have him watched day and night.'

'He always has been, Majesty. All the supporters of collaboration have been identified. When the time comes, they'll be arrested in a matter of minutes.'

'Is there still no news from the North?' Ahhotep asked Qaris.

'No, Majesty. There are probably no rebels left there.'

'Since we are alone, we shall fight alone. King Seqen's hard work is beginning to bear fruit. We now have a small army at our disposal, and our soldiers are a match for any enemy.'

'What of the boats?' asked Qaris.

'The first has left the boatyard, and they have started building the second. The team of boat-builders is also becoming battle-hardened, and will work faster.'

'According to the last message from Governor Emheb, Majesty, the rebels gathered at Edfu and Nekhen form quite a sizeable group. There is no more to fear from the Nubians. They're content with the lands granted them by the emperor, and they have no wish to have Jannas's forces unleashed upon them. And Emheb is still regarded as the very model of a collaborator, who fills the Hyksos coffers by bleeding the region dry.'

Teti rushed into the model-room. 'Come quickly, Ahhotep! Kames has been hurt.'

The little boy had cut his right hand deeply with a razor he had taken from his father's bathing-room. His cries of pain must have been heard all over the city; but there was something more serious about the wound.

'It is not normal,' said Ahhotep as she tried to calm her son.

'The evil eye!' exclaimed Teti. 'The only way to ward it off is with alum.'

'If we have any left . . .'

While her mother went off to find the precious substance, Ahhotep spoke gently and firmly to Kames. 'You are in a lot of pain and you are expressing that – nothing could be more normal. But you must also fight against it and try to overcome it. If you don't, you will never become a man.'

Kames swallowed his tears and dared to look at his hand.

'You and I,' the queen went on, 'hate the bad spirit that hurt you. We're going to deprive it of a voice. The remedy your grandmother is bringing will make it leave your flesh. Then the blood will stop flowing, and your hand will be stronger than before.'

With all the strength of his nine years, Kames talked of his future life. The future of a proud man, determined to fight and conquer.

The alum Teti applied to the wound was remarkably effective: it drove out the evil eye and quickly healed the first wound inflicted upon the pharaoh's son.

47

As far as Kebet, all went well. By making lengthy detours, the Afghan and Moustache evaded Hyksos fortresses and patrols. They drank from canals, and ate small animals they killed. And all the time they moved onward, painfully slowly but without incident.

Sheltering at a farm would have been too dangerous. In this region, they could trust no one. On each road there were soldiers and guards. Even the desert tracks were under Hyksos control.

'We'll never get there,' lamented Moustache.

'We still have the Nile.'

'Only Hyksos boats use the Nile. If we steal one, they'll intercept us.'

'I've seen cargo-vessels passing by,' the Afghan reminded him.

'Yes, carrying wheat for the emperor's Nubian allies.'

'We'll hide in a consignment and disembark when we get to Thebes.'

'Supposing the crew spot us?'

'Too bad for them.'

They had one chance in ten of succeeding, Moustache thought. It was a lot better than nothing.

The morning was beautifully warm and the sky incomparably

blue. Kames was playing ball with his friends, Teti was making pastries, and Thebes was continuing to measure out its tranquil days as though the sun's dazzling presence had postponed the threat of destruction.

Ahhotep picked up a female figurine her mother had made, following an old magical text, and placed it on a face-paint spoon. The statue had no arms or legs, but had a huge pubic triangle marked by pin-pricks. The spoon was shaped like a naked swimmer, pushing a duck before her. The swimmer was the sky-goddess Nut, swimming in the primordial ocean. She held up the earth-god, Geb, represented by the duck. Together the primordial couple had given birth to many forms of life. Surely bringing these two together would guarantee Ahhotep's fertility?

The queen left the palace and went to find Seqen. He was asleep under a calotrope, an imposing tree with five-petalled pink flowers. Because its fruit was shaped like a testicle, the tree was believed to have aphrodisiac qualities.

The queen knelt and gently stroked Seqen's forehead.

He awoke and blinked up at her. 'Ahhotep, you look radiant.'

'Sometimes I think of the timid young man who was too afraid to talk to me. You have become a true warrior, worthy of leading your men into battle.'

'The reality is not so bright. Soon we shall have been working for ten years, and we still have only a tiny army.'

'What matters is its desire for victory. Can't you feel mine?'

Seqen took her in his arms and drew her down to him. Entwined, they lay together and became one.

'At last,' she told him afterwards, 'At last I'm pregnant again.'

High Treasurer Khamudi had become even fatter and was having more and more difficulty in squeezing into his old clothes. He loathed wasting money, so he wanted to wait until the very last minute before having new ones made by the finest weaver in the capital, who would be given ample incentive not to divulge his illustrious customer's measurements.

Nevertheless, as he looked over his scrolls, Khamudi gulped down a fried pastry spiced with cumin, for today was a festival for the ruling elite in Avaris. The emperor had promised to stage an unrivalled celebration. The army would acclaim him, and Khamudi had only excellent news for him. Nubia and Egypt were prostrating themselves before their sovereign, and all resistance had been wiped out. As the Theban minister for agriculture regularly confirmed, the dying city had but one ambition, and a laudable one at that: to pay its taxes and levies to Apophis.

Only one minor problem remained, but it was a difficult one to resolve: attacks on caravans by small but very mobile robber bands. However, on the road to Wadi Tumilat, between the eastern Delta and the Red Sea, Khamudi had just had a notable success. A detachment of soldiers had ambushed twenty sand-travellers, and killed them with particular relish. Their fate would serve as an example.

'Leave your scrolls,' Yima warned him. 'The emperor is ready.'

Abandoning his work, and paying not the slightest attention to his plump wife, the High Treasurer hurried to join his master, whom he found surrounded by his special body-guards; they would protect him as he passed through the streets of Avaris.

Partly as a security measure and partly because he loathed the common people, the emperor rarely left the citadel. So his appearance in public unleashed the enthusiasm of a jubilant crowd, carefully organized by Khamudi. Anyone caught failing to cheer Apophis would be deported to the copper mines.

243

The emperor halted before the garden of an Egyptian collaborator. It was positively magical, with its cornflowers, iris, mallow, chrysanthemums and larkspur.

'Destroy all this,' he order Khamudi.

'Now, Majesty?'

'I do not like repeating myself, my friend.'

The High Treasurer summoned his own men, who trampled on the flowers and tore up the young shoots.

'I do not wish to see a single garden in my capital,' decreed Apophis, 'because the sight of flowers softens men's hearts. The sole exception is to be the garden in the citadel, which I grant to my wife as a special favour.'

'If your Majesty would be so good as to enter.'

With the approval of 'empress' Tany, the lady Yima had organized a reception at the harem in Apophis's honour. Although she loathed the fat, ugly, vulgar Tany, Yima continually heaped flattery upon her, to ward off her rages. Without asking her husband's permission, Tany had all those who displeased her killed by Aberia, who still took great delight in strangling her victims.

Fortunately, Yima's husband and the emperor remained on good terms, and she felt protected. Nevertheless, she was careful to congratulate the appalling Tany on everything and nothing, in order to remain in her good graces.

Yima and Khamudi continued to indulge themselves in the vilest perversions, knowing that Apophis would not reprimand them, particularly since they liked to amuse themselves with Egyptian women, who never emerged alive from their sadistic games.

Apophis gazed round the large reception hall, with its covered pool and comfortable chairs.

'We have a beautiful harem here, Lady Yima,' he said.

'All the credit should go to your wife, Majesty.'

'What have you to show me that is so exceptional?'

'A dance, Majesty. A lascivious dance which used to be performed by women of ill-repute in ale-houses. Today it will be performed for you and you alone, by the last surviving heiress of the richest family in Memphis. If you are dissatisfied with her performance, the lady Aberia will strangle her.'

'Entertaining, indeed,' said Apophis. 'Let her begin.'

She was eighteen years old and beautiful. Aberia tore off the girl's wrap and pushed her, naked, to the centre of the room.

'Show us what you can do,' ordered Yima, 'or else . . .'

Not trying to hide either her genitals or her breasts, the young girl stood as upright and as still as the statue of a goddess.

'Dance!' Yima screeched hysterically.

She grabbed the girl's arm and shook her; the girl slapped her.

'No one is more miserable than you,' said the prisoner with impressive calm. 'When you are all judged in the afterlife, the Soul-Eater will feast on your rotten souls.'

'The arrogance of these Egyptians is really exasperating,' said the emperor. 'Have the rebel put to death.'

48

Although Ahhotep was massaged every day and took preparations designed to prevent bleeding, the palace doctor was anxious. The prospects for the birth were still unclear, and the progress of the pregnancy was causing him concern. Ahhotep ought to have been resting in bed, but she always answered the doctor's advice with 'Everything will go well because everything has to go well. And I shall have a second son.'

Even Teti could not reason with her daughter, who had undertaken the onerous task of reopening the weavers' workshops, which had been closed for too long. Officially, this was because the young queen could not long bear to see Theban women poorly dressed, but in reality clothes were needed for the army.

The resumption of work had attracted Chomu's attention, so the weaving-women made dresses, underclothing and shawls for all to see, while at night tunics and kilts left for the training-camp. The need to deceive slowed both production and delivery, but extreme caution was essential.

Ahhotep herself had recruited four experienced female weavers who dreamt constantly of seeing the Hyksos defeated. They alone knew the truth, while their apprentices busied themselves reclothing the population. Chomu had profited nicely from the work, by hiring out some empty premises at a good rate.

One day, while the queen was visiting the workshops to check that they were properly ventilated and that the workers had suitable materials, Heray came hurrying in.

'Majesty, your presence is required at the palace.'

'Is it urgent?'

'I believe so.'

'Thebes! We're in Thebes. Do you realize, Afghan? We've done it!' To hide the fact that he was almost in tears, Moustache bent his head lower over the moon hieroglyph he was drawing on the palm of his left hand.

'It's much smaller than Memphis.'

'It will grow, you can be sure of that. Nothing is more nourishing than freedom.'

'Provided it still exists. Don't forget, the region is under Hyksos control.'

'And *you* mustn't forget that the sign of Ahhotep proclaims the opposite.'

'Don't get too excited, my friend. We've avoided soldiers, guards and crocodiles, but we must stay on the alert.'

'Let's go to the palace and tell them who we are.'

'Supposing Queen Ahhotep is in league with the Hyksos?'

Moustache was so intoxicated with excitement that he could hardly bring himself to accept the possibility. But it would have been childish to discount it.

'I'll go to the palace,' decided the Afghan. 'I'll explain myself awkwardly, like a foreigner. If all goes well, I'll emerge free and come and fetch you. If I don't, escape and rejoin our men.'

'I won't let you take such a risk.'

Moustache did not have time to develop his argument, for ten sturdy fellows armed with spears suddenly leapt out of the reeds and surrounded them.

In his heart, the Afghan admired the men's skill: although thoroughly accustomed to danger, he had not realized they were there. Their swift, decisive action was worthy of professional soldiers.

Moustache was thinking the same thing.

It was pointless to resist.

'Who are you?' demanded one of the Thebans.

Moustache held out his left hand so that the moon hieroglyph showed clearly. 'We want to see Queen Ahhotep – because of this sign.'

The soldier was unmoved. 'Why?'

'We have important information for her.'

'Your hands will be bound and you will follow us. One false move, and you will be killed.'

She was the most beautiful woman the Afghan had ever seen. Her eyes burned with a fire that would conquer any man in an instant, mingling power, tenderness and intelligence.

'I am from Afghanistan, and Moustache is Egyptian. We are the leaders of a rebel band based in Middle Egypt and we have a few contacts in Avaris.'

Teti and Qaris gasped, and Heray was astonished, but Ahhotep did not turn a hair.

She said, 'Give us good reasons to believe that you are not Hyksos spies.'

'Majesty,' said Moustache, 'we will tell you the names of our men, the places where they are hiding, and the locations of Hyksos fortresses and garrisons. We have trained many fighters, made our own weapons, and created a network of sympathizers. We cannot launch a direct attack, but we raid caravans and kill the emperor's spies one by one, so that he is far less well informed than he thinks he is.'

As the Afghan and Moustache talked, Qaris took notes. Using this priceless information, he would be able to complete his model. And he was already dreaming up plans to attack specific places.

'How can we be sure all this is not lies?' asked Ahhotep.

'We have no other way of convincing you, Majesty,' said Moustache.

'In that case, I am going to hand you over to the emperor's soldiers.'

'You can't be on their side,' he exclaimed, 'not you, Majesty. That's impossible. In the name of Pharaoh – even if there's no one alive to fill that office – I swear to you that we're telling the truth. May my soul be destroyed if I am lying.'

Ahhotep and Seqen gazed out at one of the Theban mountains' matchless sunsets. Before the apparent triumph of night, the sky took on pink and orange tints, while the river acquired a sparkling silver mantle.

'When are you ever going to rest?' asked Seqen.

'The day after the birth, if necessary.'

'The doctor has his misgivings, as you know very well.'

'Let him say what he will,' said the queen. 'I shall trust in the gods. Is the boat-building going well?'

'Too slowly – much too slowly. The carpenters have had serious problems because the wood is of poor quality. There are times when I—'

Ahhotep laid her fingers on her husband's lips. 'Several useless words – for instance "doubt" and "downhearted" – have been struck out of our language. They convey feelings which are luxuries and which only free people can allow themselves. Go on strengthening our training-camp, and don't worry yourself about futile things.'

Seqen kissed her passionately.

'For a little while,' she smiled, 'you must contain your ardour. But when you see our child, you won't regret the sacrifice.'

He stroked his wife's dark hair. 'Do you think Moustache and the Afghan are telling the truth?'

'We'll put them to the test, and if they're spies they're

bound to make a mistake. On the other hand, if there really is a rebel group in the North, it will be very useful when we are fighting to reconquer our land.'

'We're still short of weapons,' said Seqen, 'and clothing is reaching us only sporadically.'

'I shall sort things out,' promised Ahhotep. 'And I fervently hope our new guests will prove effective allies.'

Seqen smiled at her. Then his face suddenly darkened. 'Someone's been following me. I managed to lose the man in the desert, but I'm sure the collaborators are beginning to find my behaviour strange.'

'I'll find out who it is,' Ahhotep assured him. 'If he gets too close to the camp, the agreed security measures will be taken.'

49

The Afghan and Moustache were collecting flints, some light, some dark, which were harder even than metal. Although they did not balk at the task, the days sometimes seemed very long.

'We've been sentenced to forced labour,' said the Afghan.

'Don't you believe that,' replied Moustache. 'On the contrary, we've been shown the greatest trust.'

Hands on hips, the Afghan threw his companion a quizzical look. 'Would you care to explain that?'

'In our country, we use flint for razors and for doctors' instruments – and for weapons, too. Arrow- and spear-heads, blades for daggers and axes. It's an old-fashioned way, but it's cheap and effective. Everyone must think we are picking up pebbles, whereas in fact we're gathering weapons for the Theban army.'

'Why didn't Queen Ahhotep tell us that?'

'Because she wants to see if we're intelligent enough to realize it for ourselves.'

Chomu drank a cup of goat's milk. Finding it sour, he spat it out again. For a while now, he had been having stomach trouble; and he found it difficult to sleep because he kept asking himself the same question over and over again. Why had the emperor forgotten his faithful Theban subjects? After all, they were carrying out their duties punctually, and Governor Emheb had no cause for complaint.

Queen Ahhotep seemed harmless. Seqen, on the other hand, intrigued him. So Chomu had told one of his cousins, a fellow supporter of the Hyksos, to follow him.

'Well?' Chomu asked irritably when his cousin returned.

'Seqen goes hunting and fishing,' said his cousin. 'I don't follow him absolutely everywhere, so as to avoid being spotted. And the gods may bear witness that his energy seems inexhaustible.'

'In other words, he's leading you a merry dance.'

'Let's not exaggerate. But he certainly knows the desert well.'

What a fool, thought Chomu. He can't even follow someone properly. Aloud, he said, 'You must continue, cousin. I want to know more.'

'It's very tiring.'

'I will pay you more.'

'In that case . . .'

The cousin, Chomu decided, would be simply a very visible decoy. Another, more skilful, man would take over the real job of following Seqen, just when the king thought he was safe.

'Aren't you tired of picking up flints?' asked Seqen.

'We'll collect as many as are needed,' replied Moustache. 'Providing more weapons is vital, isn't it?'

The Afghan nodded his agreement.

The pharaoh surveyed the two men: Moustache, enthusiastic, strong-willed, capable of seeing things through to the end; the Afghan, cold, determined, savage. They made a formidable pair, clearly endowed with several years' experience, and Seqen had the feeling that their mutual understanding would make them unbeatable in a fight.

'Are you good hunters?' he asked.

'If you want to survive in occupied territory, you have to be,' replied the Afghan.

'Then come with me.'

Some distance from the trio as they walked into the eastern desert were ten archers, ready to act if the Afghan and Moustache tried to harm the king.

For some time, the pair had been asking him incessant questions, as if they suspected him of being more than just a high-spirited young man whose only interests were catching big fish and taking game back to the palace for food.

Seqen led them to a reed hut at the edge of the desert. 'Go in and look.'

Warily, the two men hesitated.

'What's inside?' asked Moustache.

'The answer to your questions.'

'We don't like surprises,' said the Afghan. 'As a general rule they have nothing good to offer people like us.'

'And yet your curiosity deserves to be satisfied.'

With a suspicious look, Moustache went into the hut, ready to defend himself if he were attacked. The Afghan, he knew, would not hesitate to pounce on Seqen, although the king was both taller and more heavily built.

He saw animal intestines; dozens of them, of different sizes and lengths.

'This is the main product of the hunt,' said Seqen. 'You understand why, I suppose?'

The pharaoh and the Afghan looked defiantly into each other's eyes.

'What are animal guts used for?' asked the Afghan slowly. 'They can be turned into strings for musical instruments, or . . . for bows. Flints, animal gut – Thebes is re-arming, isn't she? And you are the commander-in-chief.'

The Afghan faced Seqen, and Moustache stood behind him. If they attacked at the same time, the king would have to be swift indeed to escape unharmed; he had repeated the exercise a hundred times.

Moustache got down on one knee, and the Afghan followed suit.

'We are at your command.'

Seqen ignored the splendour of the stars shining in a sky the colour of lapis-lazuli. Mad with worry, he paced up and down the passage outside the bedchamber where Ahhotep was struggling to give birth to their second child.

The doctor had not hidden his concern. And the three midwives, although experienced, had also been nervous. 'It will be the mother or the child,' one of them had predicted.

At the thought of losing Ahhotep, the king felt a terrible pang of despair. Their love was the fire that gave him life, the air that gave him breath, the water that allowed him to survive, the earth on which he built. Without her, he could never carry on the fight. The queen was the soul of the battle, embodying the alliance of magic and will. With her, nothing was impossible.

But if their child died, she would be utterly broken.

Qaris gazed at his model with fierce concentration; Heray drank beer, even though he was not thirsty; Teti watched over little Kames as he slept. Everyone knew that Egypt's fate was being played out in that bedchamber, where the god of destiny was juggling with life and death.

It was not only that Seqen was deeply in love with Ahhotep. Each day, he found more to admire in her. In her, the pride of the queens of the golden age lived on, as if, although Egypt had been occupied and trampled underfoot, its greatness refused to be extinguished.

Ahhotep had the strength to crush the life out of misfortune; but misfortune had, like a dragon, seen the danger and was trying to stifle its adversary. Seqen was powerless to help the wife he loved and revered. He wanted to shout, to roar his indignation against this injustice, to call upon the gods not to abandon a woman who heard their voices and tried, at the risk of her own life, to pass on their words.

Looking fragile and anxious, Teti came down the passage towards him.

'Whatever happens,' he promised her, 'I shall attack. At least Thebes will die with dignity.'

The door of the bedchamber opened and one of the midwives appeared, her face haggard with exhaustion.

Seqen seized her by the shoulders. 'Tell me the truth!' he demanded.

'You have a second son. The queen is alive, but very weak.'

50

The limestone figure of Senusret I sat on his throne, gazing up at the heavens.

'Now!' ordered the emperor in his harsh voice.

With one mighty swing of his club, Khamudi decapitated the majestic statue that had so exasperated his master.

This was the tenth ancient statue he had destroyed on the forecourt of the Temple of Set. The watching Hyksos dignitaries were delighted to be present at the death of these witnesses to an extinct culture.

Apophis surveyed a sphinx which wore the face of Amenemhat III. 'Have a sculptor replace the name of this worthless monarch with my own,' he ordered. 'The same is to be done with all the few monuments I agree to retain. From now on, they will proclaim my glory.'

A select few of Apophis's servants would have the right to a crudely sculpted statue, its skin painted yellow, created by a sculptor ignorant of the ancient rites.

'Windswept, why are you smiling so scornfully?' the emperor asked.

'Because at least two of the senior officials who have just prostrated themselves before you are complete hypocrites. In public, they heap praise upon you. According to their confidences in the bedchamber, they hate you.'

'You work very well, little sister. Give their names to Khamudi.'

'No, not to him. I find him distasteful.'

'Then tell me.'

'I can refuse you nothing.' Without hesitation, she condemned to torture and death two of the men she had seduced.

'I hear,' said Apophis, 'that you have fallen in love with Minos, my Minoan painter.'

'He is an inventive and ardent lover.'

'Has he criticized me at all?'

'No. All he thinks of is his art – and my body.'

'This evening, send him to me.'

'You're not going to deprive me of my favourite toy, I hope?'

'Not yet. Don't worry.'

The emperor was not displeased with the way his palace had been redecorated. It no longer had any Egyptian features, and faithfully reproduced the main themes from the Minoan royal palace at Knossos. One of them particularly pleased him: a wall-painting of an acrobat jumping off a charging bull in full flight. The man leapt over the animal's head, sprang off its neck with arms and legs outstretched, and landed behind its tail; if the dangerous leap was successful.

One detail intrigued him. The painter's identity could not be readily guessed from his style, which was why he had summoned Minos.

The Minoan was trembling with fear.

'Are you enjoying your stay with us?' asked Apophis.

'Of course, Majesty.'

'And what about your companions?'

'We have all lost desire to return to Minoa.'

'That's fortunate, because it's out of the question. Your work here is far from finished: next you are to decorate my palaces in the main towns of the Delta.'

Christian Jacq

Minos bowed. 'You do us too much honour, Majesty.'

'Of course, you must not disappoint me.' Apophis turned to the wall-painting. 'Tell me, what is the function of this strange garden, under the bull?'

'That is the labyrinth, Majesty. It has only one entrance and one exit, and it houses a monster with a bull's head. Inside, there are many twists and turns, and the unwary visitor strays so far that he loses his mind, or else falls victim to the monster. Only the hero bearing Ariadne's thread has a chance of coming out alive.'

'How amusing. I want a more detailed painting.'

'As it pleases you, Majesty.'

Seqen held Ahhotep so tightly that she could hardly breathe. 'You are out of danger, my love. But you cannot bear any more children.'

'I wanted two sons, and I have them. What do you think of the second?'

He loosened his hold and gazed in wonder at the chubby-cheeked baby sleeping in its cradle. 'He's magnificent.'

'His name is to be Ahmose, "He Who was Born of the Moon-God", because he saw the light at the moment when the moon became full. Like his father and his elder brother, he will have only one goal: the freedom and sovereignty of Egypt.' She nestled against Seqen again. 'I thought I was going to die as I gave birth to him, and I never stopped thinking of you. If I had died, you'd have gone on fighting, wouldn't you?'

'Without you, what chance would we have had of victory? I command brave soldiers, and they're ready to die for their country, because you are its soul and its magic.'

'You must go back to the camp,' said Ahhotep. 'There is still so much to do.'

'I will, but on one condition: that you take the rest you need.'

258

'My Mother will watch over me.'

'She can't make you do anything against your will. I want you to give me your word, Queen of Egypt, otherwise I'm not leaving this room.'

'You have it – but it's only the word of a hostage.'

The Thebans rejoiced at the happy news: both mother and child were doing well. An attentive grandmother, a queen whose confinements had not diminished her beauty, two fine boys and a father who continued to adore his wife: that was the peaceful picture the royal family presented to Thebes.

The picture did not in the least reassure Chomu, because he was still worried about Seqen. A man could be passionate about hunting and fishing, but really! To leave early on the morning after his son's difficult birth, to cross the Nile, lose himself in the lonely places on the west bank, and take goodness knows how many risks to return with one paltry hare.

Chomu was now sure that Seqen was involved in secret activities. He must be followed properly this time, and the truth revealed.

After spotting Chomu's cousin, who had been used as a decoy, Seqen had pretended to head into a wadi. Then he had retraced his steps and made for the secret camp.

The Canaanite following Seqen was generously paid, because he knew how to make himself almost invisible. The king took many precautions: he stopped frequently, turned round, looked in all directions, wiped away every trace of his footprints. But the man following him avoided all the traps, and knew when to crouch or lie down flat.

So Seqen had not thrown him off the scent.

Lying flat on his belly on top of a small hillock deep in the desert, the Canaanite at last saw Seqen's goal: a camp, full of soldiers at exercise. And it was no temporary camp, either, for it contained a fort, a barracks, houses and even a small palace. So Ahhotep and Seqen were training an army, which sooner or later would commit the fatal error of attacking the Hyksos. Chomu must be warned immediately.

But as he got to his feet, the Canaanite felt a weight on the back of his neck. The weight suddenly became irresistible, and he toppled forwards. His face was plunged into the sand, muffling his shouts of terror.

Laughter sank his teeth into the back of the spy's neck. Security measures were security measures, and the giant dog carried them out most conscientiously.

51

The Persian officer, a man who specialized in lightning raids and summary executions, was in a foul temper. For more than five years, that pig Khamudi had been blocking his promotion and taking all the credit in the emperor's eyes for the bloody raids that had kept the Hyksos Empire free of rebellion.

Khamudi had devised a remarkably effective system: anyone who wished to keep his reputation spotless must go through him and pay for his services. Moreover, Khamudi claimed to have devised every new trade practice, and awarded himself exclusive rights for an unlimited time. Anyone who dared protest saw his enterprise wither, and anyone who continued to protest met with a fatal accident.

With the support of about thirty officers from his own country, the Persian had decided to get rid of Khamudi, taking care to ensure that the emperor did not suspect them. They had devised an infallible plan: to use one of the Egyptian women from the harem as soon as an opportunity arose.

And it had just done so. In order to heap more humiliation upon the daughter of some Egyptian nobles he had himself beheaded, Khamudi had had the girl brought from the harem to attend to his feet. Although they were small and fat, the High Treasurer was very proud of them and made sure that his slave treated them with the utmost respect, before forcing her to satisfy his most depraved whims.

Christian Jacq

The Persian had not found it difficult to transform the young Egyptian girl into an instrument of vengeance. Although she well knew that she would never emerge alive from Khamudi's villa, she had nevertheless agreed to carry out a mission which would give her terrible life some meaning.

The High Treasurer was in ecstasies as he read the papyrus: in less than a year, his fortune had doubled. And he had no intention of stopping there. Since no important transaction could take place without his authorization, he would increase the compulsory levies and share them out between himself and the emperor.

'The slave has arrived to attend to your feet, my lord,' announced his steward.

'Send her in.'

The young woman prostrated herself before the master of the house.

'Undress little one, and lick my feet.'

Her spirit broken, the slave did so without protest.

'Now cut my nails. If you hurt me, you will be whipped.'

Khamudi derived nearly as much pleasure from being obeyed as from torturing young girls who, after being with him, could never love another man.

The young Egyptian opened the wooden box containing her equipment. She picked up the flint knife the Persian had given her, and thought of her parents, whom she was about to avenge. One blow to the heart, and the torturer's life would be at an end. She had rehearsed the murder a hundred times with the Persian officer, so as to be certain of success.

'Hurry up, little one. I don't like being kept waiting.'

No, she wouldn't stab him in the heart. She would strike lower – much lower. Before dying, her torturer would lose his manhood.

The young girl knelt and raised her eyes, to engrave the

262

monster's face in her memory before she punished him. It was a mistake. Never before had the High Treasurer seen such a flame of hate in his slave's eyes. When she raised her arm to plunge the knife into his penis, he had time to parry the blow and felt only a burning sensation as the knife glanced off his thigh.

He punched her viciously in the face. Stunned, and with blood dripping from her nose, she dropped her knife.

Khamudi seized her by the hair. 'You wanted to kill me – me, Khamudi! You weren't acting alone, I am sure of that. I'm going to torture you myself and you'll give me the names of your accomplices. And I mean *all* your accomplices.'

The Canaanite's mutilated body was exhibited before the palace at Thebes. A large part of the population had gathered there to gaze upon his terrible wounds.

Seqen said, 'I found him in the desert. Does anyone recognize him, despite the state he's in?'

Chomu recognized a large mole on what remained of the man's left hip, but said nothing. For this was the man he had paid to follow Seqen.

'What happened to him?' asked Qaris.

'I expect he ventured too far and suffered the fate of the unwary. Monsters must have attacked him and torn him limb from limb.'

Horrified and shocked, the Thebans began returning to their homes.

'Never again ask me to follow Seqen when he's out hunting,' Chomu's cousin whispered in his ear. 'I don't want to be eaten by desert monsters.'

Even Chomu was shaken. Evidently the unfortunate man had indeed fallen victim to the gryphons and dragons that haunted the inhospitable wastes bordering the Nile. Some day, it would be Seqen's turn.

*

Aberia's enormous hands closed round the Persian soldier's neck. He was her fifteenth victim of the day, and she had been careful to make him suffer for a long time before allowing him to die.

The reprisals carried out by the High Treasurer, with the emperor's permission, were terrifying. All the plotters against Khamudi, their wives, their children and their animals had been executed in front of the Temple of Set. Some had been burnt alive, some beheaded, others stoned or put to the sword.

Khamudi, still complaining loudly of pain from his wound, watched from his place of honour beside Apophis, who had special treatment in store for the two main culprits, the Persian officer and the Egyptian slave-girl.

'Let us begin with this depraved young slut,' decreed the emperor. 'Come, my faithful friend, marvel at my new creations below the fortress. They will make you forget your pain.'

Obediently, Khamudi looked. He saw an arena and a circular wooden construction, open to the air.

'Bring the criminal forward,' ordered the emperor.

The Egyptian girl had been tortured with such savagery that she could scarcely walk. Leaning against one of the walls of the arena, she nevertheless had the strength to cast a look of hatred at her torturers, who were seated on a raised balcony to get the best view.

Apophis clicked his fingers.

A fighting bull charged into the enclosure, steam rising from its nostrils, hooves thundering.

'Jump over its horns,' advised the emperor in his harsh voice. 'If you succeed, I will spare your life.'

The creature charged. Utterly exhausted, the young girl could do nothing but close her eyes.

The Persian officer did not understand. Why had he been

thrown into this circular structure, containing a winding path interrupted by walls which formed double bends?

'Walk through my labyrinth,' the emperor ordered from the balcony above, 'and try to find the way out. That is your only chance of obtaining my pardon.'

The torture that had made him give up the names of his accomplices, one by one, had left the Persian maimed and with almost no strength. He had been given a crutch, which enabled him to walk if he put his weight mostly on his left leg, which was less badly injured.

He took a few steps forward. An axe sprang up out of the ground, cutting off three of his toes. Roaring with pain, the Persian flattened himself against a circling wall, then tried to walk round it. But as he passed, two blades sprang out simultaneously.

The first pierced his flank, the second his neck. And the man who had wanted to kill Khamudi bled to death before the eyes of the emperor and his faithful High Treasurer.

'Those two useless creatures were too damaged to give us pleasure for long,' commented Apophis. 'We shall make sure the next ones are in good condition, so that the spectacle is more compelling.'

52

The annual flood had been so slight that there would not be enough silt for all the fields in Waset. Moreover, when next spring came all the reservoirs would be empty. It was pointless to look for help to the emperor, who would not lower taxes even when severe drought threatened.

The only consolation was an abundant harvest of cucumbers; but most of those would have to be handed over to Governor Emheb, who would send them to Avaris.

This evening, Seqen was in low spirits.

'We can cope with this,' Ahhotep promised him. 'Heray's excellent management means we have good food reserves. If we ration food and water, we shall survive this difficult year.'

'That won't be enough.'

'Has something happened at the camp?'

'The soldiers want an increase in their pay. If they don't get it, they'll lay down their arms and return to Thebes.'

'Have they lost the will to fight?'

'It's been too long,' said Seqen. 'They're convinced that we'll never dare attack the Hyksos. If they're to continue such intensive training, they want better pay.'

'Have you tried to reason with them?'

'Usually I succeed, but this time I failed.'

'Don't they know their efforts will soon be crowned with success?'

'Qaris has just told me that the garrisons at Edfu and Nekhen have made the same demands. It's over. We no longer have the means to continue the fight. In a few days' time, we shall abandon the secret camp.'

Ahhotep left the palace in the middle of the night, slipping past her own guards. Crossing the sleeping town, she hurried to the limit of the cultivated lands.

At the point where the kingdom of the desert began, she hesitated. Set was the master there, and at any moment he could unleash forces so savage that no human could resist them. Monsters did indeed exist, and no sensible Egyptian would risk venturing into this hostile territory without the protection of the sun, which alone had the power to drive away malevolent creatures.

But Egypt was ruled by the empire of darkness, and Ahhotep must confront that darkness if she was to undertake it and steal away a part of its power.

The young queen left the world of humans and entered the desert, reminding herself of the words of the sages. Yes, this was the place of all dangers, but it was also the place of mountains, whose bellies contained gold and precious stones. At the heart of each misfortune, there was hidden happiness.

Ahhotep headed along the bed of a dried-up river and walked at a brisk but comfortable pace. Leather sandals protected her feet, and the moon's light enabled her to make out the undulations of the landscape.

All around her were crackling and hissing noises. A rock shattered, and the scree tumbled down the slope of a hill. The laughter of hyenas mingled with the hooting of owls, while a big snake zig-zagged across the intruder's path.

Ahhotep followed her instinct, which told her to go further, and yet further. She felt as though she were walking in the air, and all her tiredness disappeared. She reached the narrow entrance to a valley framed by menacing rock-faces. If she

267

stepped through the constricted opening, would she be cut off for ever?

The queen walked on. This time she was walking in deepest darkness, for the gentle light of her guiding moon could not reach into the depths of this ravine.

A tall man loomed up before her, a man with an ugly face and a jutting nose. He was bright red, armed with a yellow dagger which shone with evil light, and he was coming towards her, ready to attack.

Emperor Apophis . . . Yes, it was he, the coward who was persecuting the Egyptian people, the tyrant whom Ahhotep had sworn to oppose.

She did not flinch. Although unarmed, she would fight. Picking up a stone, she threw it at her enemy, but it seemed she missed. Twice more she threw. Although certain she had hit her target, she could not prevent the emperor moving forward and he did not even cry out.

A ghost . . . It was a ghost, which had risen from the empire of darkness to devour her.

Running away was impossible. Since the stones had passed right through the ghost, Ahhotep would, too. When it was scarcely more than an arm's length away, Ahhotep rushed at it, head down.

She felt as though she had been plunged into a furnace whose flames licked cruelly at her flesh. Just as she was on the point of fainting, she saw a gleam of light and concentrated all her will on it. The light grew bigger, and as it did so the pain grew less. An orange ball began to form and swelled so quickly that the night was vanquished. A new day had just been born, and the dawn lit up hundreds of trees with long, slender branches, decorated with sweetly scented green flowers.

Balanites: a real treasure-store, providing wood for making tools, oil and even a substance which purified water. Ahhotep ate a few of the yellow fruits; they were sweet and flavoursome.

Where this desert forest ended, the soil changed. In certain places water-courses seemed to flow.

The young woman knelt down to touch this new miracle, and found not water but several veins of pure silver! It had been born of the marriage between the moon-god and the desert-goddess, under the protection of Set the fiery, whose fire had made it grow in the heart of the rock. Seqen could pay his soldiers – the rebels were rich!

Intoxicated with joy, Ahhotep retraced her steps, taking care to remember every detail of her journey.

As she emerged from the desert valley she was confronted by a leopard, which stared intently at its prey. Ahhotep had nowhere to hide. Suddenly a gazelle appeared, its horns shaped like a lyre. To the queen's great surprise, the leopard showed no interest. Nor did it pay the slightest heed to a magnificent lynx, whose hieroglyph represented the word 'dignity'.

Advancing very slowly, Ahhotep saw that other animals had gathered there: a white oryx, an ostrich, a large-eared hare, a fox, a jackal, a badger, a hedgehog and a weasel. On the rocks perched a falcon and a vulture. These inhabitants of the desert gazed at the queen. But what were they waiting for? She knew that, if she did not give them what they wanted, they would not let her pass.

Ahhotep thought for a moment, and realized that she must give some proof of her magic. By confronting the darkness that surrounded the emperor's ghost, she had touched evil. In the full light of day, she must show that her soul was unharmed and that she remained, as the traditional expression had it, 'of just voice'.

So she sang. A hymn to the rebirth of the light, to the emergence of the scarab beyond death, to the mysterious form of the first sun. And all the animals – from the most ferocious to the most gentle – began to dance, forming a circle around Queen Freedom. They were enchanted by her golden voice, and she was nourished by their strength, which flowed directly from the great God. Unlike mankind, no animal had ever betrayed its celestial origins.

To concentrate on singing the words of power, Ahhotep had closed her eyes. When she opened them again, the animals had disappeared. But their footprints in the sand showed that she had not been dreaming.

And her thoughts rose, full of thankfulness and reverence, towards the Divine Light.

53

As the palace messenger was walking past a field belonging to Chomu, several of the vase-seller's men barred his way.

Behind him stood their master. 'Where are you going, friend?'

'The same place I always go. I'm carrying official messages to Governor Emheb's patrol, for forwarding to Avaris.'

'I want to see those messages.'

The messenger was outraged. 'That's impossible, absolutely impossible.'

'Give them to me at once, or we'll break your bones.'

Chomu did not look as though he was joking. The messenger had no option but to obey.

There was only one letter. Chomu broke the royal seal and read it. It consisted of a long eulogy to Apophis's infinite virtues, followed by a paragraph in which the writer stated that Thebes was sinking deeper and deeper into its torpor.

The signature gave Chomu a shock. It belonged to the former minister of agriculture – who had been dead for several years! So the palace had not stopped plotting and lying . . . With proof like this, he should have little difficulty in rallying the supporters of collaboration.

'Where is Seqen?' he asked.

'Gone hunting in the desert,' replied one of his men.

271

'What about Ahhotep?'

'At the temple in Karnak,' replied another.

'Perfect. Now I know what we must do.'

'What about the messenger?'

'He must be in league with the rebels. Kill him.'

Greatly heartened by Ahhotep's extraordinary discovery, Seqen had left for the training-camp to tell the soldiers the good news.

As for the queen, she knew that she must do something very important, something that would protect the future army of liberation. So she had gone to the temple at Karnak, where she ordered the priests to deck all the altars with flowers.

'We are going to honour the memory of our ancestors,' she declared, 'and the pharaohs in particular.'

'But, Majesty, the Hyksos have forbidden such things throughout the land,' gasped a Pure Priest.

'If you are afraid to carry out your duties, leave this temple immediately. If not, obey me.'

The priest bowed.

'Bring the ancient offertory tables up from the vaults.'

The officiating priests unearthed masterpieces made from diorite, granite and alabaster. On the stone, the sculptors had engraved different kinds of bread, sides and haunches of beef, pomegranates, dates, grapes, figs, cakes, vases of wine and milk. The flavours from this eternal banquet would rise instantly to nourish the souls of the dead.

Each image was a hieroglyph which could be read and spoken. It was the priests' task to bring them to life, so that they might have an independent existence, and ensure that the magical incantations would remain effective for ever.

'Majesty, look!' called a priest. 'There's smoke down there. A building's on fire.'

'Down there' was the centre of Thebes.

*

Moustache had so much sleep to catch up on that he slept for a good part of each day. The Afghan preferred to invent new strategies for *senet*, the Egyptians' favourite board game.

When not out hunting, the two men lodged in a small house not far from the palace. After so many nights in the open air, they appreciated the comfort of their beds and the good food which a woman neighbour cooked for them.

Deep down, mused Moustache, routine was not all bad.

'I'm thirsty, Afghan,' he said.

'You drink too much beer.'

'It helps me believe freedom isn't an illusion. If we're making weapons we will end by using them one day, won't we?'

'Neither Ahhotep nor her husband is an idle dreamer,' agreed the Afghan. 'But we cannot attack the Hyksos with nothing more than the palace guard.'

'That's strange, I was thinking the same thing. So . . .'

'So the queen hasn't told us everything because she doesn't fully trust us.'

'In her position, I'd do the same,' said Moustache.

'So would I. Ahhotep is as intelligent as she is beautiful. Moreover, a woman like that can be trusted completely. Even in my own country, I've never met anyone like her.'

'Don't forget she's married – you'd better not fall in love.'

Suddenly the Afghan stiffened, like a wild animal pricking up its ears.

Knowing how reliable his companion's instinct was, Moustache snapped out of his lethargy. 'What is it?'

'People are running through the streets. Something bad is happening.'

'The local guards will take care of it.'

'Perhaps not. I don't suppose you'd care to stretch your legs?'

'It wouldn't do us any harm.'

The first group of people was joined by a second, then a

third, led by Chomu. They were all heading for the palace.

'These people aren't brigands,' reasoned Moustache. 'Surely they're not going to—'

'Oh yes they are!'

The Afghan and Moustache took a short cut, running as fast as their legs would carry them, and reached the palace before the collaborators.

Sitting on the doorstep was an old guard, fast asleep with his spear lying beside him.

'To arms!' roared Moustache. 'The palace is under attack!'

Chomu had set fire to Heray's official residence, and had only one regret: that its owner was not inside.

The neighbours were so horror-stricken that they had not dared intervene. When Ahhotep arrived on the scene, they were still petrified.

'Is Heray safe?' she asked anxiously.

'Yes,' replied a widow, trembling from head to foot. 'It was the vase-seller, Chomu, who lit the fire.'

'What did he do then?'

'He swore that he and his friends would destroy the palace.'

Her sons, her mother, Qaris . . . Ahhotep almost fainted. If she could not save those she loved, she would kill Chomu with her bare hands. But she quickly pulled herself together, and said in a ringing voice, 'Those people are traitors. Come with me, all of you. They must be arrested.' She rushed off, followed by a motley band of old men, women and children.

When they reached the palace, they found a furious struggle taking place outside. Urged on by Moustache and the Afghan, the guards had managed to contain the attack. Heray and some of the peasants had lent their assistance, and evened up the odds.

'The Queen!' shouted one of the collaborators. 'Quick, run!'

The Empire of Darkness

But they hesitated for a few moments, and that was their undoing. Heray and Moustache seized the opportunity to kill the ringleaders, while the Afghan threw Chomu to the ground.

'Don't touch me!' whined the vase-seller, seeing that his fate was sealed.

Ahhotep's gaze was even more frightening than Heray's sword, whose tip was touching his chest.

'You have murdered Thebans,' said the queen in a sombre voice, 'and you have tried to murder the royal family. Have you any other, more serious, crimes to confess?'

'You are rebels who refuse to recognize the emperor's authority – that's the biggest crime of all,' exclaimed Chomu. 'If you surrender now, I will plead your cause to our only sovereign, and beg him to spare Thebes.'

'You will be tried for high treason,' said Ahhotep, 'and as an enemy of Egypt, which adopted you as its son.'

'Don't you understand? You and your rebels are doomed, I've sent a message to the emperor. He will be here soon and will give me my just reward.'

54

Ahhotep took Kames in her arms and hugged him for a very long time, then cuddled little Ahmose; fortunately, the children had not had time to feel afraid. If the rioters had succeeded in entering the palace, Qaris would have fled with the two boys, while Teti held back the attackers with her last few loyal supporters.

'You must show no clemency,' Teti urged Ahhotep. 'This time, Chomu and his supporters have gone too far.'

'Much further than you think: he has warned the emperor.'

Teti blanched. 'Then the Hyksos will attack at once. Is our army ready?'

'It will be.'

Shouts made the two women jump. Were other collaborators launching a new attack?

'It is the king,' Qaris reassured them.

Warned by a carrier-pigeon message, Seqen had immediately left the training-camp with a hundred men. Although afraid at first, the people of Thebes had rallied when they recognized Ahhotep's husband and many fellow citizens they thought had left for the North long ago.

The pharaoh hurried into the palace. 'Ahhotep!'

They fell into each other's arms.

'Don't worry,' said Ahhotep. 'Our family is safe and sound. But several of the guards are dead, and, had it not been for prompt action by Moustache and the Afghan, Apophis's supporters would have won.'

'Have the traitors been properly punished?'

'Heray is making sure that they can do no further harm. But Chomu sent a message to the emperor.'

'I shall prepare lines of defence immediately. They will enable us to beat off the first Hyksos attack and then counter-attack.'

'There's something vital we must do first. Mother, will you attend to it?'

'With great joy,' said Teti. 'This will be one of the most wonderful days of my life.'

'Those fellows are real soldiers,' commented Moustache as he watched Seqen's men, who had gathered at the front of the palace.

'Indeed,' nodded the Afghan. 'They're well trained and disciplined. So this is what the king and queen were hiding from us: an armed force prepared to fight the Hyksos. It is the best news I've had in a long time.'

Heray came across to the two men. 'Her Majesty wishes to see you.'

Moustache led the way, feeling rather intimidated. Neither he nor the Afghan dared lift their eyes to look at the queen, who had put on a magnificent ceremonial robe.

She said, 'I wish to thank you and congratulate you on your courageous deeds. You are both hereby appointed officers in the army of liberation.'

The two rebels exchanged looks of amazement.

'Today,' continued the queen, 'you will learn more about that army.'

The people of Thebes had assembled in front of the main entrance to the temple at Karnak. So that everyone could understand what was being said, heralds relayed the words of

Teti the Small, who spoke with an assurance that surprised more than a few townspeople.

'Thanks to the gods, Thebes is once again governed by a Pharaoh and a Great Royal Wife. I can now reveal to you that Seqen has been ritually crowned King of Upper and Lower Egypt, and that Queen Ahhotep has recognized him as such. The line of dynasties is therefore preserved, and the king and queen's rightful power has been consolidated.'

After a moment of stunned silence, the citizens of Thebes cheered their king and queen, whose names were engraved on a stele which would be placed in the temple, under Amon's protection.

When the cheering died down, it was Pharaoh Seqen's turn to speak.

'Those who advocated collaboration with the enemy have been arrested. They will be tried and sentenced. Now we must all face up to the real test of war. Our army is ready to fight, but every citizen must play his or her part. Blood, tears and savage battles are what I promise you. There is only one path open to us. Either we shall be victorious, or we shall be destroyed. And victory depends upon this: all Theban hearts must beat as one.'

This announcement was followed by a long silence. Everyone realized that the long period of false peace was coming to an end and that a terrifying war was about to begin.

Heray struck his chest with his clenched fist. 'I promise to serve Pharaoh, my country and my people, to the death.'

With one voice, the Thebans repeated his oath.

Ahhotep's heart swelled with pride. At last true hope had been born.

The emperor's new game amused him greatly, and it had become a great mark of favour to be invited to sit next to him on his balcony. Below, selected unfortunates perished one after another in the arena and the labyrinth. Watching their death agonies was a source of never-ending pleasure.

Fortunately, there was no shortage of potential victims. There were ambitious men who had annoyed the emperor, lovers who had been careless enough to criticize him in Windswept's bed, foolhardy people who refused to accept Khamudi's extortion, all the beautiful women Tany had taken a dislike to, and even a few innocent folk – strong, healthy individuals chosen at random from among the Egyptian population.

Apophis was well aware that he must soon resume the process of conquest, notably by colonizing Minoa and the surrounding islands, then destroying a clutch of small Asian kingdoms which had been unwilling or unable to form themselves into an alliance. Commander Jannas's troops needed the practice; besides, the emperor's fame must continue to spread.

Now the city of Avaris lived up to his dream: it had become an immense military base, a paradise for all the soldiers, who made full use of the Egyptian slave-girls. And the same was true of the principal cities of the Delta, Canaan and Phoenicia, wherever Hyksos order reigned.

He, Apophis, had succeeded in breaking the back of the civilization that had built the pyramids. One day he would destroy even them, stone by stone, and have a more grandiose monument built to his own glory.

The moment Khamudi stepped into his office, the emperor noticed that the High Treasurer's complexion had a greenish tinge.

'What is the matter with you?' he asked.

'My wife and I amused ourselves with some Lebanese girls yesterday evening, and we made the mistake of sampling some wine from their country.'

'Was it an attempt to poison you?'

'I don't think so, but the girls will make pretty victims for the bull. Majesty, I have to inform you of a serious incident.'

Apophis frowned. 'Serious . . . I trust that is an exaggeration.'

'You alone must judge. I have just received a message from Thebes, consisting of these simple words: "The hippopotamus is preventing the emperor sleeping. The noise it makes offends the ears of the people of Avaris."'

'What does that nonsense mean?'

'It is a code established with our informant, the minister for agriculture. It means that there have been disturbances.'

'An insurrection in Thebes? That's highly unlikely, is it not?'

'One would think so, but the message is quite clear.'

'Is this insignificant minister simply trying to get himself noticed?'

'That is not impossible, Majesty, but let us suppose that he is right. Hasn't the time come to crush Thebes once and for all?'

'I'd completely forgotten that moribund little town. Probably a handful of ruffians tried to steal some wheat, and your little minister wants to get into our good graces by denouncing them. But you're right: we had better check.'

'Shall I send Jannas?'

The emperor smeared pomade over his nose and ankles, which had been swelling up for several days. 'No, we'll be more subtle than that. We'll send an envoy there. If a revolt is indeed brewing, the Thebans will kill him, and our response will be instant and decisive. If they don't kill him, we'll know the minister was making up stories and we'll choose another informant. It is pointless to tire our best soldiers for nothing, when new conquests are in store for them.'

55

'Only one boat?' Seqen was astonished. 'It must be a decoy.'

'It seems not, Majesty,' said Heray. 'The lookouts say it's an unescorted civilian boat.'

'If it drops anchor here, we must destroy it.'

'May I advise patience? Even if there are Hyksos hiding on board, there can only be a few of them, and we'll make short work of them.'

'But why should the emperor's response be so restrained?'

'Perhaps he's sending us an ultimatum,' suggested Ahhotep.

'Demanding that we destroy Thebes ourselves and then surrender? Oh yes, of course, you're right.'

'There is one simple way to find out, Majesty,' ventured Moustache. 'I could go aboard.'

'But you'd be risking your life,' said Seqen.

'With the Afghan and fifty men behind me, I shall feel quite safe.'

The envoy was the most important wine-trader in Avaris. Khamudi had entrusted this mission to him in the hope that he would not return alive. Even if he did, his fate would be scarcely enviable. During his absence, in fact, the High Treasurer would seize his accounts and falsify them with all kinds of irregularities which would lead the fraudster to the labyrinth. And his business would fall into Khamudi's lap.

The merchant was a man of sixty, who loathed travelling, especially by boat. But one did not refuse a mission imposed on one by the emperor. The new envoy had been ill all the way down the Nile and had had to lie down in his cabin; as a result, he had seen nothing of the beauties of the countryside.

Knowing that he was in Thebes, a lost city in a far-off province, gave him no satisfaction apart from the knowledge that he had reached his destination. He managed to get up, drank a little water, and went on deck.

'An emissary from the Queen of Thebes wishes to see you,' the captain informed him.

'Show him into my cabin.'

'Am I to search him?'

'There's no need. No one would dare attack a Hyksos envoy.'

As Moustache went aboard, he made sure that no soldiers were hiding ready to attack.

From the look of the envoy, it was clear that he would be unlikely to survive another journey.

'I am the envoy of Emperor-Pharaoh Apophis, our all-powerful sovereign, and I bring your queen a message from him. Take me to the palace immediately.'

An entire squadron of soldiers was assembled at the foot of the gangplank. The envoy stared at them in astonishment.

'Merely a security precaution,' explained the Afghan.

'Is there trouble here?'

'No, but one cannot be too careful.'

There was no risk of the envoy meeting any collaborators, for Chomu and his henchmen had been executed two days before, following a trial during which no extenuating circumstances had come to light.

The envoy thought Thebes looked rather poor, but it was clean. There were no soldiers on the streets, merely old men sitting on the doorsteps of their houses, children playing, women returning from the market, dogs fighting over a rag while a cat watched from the safety of a nearby rooftop. He saw nothing to suggest that the modest city posed a threat to the emperor.

Seeing how shabby the palace was strengthened that first impression. As for the two elderly guards who bowed as he passed, they were armed with spears so ancient that they would snap at the first blow.

Holding her two sons by the hand, Ahhotep greeted the diplomat at the entrance to her small audience chamber, which the envoy thought was positively decrepit.

'Welcome to Thebes,' she said. 'Your visit is a great honour for us, an honour we had never dared hope for. Unfortunately we have little in the way of comforts to offer you, but you may be sure that my husband and I will do everything in our power to satisfy you.'

Ahhotep seemed so fragile that the envoy was quite moved. Forgetting the manly words that every good Hyksos should address to a defeated Egyptian woman, he stammered a few words of thanks.

'How long are you planning to stay among us?' she asked.

'Just long enough to deliver the emperor's message to you.'

'My husband, Prince Seqen, will be delighted to hear it. Children, go back to your grandmother. I must attend to our guest.'

Dressed in a tunic which had seen better days, Seqen had the greatest difficulty in respectfully greeting his enemy, whom he would rather have strangled. But he accepted Ahhotep's advice, and was determined to deceive the envoy in order to gain a little time.

The envoy said, 'I will be brief and precise. The emperor is disturbed by the noise your hippopotamus is making. Do you follow what I am saying?'

Ahhotep had no difficulty in decoding Chomu's message.

283

'To the east of Thebes,' she said, 'there is indeed a pool where the hippos like to play. But how could their cries have reached the ears of Apophis?'

'Enough riddles, Princess. There are rebels in Thebes, are there not?'

The queen assumed an expression of consternation. 'There were, that's true. A small group of troublemakers led by a vase-seller named Chomu.'

'I order you to hand over these rebels to me.'

'We executed them, on the advice of our minister for agriculture.'

'Ah, that's excellent. May I congratulate him?'

'Unfortunately, he has just died. He will be very difficult to replace – his loyalty to the emperor was an example to all Thebans.'

'Good, good. And are you sure there are no rebels left in Waset?'

'The public executions will have served as a lesson,' said Seqen.

'Our cook has prepared you a good meal, with meat and cakes,' smiled Ahhotep. 'We hope that you will do us the honour.'

'Certainly, certainly. Will there be wine?'

'We have reserved the very best for you.'

Having a Hyksos in their grasp and letting him leave unharmed . . . As he stood on the banks of the Nile, watching the envoy's boat disappear round a bend, Seqen seethed. But he had to admit that Ahhotep was right. Convinced that Thebes was utterly harmless, the envoy would not recommend the emperor to take immediate action. So the carpenters would have time to finish the last boat they were working on.

'I'm glad the envoy is safely on his way, Majesty,' said Qaris. 'He seemed delighted with his brief stay among us.'

'And there was no trouble in the city?'

'No, Majesty. No one tried to approach the Hyksos, and the entire population is with us.'

The Theban army's two newest officers joined the pharaoh.

'You saved my sons,' he told them, 'and I shall be grateful to you for ever. During the war, many men will die. Do you want to leave with the army or stay in Thebes and command the palace guards?'

Moustache scratched his ear. 'We've had a good rest here, but I was born in the North and I'd very much like to go back there.'

'I'm a foreigner, Majesty,' said the Afghan, 'and when we have defeated the Hyksos I want to return to my home.'

'Very well. You shall each command a forward detachment.'

Moustache looked discomfited. 'If we add up the palace guards and the real soldiers you've brought to Thebes, Majesty, that still doesn't amount to an army. Even if we add the Northern rebels, whose numbers have scarcely increased according to our information, we still won't have a big enough force to pierce the Hyksos breastplate.'

'You have still not seen everything.'

A secret training-camp, with permanent buildings and a real army of well-trained men eager to fight. The Afghan and Moustache could hide neither their astonishment nor their pleasure.

'Wonderful!' gasped Moustache. 'So we didn't collect all those flints for nothing.'

'I'm going to introduce you to the other officers,' Seqen told them. 'A perfect spirit of comradeship must unite us.'

'First, Majesty, the Afghan and I would beg a favour of you: let us train with your footsoldiers, so that we can teach them a few cunning blows they can use in close combat.'

56

Grey clouds had drifted in off the sea. Now they hung in the sky above the fortress at Avaris, making it look even more sinister than usual. The envoy did not even glance up at them; he felt queasy and suffocated at the prospect of reporting to Apophis.

'Were you well received?' the emperor asked him.

'I could not have been treated better, Majesty. Thebes is a poverty-stricken, defenceless town, which poses no danger. Princess Ahhotep and Prince Seqen are concerned only with their little family and have no wish to do us harm.'

'Did you speak to the minister for agriculture?'

'He has just died. But you may be assured that the sound of the hippopotamus will no longer disturb you. The region is perfectly calm.'

Apophis stroked his blue porcelain flask on which the map of Egypt was drawn. His index finger touched the province of Waset, which shone with a reassuring red glow, proving its submission.

But he had an unfamiliar twinge of anxiety, so he pressed harder. And the light faltered.

'You imbecile, you let yourself be deceived.'

'Majesty, I can assure you that—'

In view of the envoy's age, the trial of the bull would offer no amusement. So it would have to be the labyrinth.

The Empire of Darkness

*

High Treasurer Khamudi and Commander Jannas had been summoned urgently to the secret room in the citadel, where no indiscreet ears could overhear their conversation.

'Something out of the ordinary is happening in Thebes,' said the emperor. 'Our envoy noticed nothing, but I am convinced that rebels are plotting secretly.'

'My informants have not seen anything, either, Majesty,' said Jannas. 'Waset is one of the wealthiest provinces in Egypt, but most of its produce is delivered to us. Perhaps a palace revolution is brewing, but does it really matter in the slightest if Queen Ahhotep is replaced by someone else?'

'This uncertainty annoys me. Thebes annoys me. Hyksos sovereignty must not be contested anywhere, to even the slightest degree – particularly not in Egypt.'

'Do you wish my troops to occupy the town?' suggested Jannas.

'Thebes must be destroyed,' decided Apophis. 'And close by, fortunately, we have just the man we need. Give Governor Emheb the order to raze that insufferable city to the ground.'

'That's impossible, Majesty,' said the High Priest of Karnak.

'Why?' asked Ahhotep angrily.

'Because the gates of the four directions are closed. Until they open, any attack will be doomed to total failure.'

The queen could not ignore the gods' warnings. 'How can we induce them to open?'

'According to tradition, the royal couple do not truly reign until they have crossed the papyrus forest to the north of Thebes. But it must be infested with snakes and crocodiles – to go there would be to risk your lives.'

'The gods' will must be done, no matter what it is.'

Teti was strongly opposed to their going, but Seqen agreed without a moment's hesitation: his soldiers' nerves were on a knife-edge, and the strain of waiting was eating away at their

287

resolve. Ahhotep entrusted her sons to their grandmother's keeping, and the queen and the pharaoh left the palace. Unarmed and alone, although the papyrus forest was so dangerous that not even the most experienced huntsmen would go there, they look a light boat and set sail.

As the boat slowly approached the forest, dozens of birds, the companions of Set, fluttered up into the sky. Ahhotep rubbed several papyrus stems together. The sound made the heavy silence fertile, and calmed the hostile powers that were eager to devour the intruders' souls.

The couple entered the forest, where darkness reigned even on the sunniest day. The small, quivering sounds of a different world brought fear to their bellies.

Suddenly it was there, huge and burning bright: a female royal cobra, called in sacred writings 'the Slaughteress', 'the Goddess of Stability', 'She Who Streams with Light', 'the First Mother Who was at the Beginning and Knows the Borders of the Universe'.

Ahhotep looked into the snake's eyes. 'You may kill me, but I do not fear you, and you are the lady of the heart's blossoming. Give me your flame, so that I may destroy in order to create.'

The cobra swayed back and forth, and from left to right, then wound itself round a papyrus stem before vanishing.

Ahhotep found that she was alone in the boat. 'Seqen, where are you? Answer me!'

The fragile boat had hit an islet in the heart of the forest and, thinking they had found safe refuge on dry land, he had disembarked.

Before he could answer his wife, he saw two enormous crocodiles coming towards him; he had no chance of escape.

'Lie down, Seqen, and don't move.'

The king did as she said, but the crocodiles kept coming.

Certain he was about to be eaten, Seqen thought of Ahhotep's face and closed his eyes. The two monstrous creatures stood on either side of the king, their heads against his. They placed their forefeet on his shoulders and their back feet on his ankles, thus recognizing the King of Egypt as one of their own: a being who could rise from the depths in an instant and close its jaws upon an enemy.

'Three of the four gates, East, West and South, are open,' said the High Priest of Karnak. 'But the North gate is still closed.'

'What new ordeal are you setting us?' asked Ahhotep.

'The texts are silent, Majesty. The decision must be yours alone.'

'We must attack,' declared Seqen.

'Our army is moving northwards,' objected Ahhotep, 'but the people of the North are refusing to support us.'

'Then what more do the gods ask?'

'That is for us to discover. As long as we are deaf and blind, how can we hope for victory?'

'My men are pawing the ground with impatience. If we stretch the rope too far, it will break.'

When they returned to the palace, they found Emheb waiting for them. Though usually so calm, today he was in a state of great agitation.

'Majesties,' he said, 'I have just received an order from Commander Jannas: Thebes is to be razed to the ground.'

'So Apophis did not believe his envoy,' said Ahhotep. 'Are your troops ready to fight, Emheb?'

'They're eager to do so.'

Heray came hurrying in and said, 'Majesties, come quickly. Come and see!' His voice was so authoritative that without protest the royal couple and Emheb at once followed him to the riverside.

'Look at these eggs,' said Qaris.

'The teal have started to lay,' said Emheb. 'They're at least three weeks early, which means the annual flood will begin much earlier than usual, and we shan't be able to launch our boats until its ferocity abates.'

'In other words,' said Seqen, 'we can't possibly attack immediately.'

'No, but perhaps we can turn these unusual events to our advantage,' said Ahhotep. 'We must find out why the North is still hostile. Emheb, you must write a report for the emperor, saying that you have carried out your mission with great zeal, that Thebes has been destroyed, and its prince and princess are dead.'

'Will he believe me?'

'Yes, if you send him my crown, my robe and Seqen's tunic, soaked in blood.'

57

'A worthless crown,' sneered Apophis, 'a pauper's dress and a heathen's tunic. The relics of dead Thebes aren't worth keeping.'

'Governor Emheb's report is cause for celebration,' said Khamudi. 'His soldiers destroyed a town full of people too cowardly to fight. Everything, including the corpses, has been burnt. On the site where the city of Amon used to stand, the governor suggests building a barracks.'

'An excellent idea. All the same, send an observer to confirm the report. And tell him to bring this man Emheb back with him when he returns. I want to meet him and congratulate him.'

'We shall need a little patience, Majesty. The flood is particularly strong this year, and river travel will be impossible for some time.'

'By the way, I have a new candidate for the labyrinth,' said Apophis.

He was smiling. A consultation with his blue flask had reassured him that pitiful Thebes had indeed been burnt to the ground.

The royal palace and several houses actually had been burnt, watched in horror by the people of Thebes.

'Why did you decide to do it?' asked Seqen in astonishment.

'Because an enemy as formidable as Apophis has senses

more acute than those of ordinary people,' replied Ahhotep. 'He had to have some proof, even at a distance, that our city had truly been destroyed.'

That very morning, Teti, Kames and Ahmose had left for the training-camp where they would live from now on.

Ahhotep and Seqen went to the temple at Karnak, where the High Priest greeted them.

He said, 'I have gazed once more at the corners of the sky. Three of the four gates are open and favourable. But the North remains stubbornly closed, and no incantation can unlock it.'

'Is it true that there is a closed shrine within this temple?' asked the queen.

'Yes, the central shrine of Amon. But, as you know, it will not be opened until the day Egypt wins back her freedom.'

'Amon is the god of the life-giving wind, the north wind. It is Amon who is demanding that we break through this prohibition.'

'You must do no such thing, Majesty,' said the High Priest, horrified. 'That would be an insult to destiny.'

'I am convinced the opposite is true. It is because we have stayed passive that Egypt is still enslaved. Only Amon can open the road to the North for us.'

'The master of Karnak will strike you down!'

'I am not his enemy.'

With the greatest reluctance, the High Priest led Ahhotep to the closed shrine. She meditated for some time before the door, then drew back the gilded wooden bolt, imploring Amon, 'the Hidden God', 'the Unchanging One', upon whom all creation rested, to come to her aid.

Half opening the door, the queen slipped inside the little shrine. A single ray of light entered it, just sufficient to make out the statue of Amon seated on his throne. In his right hand, he held a curved bronze sword coated with silver and encrusted with electrum. On its hilt it bore a gold lotus.

'We have need of your sword, O Lord Amon. It will give us the power to defeat the emperor of darkness.'

Ahhotep laid her hand on the stone hand, though she knew she might not be able to withdraw it again. The granite was not cold. An ageless energy flowed within it. She waited.

After what seemed an age, Amon consented to entrust the sword to her: from it there began to flow an intense light which illuminated the shrine.

Ahhotep withdrew, walking backwards with her head bowed.

When she emerged and held up the sword of light, as dazzling as the midday sun, Seqen and the priests covered their faces.

'The door of the shrine is to remain closed until we have won total victory,' said Ahhotep. 'Henceforth, Pharaoh, you have a weapon, and the road to the North lies open.'

In front of the palace at the training-camp a small garden had been planted, and it was beginning to look lovely, with tamarisks and palm-trees growing around an arbour.

In the shade of the trees, briefly oblivious to the frantic activity raging around them, Ahhotep and Seqen shared a moment of happiness which was all the more intense because they must soon part.

Both knew how much was at stake. But it was the pharaoh's task to lead his troops into battle, and the queen's to govern Thebes in his absence.

'I want so much to live,' he told her as he caressed her wonderful body. 'I want so much to love you until old age carries us away to the other side, to become so completely one with you that even death cannot separate us.'

'Death can never separate us,' she promised him. 'If you die fighting the darkness, my hand will pick up your sword, and your strength will dwell within me. You shall be the only man in my life, Seqen. I swear it upon the name of Pharaoh.'

293

Their bodies entwined, they gazed up at the immense sky and into the far distance. Why had the gods chosen them to carry out this superhuman task?

They could hear people in the camp calling out to one another, and officers trying to impose order on their excited men.

'I think I'm needed,' said Seqen.

Seqen had appointed a captain named Baba to lead the troops from Nekhen. Emheb would command his Edfu men.

'May I present my young son, Majesty?' asked Baba.

'My name is Ahmes, son of the lady Abana,' the boy said proudly, 'and I'm going to kill hundreds of Hyksos.'

'Aren't you a bit too young?'

'I already know how to use all the weapons, Majesty, and I'm not afraid to fight in the vanguard.'

'Egypt needs men like you, Ahmes son of Abana.'

Seqen took the time to say a few words to each soldier. Their faces were sombre, often full of anxiety. No one underestimated the Hyksos, who moreover had the advantage of numbers. Anyone who thought about it came to the conclusion that the little Egyptian army would be wiped out. But the queen's presence had dispelled many men's fears, and there had been no desertions.

A small hand slipped into the pharaoh's. 'I want to go to war, too.'

'Ahmose!' Seqen picked up his four-year-old son.

'He's right,' said Kames with all the confidence of his fourteen years, 'and so do I. Since we came here, we've trained every day with the soldiers.'

The king set Ahmose down and embraced both his sons. 'This is how the two crocodiles gave me their power; and I am giving you mine. If I don't come back from the battle, it is up to you to continue the struggle under the authority of the Queen of Egypt. Do you understand?'

Kames and Ahmose gave their solemn oath.

'But you will come back, won't you?' asked the latter.

In the middle of a most delightful evening, Khamudi was dragged away by Jannas himself. The commander had forced the door of the villa where the High Treasurer and his wife were teaching perverted games to terrified young girls.

Jannas was disgusted but chose not to see anything, since the emperor tolerated these obscene practices.

Khamudi was sweating profusely and ordered a servant-girl to mop his brow. 'What is so urgent, Commander?'

'Our trading-ships have been attacked by pirates based in the Thera islands.'

'Thera's in the southern Cyclades, isn't it?'

'Yes.'

'We ought to have cleaned up that part of the world long ago.'

'I thought it would be unwise to wake the emperor at this late hour, but I felt I must alert you at once.'

'You were right. I thought those damned pirates had been dealt with, but their greed was too much for them. They won't survive this mistake. And if the Minoans have helped them in any way at all, they will pay very dearly for it. We must go to the palace quickly. But first, wouldn't you like to try one of these little beauties?'

'Certainly not,' said Jannas.

'But they're so delicious. You don't know what you're missing.'

The emperor's icy rage made even Jannas afraid. He was ordered to leave Avaris immediately with several warships and to exterminate every last one of the pirates.

As for Khamudi, he was instructed to send troops into Syria, Canaan and Phoenicia, to show that no one could attack the Hyksos order and live.

295

58

Rascal and the other carrier-pigeons left for the North, bearing messages to the rebels who were to link up with Seqen's army. Aboard their transport vessels, the soldiers watched the birds fly off towards Lower Egypt. That land was so near yet so distant, and only the sacrifice of many lives would win it back.

In the palace, in great secrecy, Ahhotep had made Seqen touch the sceptre with which she hoped one day to measure out their country. Now, on the flagship, in the presence of all the officers, she crowned him with a diadem bearing a gold uraeus. The female cobra would spit fire, lighting the pharaoh's way and burning his enemies.

Admittedly this was only a lesser substitute for the traditional Red Crown of Lower Egypt and White Crown of Upper Egypt, which the emperor had stolen and seemingly destroyed.

Qaris and Heray placed the model of Egypt in the king's cabin, in the hope that day by day he would extend the boundaries of freedom.

And now it was time for the last kiss and the last embrace. Ahhotep wished that she could be simply a loving wife, mother of two fine boys and an ordinary Theban woman; but the empire of darkness had decided otherwise.

'Sail northwards, Pharaoh, break through the blockade at

Kebet and travel as far as you can. As your victories are proclaimed, hope will be reborn throughout the land.'

'There are boats coming,' a river-guards officer at Kebet told his colleague, who was dozing under a palm-tree.

'It'll be a merchant fleet from the north. Nobody bothered to tell us.'

'No, they're coming from the south.'

'You've drunk too much date wine.'

'Get up and see for yourself. There are several of them.'

The man snapped out of his doze, and gaped at the incredible sight. 'Quickly, man, the boats!'

The guards hastily created a floating barricade. Its very presence would be enough to deter the culprits from continuing on their way. They were probably Nubians, or perhaps traders from the Great South who were trying to evade taxes.

'Halt in the name of Emperor Apophis!' shouted the officer.

Those were the last words he spoke. Seqen's arrow embedded itself in his throat – the pharaoh had been determined to kill the first Hyksos who tried to bar the way.

Within a few minutes, the Egyptian archers had wiped out their opponents, then they broke through the blockade with ease.

'Aren't we halting at Kebet?' asked Emheb.

'No,' said Seqen, 'because we don't entirely trust Titi, the town's mayor. He'll ally himself with the stronger side.'

At Dendera, the pharaoh's fleet encountered two Hyksos war-boats. Caught off guard by this surprise attack, their crews had no time to organize themselves and put up only feeble resistance.

'Our second victory, Majesty,' said Captain Baba.

At Abydos, there were five Hyksos boats. One of them sacrificed itself in order to slow the Egyptian advance boats, while the other four turned broadside on.

297

Christian Jacq

This time, the fight was a real test for the army of liberation. But the Hyksos, too confident of their own superiority, made the mistake of firing their arrows without taking cover, while the Egyptian archers protected themselves with shields.

Emheb's ship ploughed into the side of an enemy boat, and his soldiers from Edfu rushed to board her, while those from Nekhen seized the Hyksos captain. His capture disheartened his sailors, who suddenly had no one to give them clear orders.

'Give no quarter!' shouted Baba, spearing an Asian officer who was trying to regroup his men.

From that moment, the outcome of the fight was in no doubt. The soldiers trained by Seqen completely overran the enemy.

'Four more boats for our fleet, and plenty of weapons we can put to good use,' noted the Afghan, wiping enemy blood off his arm. 'We are becoming a proper army.'

Rascal alighted on Qaris's shoulder.

'It's a message from Pharaoh Seqen, Majesty.'

'You read it first,' said Ahhotep, 'and tell me only the good news.'

Dry-mouthed, Qaris deciphered the coded text, which Seqen himself had written. 'Our army has broken through at Abydos – it's our third victory. The fighting is fierce, but our soldiers acquitted themselves admirably.'

'What about our losses?' asked Ahhotep anxiously.

'Very light. A boat is bringing the wounded home.'

'Make sure everything is ready to treat them.'

'You can rely on me, Majesty.'

Ahhotep herself had taken command of the soldiers who had remained at the training-camp. At first they had been furious at not being allowed to leave with their comrades, but they soon stopped complaining. After all, serving the queen and protecting the royal family was a noble duty.

Without sacrificing any of her grace or femininity, Ahhotep was proving adept at handling the sword and the bow. Many strong fellows, confident that they would easily defeat her, had found themselves unexpectedly floored, for Ahhotep was adept both at dodging blows and at devising unusual holds.

Kames had become a young man. He took part in exercises with such fervour that he had already hurt himself several times; but he bore the pain with great fortitude. Little Ahmose always watched his brother, occasionally with great alarm; his grandmother tried in vain to make him look away.

'This is not a proper way to bring the boy up,' she scolded Ahhotep.

'Can you suggest a better one in time of war?' her daughter asked.

'Of course not, but it is still not a proper upbringing. The sons of a king must know the great classical texts and have a good general education. Kames is backward in his reading, so I want him to work with me for at least an hour every evening.'

'Granted, Majesty.'

Khamudi was ill. His skin was covered with a rash and he had dreadful pains in his belly. But he could no longer put off telling Apophis about the message from his new Theban informant, the agriculture minister's replacement.

At first, he had thought the spy had simply fabricated the story from some minor incident at the Kebet frontier, to curry favour in Avaris. But now the spy said that Hyksos crews had also been killed at Dendera and Abydos. He couldn't possibly give the emperor such news. And yet urgent measures must be taken to halt the rebels.

Alas, Jannas was away hunting pirates in the Cyclades and the best troops were sowing terror in Canaan and Phoenicia.

Still, there were enough regiments left in Egypt to crush the vermin who dared to nibble away at the Hyksos Empire.

A burning sun was beating down on the citadel, and the heat made Khamudi feel even worse. Although it was still morning, it was already unbearably hot. Climbing up the palace steps was torture.

When the emperor received him, Khamudi swallowed hard several times.

'There is nothing more hateful than summer,' said Apophis. 'Fortunately, these thick walls hold in a little coolness. You should slow your pace, my friend. From the look of you, you are having too many busy nights.'

Khamudi took the plunge. 'We have been attacked in Upper Egypt.'

The emperor's eyes were as piercing as a knife-blade. 'Where exactly?'

'At Kebet, Dendera and Abydos.'

'By whom?'

'The Thebans.'

'Who is commanding them?'

'Seqen, Queen Ahhotep's husband. He claims to be' – Khamudi swallowed again – 'the pharaoh.'

'Is he still moving north?'

'I don't yet know, but it seems likely.'

'The rebellion is to be crushed, and this man Seqen is to be brought here to me, dead or alive.'

59

Since Abydos, Seqen's army had travelled for several days without meeting any resistance. It was almost as if the Hyksos had retreated as soon as they heard of the Thebans' first victories.

'I don't like it,' said Emheb.

'Perhaps our surprise attack was such a shock that the enemy doesn't know what to do?' suggested Baba.

'No,' said Seqen. 'So far we've faced only small forces, which were used to keep order in the provinces. I think they're now massing their troops somewhere, with the aim of halting us in our tracks.'

From nowhere a storm blew up, as violent as it was sudden. A furious wind snapped branches, twisted the palm-trees, blew desert sand over the fields and whipped the waters of the Nile into rough waves.

'Drop anchor,' ordered the king.

The storm lasted for several hours, during which the soldiers sheltered as best they could, their heads resting on their knees. It seemed that Set, Apophis's protector, was angry and had a terrible fate in store for them.

As soon as the sky and the river began to grow calmer, Moustache ventured on to the bridge of his ship to check that it had not suffered too badly.

And then he saw them: about twenty Hyksos warships, anchored off the town of Qis.

'This time,' he told the Afghan, 'it'll be a bloodbath. We aren't going to take these fellows by surprise.'

'That depends, my friend. They are probably expecting us to mount a frontal attack, so we shall advise the king to do something else.'

The best Egyptian archers, including young Ahmes, son of Abana, fired hundreds of burning arrows at a speed which only well-trained men could have sustained. Most reached their target: the Hyksos sails, which the crews had omitted to lower. They soon caught fire and, aided by the wind, the fire spread to the masts, despite the sailors' efforts to put out the blaze. Not a single ship escaped unscathed.

'They are jumping on to the riverbank and running away,' said Baba excitedly. 'Let's chase them and kill them.'

Seqen gave his assent, and the Egyptians disembarked. This was a fine opportunity to destroy one of Apophis's warbands. Led by Baba, the Thebans cut down many sailors with their axes, spears and swords. Victory was in sight.

Suddenly they halted in their tracks, and the shouts of triumph died in their throats.

'What is it?' asked Seqen, hurrying back to the bow of the ship.

'We've fallen into a trap,' said, Emheb.

The Thebans were now faced with a very different army.

'I have never seen anything like this,' confessed Baba. 'I've never seen contraptions like that or animals like those.'

They were chariots, drawn by horses.

Nor was that all. The Hyksos had bronze swords, much stronger than the Egyptians', more powerful bows, better armour and helmets. The enemy was superior in every respect.

'This is a bad time to die,' said Moustache.

'At least,' said the Afghan, 'This way we shan't feel so badly about this old land.'

Seqen's soldiers were terrified.

'We must retreat, Majesty,' urged Emheb.

'No. We'd be slaughtered like cowards.' The king turned to his men. 'We have dreamt of this battle for many years. Apophis is the one who is afraid. He thinks we're going to scatter like sparrows, because up to now no one has dared take on his elite troops. So we shall be the first – and we shall prove that the Hyksos are not invincible.'

All the soldiers brandished their swords in agreement.

The sound of chariot-wheels and horses' hooves striking the stony ground raised a deafening clamour.

'Attack!' ordered Seqen, pointing the Sword of Amon at the chariots.

The first Egyptian line was cut down. The Hyksos archers and javelin-throwers decimated the second line, and only the energy of despair enabled Seqen to prevent a rout.

Cutting off a charioteer's arm and slitting the throat of the archer who stood beside hum, the pharaoh managed to overturn the chariot. This unexpected success inspired Baba and the soldiers from Elkab, who succeeded in immobilizing several others, though at the cost of many men.

When they saw Hyksos breastplates spattered with blood, the Egyptians realized that the enemy was indeed not invincible, and the two sides began to be more evenly matched.

'Look, there on the enemy's left flank!' shouted Moustache as he disembowelled a Persian. 'Those are our men.'

Alerted by the carrier-pigeons' messages, other rebels had come to join the battle. Their attack took the Hyksos by surprise and disrupted their advance.

'The king!' roared Emheb, who had just killed two Anatolians. 'The king is alone!'

Seqen had fought with such fury that his bodyguards could not follow him. Trapped in a circle of chariots and foot-soldiers, he was trying to parry attacks from all directions.

Sliding under his guard, a short Canaanite caught him a blow below the left eye with an axe.

Ignoring the pain, Seqen plunged his sword into his enemy's chest. But another Canaanite sank his dagger into the king's forehead. Blinded by the blood pouring down his face, the king swung his sword at empty air.

Baba eventually broke through the circle, killed the second Canaanite and, for a moment, thought he would succeed in rescuing Seqen. But a spear caught him in the back, while an Asian officer smashed his heavy axe down on the king's head.

Dying, the pharaoh sank down on to his right side. A Syrian crushed his nose with club and finished him off with a final blow to the base of the skull.

Enraged by the deaths of his father and his king, young Ahmes fired arrow after arrow. One by one, he killed their killers, while the Afghan and Moustache mounted a furious charge and at last managed to reach Seqen.*

In Thebes, Ahhotep searched the sky in vain for carrier-pigeons. She no longer dared to count the days since the birds had last brought news from the front.

This evening, after reassuring her mother, her children and the soldiers, she was exhausted. This lack of news gnawed at her soul, but she was the queen and she had no choice but to bear it.

The sun had not yet set, and the soldiers were attending to their usual duties in spite of the heat. Kames was teaching his little brother how to handle a wooden sword, Teti was reading prayers to Amon, and Qaris was watching over the wounded, whom the queen visited every morning and evening.

'There's a boat coming, Majesty,' said Heray. 'I'll go and ask for news.'

* The mummy of Pharaoh Seqen-en-Ra has survived, and can be seen in Cairo museum.

'No, I want to be the first to know.'

They hurried down to the quay, the soldiers from the camp close behind the young queen.

It took an age for the boat to reach the quay and moor. The first person to walk down the gangplank was Emheb, who looked haggard and drawn; he had aged ten years.

He bore the Sword of Amon and the royal crown, both spattered with blood.

The queen went towards him.

'We reached Qis, Majesty,' said Emheb, 'and there we met an elite regiment of Hyksos. Thanks to the pharaoh's courage, we were not defeated.'

'Seqen . . .?'

'The pharaoh is dead, Majesty. We have brought his body back so that it may be mummified. The wounds are such that it would be better—'

'I want to see him. And the embalmers are to leave the wounds for all to see, so that future generations will know how this hero died, fighting the first battles in the war of liberation. May his name be honoured for ever, as the name of a true pharaoh.'

Emheb had a lump in his throat as he watched her. 'Forgive this pitiless question, Majesty,' he said with difficulty, 'but thousands of men await your answer. Are we to surrender to the emperor, or are you resolved to take command of our army and continue the fight?'

Ahhotep went on board the ship and gazed down for a long time at the disfigured body of the man she had loved so much and whom she would love beyond death. Soon she would have to explain to her sons why they would never see their father again.

She kissed his forehead, then went to the prow of the boat. All eyes were upon her.

'Give me the Sword of Amon and the king's diadem,' she ordered Emheb.

She put on the bloodstained crown and pointed the sword northward.

'As soon as he is old enough, Kames shall succeed his father and become our new pharaoh. Until that moment, I shall act as regent and we shall continue the fight against the empire of darkness. May Seqen's soul shine among the stars and guide us on to the path of light.'